THE OAKS ON THE GLEN

The Oaks on the Glen

By Ginny Davis

Copyright@2021 Ginny Davis

ISBN# 978-1-7369065-0-7

Author: Ginny Davis

Editor: Valerie L. McDowell

Illustrations: Andrea Churchville

Publisher: Power2Excel

Dedication

This book is dedicated to my sister, Lisa. My best friend, partner in crime and my trusted cohort whenever I feel like walking into the deep, dark woods.

Much love and gratitude to my sister-friends, Davonna, Erin, and Rolanda for keeping me sane and being supportive during this interesting and slightly terrifying period in my life.

I love all of you strong, beautiful, intelligent women. Thank you for always being in my corner.

Contents

Introduction 1

Chapter 1
Dena 7

Chapter 2
Larry and Annette 13

Chapter 3
Valarie, Elise and Jack 19

Chapter 4
Empty Unit and the Kid 27

Chapter 5
Dena 35

Chapter 6
Larry and Annette 39

Chapter 7
Valarie, Elise and Jack 41

Chapter 8
All 45

Chapter 9
Dena and the New Neighbor 49

Chapter 10
Elise 61

Chapter 11

Larry and Annette...67

Chapter 12

Valarie and Elise 69

Chapter 13

Dena..71

Chapter 14

Annette and Larry..73

Chapter 15

Dena..77

Chapter 16

Kelly..89

Chapter 17

Dena...101

Chapter 18

The Couple on the Hill 105

Chapter 19

Kelly...119

Chapter 20

Dena's Place 123

Chapter 21

Bonnie and Malcolm 127

Chapter 22

Dena...173

Chapter 23

Kelly...175

Chapter 24

Up on the Hill...177

Chapter 25

Bonnie..181

Chapter 26

Thanksgiving..209

Chapter 27

Dena...233

Chapter 28

Kelly...235

Chapter 29

Bonnie, Malcolm, Micah, Michael, Janae and Katie.........237

Chapter 30

Kelly's Thanksgiving....................................275

Chapter 31

Dena...283

Chapter 32

Bonnie Without Malcolm............................313

Chapter 33

Lethar...325

Chapter 34

Epilogue...327

Introduction

The entity tried to leave again today. He waited until the sun was about to set in the sky. His powers were usually strongest in the early morning hours, yet lately it seemed as soon as the sun rose its powers disappeared. So, he waited until his powers were somewhat renewed and he left the unit.

He stretched and stretched as far as possible to escape the hold that his home had on him.

There were so many buildings to navigate around. He made it down the lane, where there were apartment buildings on one side and woods on the other. With the sun slowly sinking in the sky, the evil being made it past the wrought iron gates that guarded the entrance to the apartments and the buildings within. He looked back as he always did; for some reason the being never expected to make it through the gates. He made it to the small road called North Park Lane, just outside of the gates that lead to the six-lane highway beyond the apartment buildings. He glanced back a second time, always doubting he would make it any further. He noted the name of the complex as he always did, desperately hoping this time would be the last time he would see the name, "The Oaks on the Glen."

Which way should he try this time?

The presence began to feel lonely as well as doubtful since he had left his companion behind. He would come back for his partner of sorts as soon as he had the strength. At least he felt he would come back. If he found a better partner along his travels, then the future would be uncertain for his companion. His loneliness turned to disdain and coldness in the wake of abandoning a creature that had been completely loyal to him.

He often tried to go in the direction in which traffic flowed the most. The being could see the people riding in their cars to and fro, from way above the tree line. He could rise above the tree line to survey the area but had to travel beneath it to attempt escape.

He decided to go to the left--west--as most of the cars were heading that way.

The air was foul with a sweet smell and the day was warm and still somewhat bright. He could feel the goodness hanging in the air, like a thick, sticky sap. Lethar detested goodness and longed for the dark and the dank. The maliciousness of men and women was where he thrived. There was no darkness to be had today.

Lethar turned off the small road heading west and navigated a series of turns down other streets to get to the main road. Right on Hickory, left on Old Creek, left on Sycamore, and then straight until hitting Gallatin Road. He willed that the constraints of the host home would let him leave. Maybe the constraints were sleeping or had given up on keeping him contained.

He stretched down Gallatin Road, passing stores and restaurants, leaving an almost invisible trail of cold and darkness. He was very aware of the small world he was contained to; he understood the barriers and the rules that he was to abide by and yet Lethar needed to see if those barriers and rules really existed.

So far, the principal rules had held him in place.

He noticed that some of the drivers would hesitate after he passed by. This was normal for him. Sometimes a car would lose control, or the traffic lights wouldn't work properly, causing a collision. In most cases, the damage was minor, and no one was seriously hurt. Unfortunately, Lethar's powers grew from pain and destruction.

So down Gallatin Road he proceeded, past brightly lit fast-food restaurants, clothing stores and gas stations, each of which gave off a different smell and energy, sometimes pleasant, sometimes not so pleasant. Today, there was more of the former rather than the latter. Today, everything was against his favor. Even the sun seemed to be moving at a slower pace as it lowered in the sky. This day was not so pleasant for Lethar. There was joy in the air and joy weakened his already stretched and depleted powers. He moved slowly and steadily in an effort to conserve power and strength.

He passed by a building known as a shopping mall. It had been a popular place a few years ago, filled with people. Sometimes, Lethar would stop here and feed on the pain of the people inside. Sometimes, a fight would start after he fed. Sometimes weapons were involved. More often than not, people were robbed, or the shops were robbed. Because of this, the mall was not as popular as it used to be and there were fewer unhappy people to feed on. Fights stopped, robberies stopped, and people returned. People felt safe and happy. This was not pleasant for Lethar.

Happiness and feelings of safety spread faster through people than they knew. It made it nearly impossible to feed. And on a day, such as today, he might as well have settled on starving.

He kept moving, still on Gallatin Road, past family-style restaurants and auto dealerships. Past churches, schools, doctor's offices, and attorney's offices. These offices were a favorite. So much pain to feed on in both cases, yet there was nothing to feast on from either today. How was that possible?

Still, he kept moving and stretching, strength again fading, passing shopping centers, gardening stores and auto shops. He passed a field where swarms of butterflies seemed to float happily and colorfully just above the grass and bushes. Lethar finally reached the large cemetery and thought, "This is where my time away will come to an end." There was absolutely nothing to feed on. The sky was bright, the trees and grass were green, and all was filled with a different kind of joy and contentment all around. The contentment of loss, of understanding loss, of knowing that loved ones had moved on and were probably in a better place. All the energy around Lethar was happy, even in the cemetery.

He fought to keep going. Stretching just beyond the cemetery was Briley Parkway. He had reached out this far before but knew that he would reach no further today. And in an instant, his power was depleted. He snapped back in mere seconds to his home base, much like a rubber band. What took many minutes to travel was taken away from him in less than a minute. He was back in the lonely, abandoned apartment with nothing to feed on.

✦

The unit has been empty for weeks, as had the unit next door. The silence was slowly destroying him. And the journey had taken away all his strength. The best that Lethar could manage at this point was to linger. Linger and rest until some strength could be regained. It had been so long since he had properly fed, weeks since the boy had left. How had he let the musical boy slip away? Well, maybe not slip away exactly but, still the boy was useless to him now.

Lethar recalled the boy was almost broken, more than halfway out of his mind, using music as a deranged weapon; it was glorious and completely in Lethar's control. Or so he thought. He must have missed something, but what could it have been?

Lethar vowed to be more cunning next time. He would wait out the pain and feast much more slowly. Or at least he would try. He would rely more on his companion in making complex and calculated moves. But for now, he would wait. And so, he waited, barely a mist of a shadow of his former self. Waited for the new tenant. Waited to feed.

CHAPTER 1

Dena

Dena sighed as she moved around while shuffling the heavy brown boxes. It was hot outside and even though the air conditioning was on full blast, so much hot air had come in from the outside with the movers going back and forth that the temperature was warm and muggy inside her new home. She paused for a moment to take a sip from an iced cold glass of water. Her throat was dry, arms and legs sweaty, forehead moist. The water gave her a welcoming chill. Her pause turned into a much-needed break while she surveyed her new apartment. It was a box... the one-bedroom unit was shaped quite literally into a square. No halls to divide rooms properly, just walls that sectioned off spaces to make them into comfortable rooms. The front door opened into the living room, which was large. The carpet was a light beige color, and the walls were a kind of dark cream color. There was an alcove set in the wall for her entertainment system. Big enough for a 46-inch TV. Her 42-inch TV fit nicely. To the right was a decent-sized bedroom. Her queen-sized bed fit quite well, but when the two nightstands were added the space was tight.

There was not enough space to open the closet all the way with the nightstand in the way. Her cherry wood dresser stood against the wall opposite her bed. She left the area in front of the windows free. She loved light and was trying everything she could to maximize the light in the space. She left her footlocker on the floor in front of the bed, opting to use it for closet overflow. The bathroom had two entrances, one from the bedroom and one from the area across from the kitchen. The bathroom was long with a single sink, and a standard white bathtub. She would have preferred a garden tub, but this would have to do. The tiles on the floor were white and cool. Outside of the bathroom entrance near the kitchen was a built-in computer hutch she planned to use as an office. The kitchen had a black laminate bar countertop. The appliances were white - nothing to brag about. The floor had a beige patterned tile. Through the kitchen was the laundry room. Dena debated getting bar stools or a small dining room set.

She was okay with the size of the apartment. It was roomy enough for just her, but she wished that she had checked out the location first. It was on the first floor, and she had a wonderful view of a wooden wall and some landscaping. It was not a basement apartment, but it felt like it was because when she looked out the living room windows, she would see the wall. Above the wall were other units. Then there was the mini breakdown she had when she saw how small her bedroom closet was. And then the aftershock mini breakdown when she realized that she didn't have a coat closet for guests as she had seen in the model. She paused and breathed slowly in and out. She laughed at the New York City girl in her having a meltdown over closet space. She giggled quietly, noting that she was from the Midwest. "What was with the mood swings", she thought? Oh well...it's close to work and she would save a ton of money on gas and cut down on wear and tear on her car.

Thankfully, the bedroom was done, her new living room furniture had arrived already. The cable company was on the scene finishing up the home entertainment system and Wi- Fi. Dena pulled out artwork, candles, and knick- knacks to be placed in the living room. She had been chatting with the friendly cable guy while he worked; he had suddenly become quiet. She guessed he had run into something difficult while completing the install. She quickly learned that getting a cell signal in her apartment was next to impossible, so she bit the bullet and had an actual hard -wired phone put in. "How retro," she thought. But it had to be done or how would anyone get in touch with her while she was at home? The cable man lifted his head. He was in his forties, salt and pepper hair, slender with a moustache. "Well, I can't get the Wi-Fi to connect for some reason," he said perplexed. "Maybe the router is bad," he shrugged. Lightning-fast anger took over and Dena suppressed the urge to defiantly ask how come he didn't know for sure the router was bad, but this was the first real hiccup in her move, how much trouble could one little call to the cable company be? Trouble and worry for another day: her internet worked even though it was a hard- wired system. The cable and phone worked so that was good enough. She said goodbye to the cable man and went back to decorating her new place.

She was able to connect to the music stations available on cable, so she tuned into one of the few jazz stations while she worked. She hummed along to the songs she knew while unpacking and cleaning. The music was soothing and light for the most part.

There were a couple of songs that she didn't recognize, and they seemed to have a religious tone to them. She hit the info button on the TV to identify them and was shocked to find that she knew the songs. She listened for a moment to catch the melodies and began to hum or sing along.

She felt a chill after a while and went to turn the air off. She figured she had turned it down too low with all the excitement going on. She remembered that when she picked up her keys and was able to get her first look at the actual unit that the place was freezing cold. She thought the workers getting the place ready were probably working in overdrive and turned it down too low. June was supposed to be warm, not sweltering she thought, but here in the south you go with the flow. She loved the extended summers in greater Nashville. She noticed how chocolate her skin had turned from her laying in the sun to even out her tone. Her muscles were defined, she was shapely, thick, home-grown, or whatever terms were used by the current urban musicians. Her short, dark brown hair had lost much of its curl from the humidity. Dimples accented a face with baby doll brown eyes and high cheekbones. Her smile and voice were warm and comforting and she had an infectious laugh. She moved from the thermostat and turned on some smooth jazz so that she could continue furnishing her apartment and unwind from the stress of moving. Her sister would be coming by later to help her put contact paper in the cabinets. Dena wanted to have a nice snack ready for her upon arrival. So much to do.... she ran to the newly installed phone to call her sister so that she would have the new number.

An hour later, her sister arrived. Dena and Liz worked on the contact paper for the kitchen cabinets and did some touch up cleaning in the rest of the apartment. It turned out to be light work and the two were finished in no time. They sat on the couch with their lemonades, waiting for the hot snacks to be ready. The music on the jazz station continued to play light and soft. Dena noticed Liz shiver and she went to check the air again. The temperatures looked fine, so she checked to make sure that the system was off again hoping that would help. "I'm going to have to call maintenance if I can't get this figured out," said Dena. "Well, you are in the middle unit, maybe you're getting the air from the other units," said Liz. Dena hoped her sister was right, but she still took notice of both of their goose bumps. The timer on the oven went off and Dena went to grab the snacks. The girls sat and chatted and laughed. Then they talked about the upcoming visit from their parents. "This is going to be a tight space for the four of us, huh Liz?" "Yeah," agreed Liz. "Especially with only one bathroom but, it's only for a few days." The two sisters went back to snacking and talking for quite some time. Dena bought out a comforter for them to snuggle under while they chatted away the afternoon.

CHAPTER 2

Larry and Annette

A nnette sat in the master bedroom watching or not watching some show on TV. She was reading and enjoying the peace of a Saturday afternoon. There had been quite a ruckus this morning when the new neighbor moved in. Annette had spied on her from the balcony. She observed a cute, chubby black lady. Annette could tell that she would be a quiet neighbor. There was just her and the moving men, no huge speakers, or shelves to hold huge speakers. Annette and her husband Larry had moved in almost a year ago. Things had been intense with the move and with selling their old house. They had decided to move into an apartment to save money for their new home, which was just now starting to be built. She hoped the new home would be done by late fall, but you never can tell with construction. At least, there would be peace with the presumably quiet new tenant moving in, or so she hoped. It was quiet when they first moved in and then the so-called "musician" moved in downstairs and shortly after the move-in peace, became a memory.

The last tenant likened himself to be the next Gospel-Billy to hit the scene and the musical noise was unbearable. He usually quieted down by nighttime but there were more than a few nights when he was blasting away until 1am. Annette guessed he had to work his regular job on the peaceful nights. But there were few Saturdays and Sundays that were peaceful with Gospel-Billy around. She couldn't understand how a man could take a beautiful hymn and twist it into something that lost its true meaning and had no sense at all. The only constant about the racket was the volume: loud! It was the source of many arguments between her and her husband Larry. Arguments that would start about the music and then drift off to why the bills were so high, why her mother or his mother never came to visit since they had moved so far away, why did she keep moving his wallet, shoes, or socks or why he kept moving her books, throws and pictures. Or the most laughable argument of all - why did the cat have to shed so much fur? Indeed! The stoked flames of heated unrest grew with the raging hot spring that was upon them. For one instant, during a particularly malicious argument, she had almost reached for a vase and chucked it at her husband of eight years. The urge passed as quickly as it came. That day she conceded that whatever silliness indeed that almost brought her to do harm to her husband was silliness indeed. She loved him, and he loved her. And this was just how marriage went after a time, right?

Gospel-Billy left about three weeks ago, and it seemed that their arguments left with him. There was peace and harmony. Quite a bit of romance, compassion; it was like a honeymoon of sorts. There had even been long nights of soft conversation in front of the TV as well as nights of long-lost passion in the bedroom, kitchen and surprisingly in the guest bathroom one night. Annette was content. She dug into her book and buried herself in its world.

Larry sat at his desk in the second bedroom. The bedroom was half guest room, half bedroom. He didn't know how Annette had done it but, she managed to find matching wood furniture for his office and the bed. It looked like the perfect place for a weekend warrior who occasionally had to stay the night at the war. He thought to himself that she was really a creative person at times. His fondness for her over the past few weeks had grown. Well, grown was the wrong word. It was as if it had faded away some time ago and now it had come back almost instantly. That Gospel-Billy had caused so much tension he couldn't think at times. Larry would plan to use his home office for light work on the weekends but the noise from the downstairs neighbor was so horrible he would often have to drive to the office, which he absolutely hated. He would have to take off his sweats or pajamas in case one of the corporate officers might come in and see him. Larry was always professional during the week and felt the weekends were designed for him to let his hair down. He preferred working at home as much as possible. It was relaxing and casual. He could listen to music of any genre at a moderate level and wear what he wanted even if it was just his boxers. And you would think that the office would be empty on the weekend but, he would always run into some junior partner or executive on the rise hanging around the office on the weekend. These men were much older than him and he guessed that they hated to go home. Why else would they be in a dimly lit, cold office every single day? Larry sighed with relief while going over his notes. He had a big meeting with a new client on Monday and he of course wanted to be well prepared. He wasn't sprinting up the corporate ladder, but his climb was steady if slow. His notes were concise and light. They were sure to win over the client. Larry leaned back and rested his hands on the keyboard. He couldn't get over the sense of peace that had come over him the last few weeks. He remembered back to a time a couple of months ago where he thought of his sweet loving wife as a shrill, frigid banshee. He knew that he was as much to blame for the arguing as she was, but for some reason he felt that on more than a few occasions, it seemed he had purposely started the arguments. He would hurl horrible verbal assaults at his wife not knowing where the anger was coming from. He only remembered that they seemed to start when the wannabe gospel rock star downstairs started playing that garbage he called music.

Larry loved religious music and to hear that hack butcher songs like *Nearer My God To Thee* or *Amazing Grace* was enough to make his eardrums cringe. Larry stretched out his long, skinny legs and examined the pale pink skin exposed by his long cotton shorts. He desperately needed some sun. He finished his notes and re-read them to make sure they were perfect. He shut off the computer and went to find Annette.

He was starving, he thought as he left the office, running his fingers through his thick brown hair. He would ask Annette for a lunch date and maybe they could lie out by the complex pool and get some color, maybe go by the storage unit to get their picnic basket. Make the most of this wonderful day. He wanted to surprise her with news from the builder. They were going to start pouring the foundation on Monday and he was sure that she would be just as excited as he was. The two-bedroom apartment was spacious, but nothing like having a home with a two-car garage, four bedrooms, a backyard and pool of your own. Maybe then both sets of parents would come by to visit. Annette was very close to both her mom and his, and not being able to see them seemed to heighten the tension between them over the past few months.

Larry found Annette dozing in a chair in the master bedroom. Her long, light brown hair caught the light and ignited something in Larry. Her skin seemed to be begging for his touch. He had to have her now. He walked over to her quietly and gently kissed her on the forehead. She opened her bright green eyes and smiled at him. She looked into his brown eyes and something in that gaze made Larry lose control. He kissed Annette and wrapped his arms around her. In seconds they were on the floor going at it like horny teenagers. In between gasps and moans he asked her if she would like to have a lunch date with her husband today. She laughed and said, "We better hurry before he gets home!" They both laughed, and it ignited their love lust again.

CHAPTER 3
Valarie, Elise and Jack

Valarie and Elise were just getting back from a softball game. Both were exhausted from the heat but elated that their team had won. Elise played second base for the local junior high school team. Valarie, her mom, was at every game cheering her on. She was amazed at how long and lean her daughter had become over the school year. She noticed today that Elise was becoming a young lady. She would have to get her a bra before the summer was out. Valarie and Elise walked down the short hallway, and Valarie stopped in the kitchen to grab a couple of waters out of the fridge.

Elise started peeling off her gear and walked past her mom to the laundry room to throw it in the washing machine. Elise added soap and adjusted the setting on the washer. She took the cold water her mom gave her and rubbed it across her forehead. She was still high off the win which put her team in the semi-finals, but she was anxious to wash off the grime from the field. She walked out of the kitchen in just her panties and a tank top which were moist from sweat, and headed toward her bathroom. Elise liked the new place. They had been here for just a few months, but she had made quite a few friends in the complex. She made a lot of those friends while walking Jack their black lab. Jack was currently crated and napping. He was a very relaxed dog, well behaved and he was still just a puppy. He didn't bark or beg to be let out for the most part. He seemed at ease in the crate and stayed close by it unless he knew they were going for a walk. Then he was uncontrollable and excited beyond belief. Elise peeked into her room to see if Jack was asleep in the large crate in her room. Sometimes he would start to mewl when he heard them come in...but all was quiet in the crate today. Elise turned on her tip toes and entered the bathroom located to the left. She turned on the shower and waited for it to get warm. She looked at herself in the mirror and wondered if her mom noticed that her boobs were coming in. She was excited that her mom would have to buy her a bra soon. She hopped in the shower and thought about the game blow by blow – it was an incredible win and she wanted to savor every second.

Valarie sipped the cool water from the bottle and looked around the kitchen. She needed a few minutes to unwind and to wait for the washing machine to stop so she could tend to Elise's uniform. She figured that she would make lunch and catch up on some reading while Elise walked the dog. There were leftovers in the fridge that would do nicely. Valarie put on a pot of water to make some Southern Nectar or sweet tea as it's called by the natives.

Valarie and her daughter had moved in about six months ago. They left their home in Ohio to get away from her ex-husband who somehow had found out where she lived. While she and her daughter were out one evening, he broke nearly every window on the lower level and spray- painted obscenities where the neighbors could see. Luckily, one of the neighbors saw him skulking around and called the police. The police came to the quiet neighborhood immediately and promptly arrested Nick, who had violated an order of protection and his probation by coming to the home and crossing state lines to do so. Valarie went to court to testify against Nick. She was worried that he would get off again because he came from a wealthy family. But the jury gave Nick the max which was three years. he was also ordered to pay for the damages to the home and his child support was increased due to the amount he had accrued in his personal savings and checking. He was absolutely infuriated, but Valarie and Elise were happy to be rid of him. They hoped that he would forget about them while he was locked up. It was quiet for some time, then the holidays came, and they had a big family dinner at the house. The windows had been repaired months ago and the spray paint removed. Valarie went to check the mail the day after Christmas and found a couple of late Christmas cards.

For some reason, the cards made her very nervous. She took them up to her room and looked at them closely. No return address, but they were postmarked from Chicago.

She thought maybe an old co-worker had sent something to her but why send one for her and one for her daughter? She opened the envelope addressed to her. Inside was a card with Santa petting a reindeer on the front. For some reason this made Valarie even more nervous. Her hands started to shake as she opened the card. The inside was covered and crowded with handwriting except for the picture that was taped inside. The picture was a few years old, and it was of Valarie and Elise but what frightened her was the bloody thumbprint on both her and Elise's foreheads. And the words inside the card were hard to make out except for three which were repeated in heavy writing: Mine, Forever, Punish. Valarie closed her bedroom door and placed a call to the police in Chicago, and to her attorney.

The next morning Valarie took both the unopened card and the one she had opened down to the police station as her attorney instructed her to do. Valarie made up an excuse to her daughter and her sister the next morning so that she wouldn't have to worry them. Thank goodness her sister Gabby had decided to stay a couple of days so that Elise wouldn't be alone. Her husband had not escaped but he clearly had someone working with him on the outside so that he could continue to terrify her. After a short wait, while sitting on an uncomfortable bench the police called her up to the counter where she opened the card addressed to her daughter. Inside was the same card with Santa and the reindeer. Inside the card was the same crazy scribbled writing and the same picture with her and Elise with the thumbprints on the foreheads...but there were two additional thumbprints as close to the crotch area as the sender could get. Valarie started to tremble, her knees became weak, and she gripped the old wooden counter to keep her balance. The officers went to work jotting down as much information as they could from the envelopes and cards. Elise walked shakily back to the bench and sat down. Her head was spinning. How? Why? Are we safe? When? She thought she might truly faint; so she began to focus on a lamp until the room slowed its spin. A female officer gave her a cup of coffee and Valarie managed not to spill too much of it on her wool coat. But then her stomach started to churn; she got up and set the cup down firmly on a desk and bolted for the bathroom which fortunately was nearby. Valarie dry heaved into the toilet for a few moments and her head began to pound again.

The pounding became louder and louder until a voice sprang from it screaming, "PACK UP AND LEAVE NOW!" With this mental release, her head begin to calm, and her stomach began to get under control. She went to the mirror and looked at herself. She wasn't a total wreck. Her long brown hair was drawn into a messy but chic ponytail. Her big, dark brown eyes looked a little tired but that was understandable. She turned on the cold water and rinsed out her mouth and washed her face. Move again? She had moved from Chicago to Dayton to put space between her and her ex-husband and obviously it hadn't worked, in fact he seemed even more angry and determined to not only make her life a misery but Elise's as well.

This time Valarie would be smarter. Thank goodness she worked for an international company with offices in or near all major cities in the world. She would call her boss who was still in Chicago in the morning; he had been very understanding about her ex-husband and she was sure that he would help her again. This time she would not have any contact with her ex's family. She could see how his crazy sister or whomever had been enlisted was able to do his dirty work so this time she would cover her tracks. Nick may have come from money, but she doubted that his money could buy much considering his disturbing behavior. His wealth came from his parents, and she didn't think they would jeopardize their standing in the community and their relationships with colleagues to stand behind their son. Maybe by the time Nick's prison sentence was up he will have moved on. Valarie Alvarez (soon to be the former Adriana Valarie Perez-Hernandez) gazed at herself in the mirror a moment more. She saw the determined look that her mom will sometimes have while working on a piece of art. Everything became clear and she knew she would have to act fast. She left the bathroom and began her journey to becoming Valarie Alvarez.

Everything from that point on moved smoothly. Talking to Elise was much easier than expected. Elise understood that she couldn't have contact with her new friends or old friends anymore. Elise had just started to make delicate friendships but figured if she could do it once she could do it again. She knew her dad was coming off the rails, probably going stir crazy in prison and needed to get them back under his thumb some way. Elise understood. Safety first and foremost. Valarie's boss, although sad to lose her in his division, was much more concerned about Valarie and Elise's (formerly Isabella Elizabeth Hernandez) safety. He had been thinking of mentioning a higher position to Valarie but was not sure if she would be interested since it was out of state, and she had seemed to be just settling into Dayton. The position was with a sister company which had just been acquired. It was a promotion with a significant salary bump and her moving costs would be covered if she took the position. He went to HR and explained the situation regarding the name change and gave Valarie his highest recommendation. Her first day at work would be in February... plenty of time for her to move and get settled.

The house sold almost as soon as she put it on the market. She donated almost all the furniture to various local charities, she turned her car back into the dealer. She would purchase a new car once she got to Nashville and her banking and credit information were set up with her new name. She sent all jewelry and relics associated with Nick back to his parents. The Hernandez's traveled frequently, especially during this time of year. It might take a month or two before they were home to open her package. They were distant but supportive of Valarie during her marriage to their son. The only one who seemed to think she was in the wrong was Nick's older sister, Elena, who believed that a marriage was truly until death parted the couple... one way or another.

By mid-January, Valarie, her sister Gabby, and Elise were riding in the back of her parent's SUV heading to a new life in a new city. Her brother stayed behind to make sure that her tracks were covered. Mr. and Mrs. Perez told family and friends that they were taking the girls (daughters and granddaughter) and driving to Orlando to see this Disney World that everyone was so jazzed about. They planned to return home in a month. That's what retirees do... spoil their children and grandchildren. There were plenty of cities between Ohio and Florida. It would take Nick some time to figure out where they were. But first he had to get used to where he was staying. The judge ordered that he be moved to another prison further west...some place in Draper, Utah. His transfer was rushed due to the severity of the implied threat. Valarie was sure her brother Benjamin had something to do with that. He was, after all, the accounting manager for the prison system in Chicago.

It all seemed so far away, almost surreal. But this was her new reality and she had embraced it happily. Seeing her family was a bit trickier, but there had not been any more threats or incidents since the move. Nothing but peace for the most part...except for the loud noise of the previous neighbor. Valarie was thankful that she and Elise were gone most Saturdays and Sundays. She was also thankful that there was a bedroom between them and Gospel-Billy's living room. Although on some nights the music was so loud that she couldn't sleep in her bedroom. Thank goodness she had purchased a comfortable living room sectional. She was able to sleep there when the noise got to be too much.

Valarie came out of her daze when she heard the buzzer on the washing machine go off. She had finished the tea and lunch was being kept warm in the oven. She heard Elise fumbling around in her room while she was hanging up the uniform to dry. "Mom, I'm gonna take Jack for a walk before we eat! I will be back in about 30 minutes!" Relief. That will give the tea some time to get cool, she could squeeze in a cold shower and maybe she would even get in a quick nap before working on the rest of the laundry. She put in the next load of laundry and walked quickly to her bathroom just off the living room. She smiled as she thought about how wonderful the water would feel on her skin.

CHAPTER 4

Empty Unit and the Kid

The unit on the corner next to Dena's apartment was empty. She noticed it when she was moving in. Dena knew that it was a three-bedroom unit. She could see the inside since the blinds were open. She figured that new neighbors would be moving in soon. She had heard rumors about the previous tenant of her unit. Apparently, he blasted horrible religious music till all hours with no regard to anyone else. Dena wondered if the former tenants in the unit next to her were forced to move due to the noise. No one mentioned what happened to Gospel-Billy either. She guessed that everyone was glad to find out he was gone. She noticed that there were some look-i-loos as she moved in, but none of her new neighbors approached her directly at first. She talked to a neighbor that was moving out of the building above the wall on the hill and was able to get some details. Evidently the old tenant made so much noise that they could hear it up on the hill. In fact, it forced most of them off their patios and balconies on warm days and it came to the point where no one could enjoy a nice breeze through an open window. This Mr. Billy person had made quite a few enemies. The police had been called several times during the day and it sounded like he finally agreed to leave. No one was quite sure on that. All that was known is that the front door was left wide open and most of his belongings were gone one morning. That was about two months ago.

Dena checked the apartment thoroughly to make sure that Mr. Billy hadn't left any damage. But everything seemed normal, just minor issues that the management company fixed quickly. The only problem was in the laundry room which was on the same wall as the empty three-bedroom unit. There was a strange odor that wafted through the other unit into hers. She cleaned the floor and sprayed disinfectant several times, but the odor was still there. It smelled like stale, cooked cabbage. She couldn't understand why the smell was only noticeable in the laundry room when the entire living room wall was shared by the neighboring unit. She was even more puzzled when she glanced into the open blinds of the empty unit and saw that the kitchen was not one of the rooms that shared a wall with her unit. She kept trying to figure it out and the best reason she could come up with is that maybe the odor was coming from the unit above her. Very strange. She wound up keeping an open box of baking soda above the dryer and one of those air freshener thingys to cut the smell. It was much less noticeable after a few days.

Larry and Annette had very little contact with the unit at the end on the lower level. They had seen a couple of young men living there... most likely college roommates. They seemed very nice, quiet, orderly...but who knows? There were a couple of late-night parties that took place in their apartment, but Larry and Annette figured it was payback due to them having to combat the noise from Billy. They left quite suddenly as well...about a week or two before Billy left. Larry and Annette were awakened one early morning by the sound of a small band of movers consisting of a small van and at least two large pick-up trucks. The place was empty within two hours flat and it looked like the two roommates were going to the same destination. The mood of everyone seemed to be one of liberation. Probably had to leave because of the noise from Billy. It was a shame that good people were leaving because of one inconsiderate person. Annette had called the office several times regarding the noise, and she knew that the neighbors on the hill had been bothered by it as well. She knew that the police had been called a few times, but she didn't know if he had been cited. She also wondered to herself and to her husband if anyone had confronted Billy. Larry lied and said he didn't think so. Annette didn't pick up on it or maybe she did. She went back to bed and Larry stood watching from the balcony as the neighbors moved out.

Larry had confronted Billy about a month ago. Annette had gone to visit a friend in Murfreesboro overnight. Both were looking forward to a night of peace away from each other. Larry was pretty sure that Billy would be at work on this particular Saturday and had planned a peaceful day of watching college basketball reruns and video gaming. He had just settled in for an early afternoon nap when the pounding noise of ripped gospel jolted him out his slumber. Rage consumed Larry in an instant and before he knew it, he was scrambling down the stairs in his house shoes and into a gathering thunderstorm. He didn't remember running but he made it to Billy's doorway in what seemed like seconds. The noise was countless times worse up close. The balcony from the unit above covered him from the rain while he banged on the door three times with both his fists. He had no idea of what he would say or do; his anger was a bright, sharp red and it was starting to ooze out of him like lava. The door opened slowly and what Larry saw shocked him. A kid, white, rail thin, shaking, deep dark shadows under bloodshot eyes covered in sweat. His sweats were hanging from his frame, and he had brown ragged hair that looked like it was breaking off in some places. Sunken cheeks, and there was a smell that Larry couldn't place. The first thing his mind grabbed for was weed, but that wasn't it. It was a strong smell but nothing like marijuana, nothing like piss or feces. And the smell wasn't Billy, it was coming from inside the dark apartment where the noise was still blasting. It was like a wild animal smell but if Billy had a pet, it was nowhere to be seen.

Larry and Billy the Kid looked at each other for a long time. Larry thought that Billy wanted to say something but couldn't form the words. The kid was terrified, and Larry's disgust eased, and the anger was gone. Although he wasn't a father or a cop those instincts took over. "Come out here and talk to me for a minute man." The kid looked down almost sheepishly, took a couple of steps outside and pulled the door closed behind him which did little to cut down on the noise, but at least he could hear what Larry said. "What is going on in there? You know you are disturbing everyone in the area? You know people can't sleep?" The kid continued to look down at his bare feet. This was not at all what Larry was expecting, he was prepared for battle, an argument that would lead to blows and a possible arrest. His anger was replaced by confusion and pity because Billy the Kid b.k.a. Gospel- Billy was nothing but a terrified kid. He must have been high on something. He wouldn't speak so Larry continued. "Look dude, everyone around here just wants an afternoon of peace and quiet for a change. Can you keep the noi-music down every now and again? Give us a chance to refresh with some time off from your musical stylings?"

The kid looked up, opened his mouth, and then closed it. "Kid, are you in some kinda trouble? Is there someone in there bothering you?" No response. But the kid's body seemed to scream, "Help me!" Larry took a step closer to him and mouthed, "Do you need the police?" Billy shook his head no. Larry tried another approach. "Okay kid, do me this favor...I will give you $80 to call it a night. Go out and hang with your friends or something. Go to a movie and get something to eat. Heck, get a room at the Comfort Inn or something if you need one." Larry reached into his back pocket and pulled out the money and handed it to the kid. The kid raised his head and looked at Larry, he made no move to take the money, and he was still shaking. Larry looked into the kid's eyes and for a moment he thought he saw a hand reaching out to him beckoning for help. Suddenly thunder crashed around them, and lightning struck hard and sharp. The wind started to blow so hard it forced the apartment door back open. Larry and the kid turned and watched the door open. The kid slowly reached to pull the door shut, but before he could reach the doorknob the door shut so fast and hard that the knocker on the door banged back against the door on its own.

The kid nearly jumped out of his skin. Larry took the kid's hand and gave him the money. "Just go in and turn the music off. I will wait here while you do it." The kid nodded and moved slowly toward the door. At first neither of them thought the door would open, but it did. The kid went inside, and Larry could hear him moving quickly through the rooms picking up and putting things down. The music was killed, and sweet silence filled the air. The wind died down and the kid was back outside the door in less than three minutes. He had a backpack and keys in hand. He locked the front door and turned to Larry with watery eyes. He whispered, "Thank you." Larry watched the kid turn and walk down the path to the parking lot. Larry wanted to call after him and ask him what was going on. Why were his eyes so frantic? Did he have someone else he could stay with? That look in his eyes, what was that? Who/what shut the door?

Suddenly, Larry felt cold, and he began to shiver. His mind vaguely wrapped around remembering that cold air seemed to shoot out of the unit door whenever it opened. Larry stepped back out in the rain and started trying to rationalize what happened. Someone else was there...someone bothering the kid. But why was the music up so loud? And why was it okay to turn it off? He stopped his mind from thinking crazy thoughts. The kid is on meth or someone in the apartment is on meth. But meth doesn't smell like that. The apartment was clean and furnished. Plus, he had seen the cops there on at least two occasions and no one was arrested. He got back to his place and dried off. He grabbed a blanket and lay down on the couch to get in that nap he so desperately needed. But when sleep came so did some strange dreams about hands and things that weren't there. The rain poured outside. He hoped the kid made it to a safe place that night. He thought he would go and check on him in a couple of days. But Larry never saw the kid again. He heard the blasting noise again two days later and made up his mind that he would go talk to the kid again that weekend. But whenever he made up his mind to go and talk to him, something would always convince him to stay away. Unknown to him at the time, the college kids would move out soon and shortly after so would Billy.

He never told Annette about the visit, and he didn't know why. He didn't know why he lied to her about it when she asked. But it seemed to him that what happened that day needed to stay a secret. Maybe he was ashamed that he didn't do more to help someone who was obviously in trouble. Oh well, why worry? "Babe let's just enjoy the peace right now." he had replied at the time. And of course, an hour later the horrible music started, and all thoughts of peace faded quickly away. Not long after the noise started Annette and Larry got into a horrible argument about boarding the cat because the shedding was out of control. Thankfully, the arguing and noise stopped two weeks later.

Then there was the big riddle of what actually happened to the kid. There were no moving vans or trucks that came to take his things away.

Larry got a glimpse inside the apartment and noticed it did have furniture and a lot of heavy music equipment; once it was discovered that the kid was gone, and the door was wide open, everyone just assumed that he moved out in the middle of the night. He wasn't evicted...no marshals or sheriffs showed up to force him out. The place was a wreck from what he overheard from the office staff. Papers and smells and broken furniture left behind. But that was strange because the furniture looked fine to Larry from the glimpse he got inside. Did the kid just walk away? Larry didn't remember him having a car. No way could he have carried any of the equipment on his own.

CHAPTER 5

Dena

Dena had pretty much settled in and liked her new place a lot. She hadn't quite figured out what was going on with the air conditioning. It seemed to happen just in spurts, so it wasn't too big of a deal. She was so excited about saving gas money and happy to be closer to downtown Nashville. Her drive to work took about 7 to 10 minutes. She could come home on lunch hours and do a load of laundry or nap or even drop off groceries. The only problem was with her upstairs neighbors...they sounded like elephants moving across the floor. It wouldn't have been so bad except they got up at 4am every morning, opening and closing doors and drawers with such fierceness that it made the ceiling rumble. They also argued from time to time...nothing too serious. But it was enough to annoy Dena and she could easily find someplace else to be most times. She would sometimes take a walk or grab a comic book and lay by the pool, go to the onsite gym which wasn't much to speak of, and she eventually stopped going there after a couple of weeks. The gym at her job was close by and she would drive there sometimes and get in a quick workout.

Late one night, about a month into her arrival, there was quite a lot of banging going on. It finally quieted down at about 2am but by then Dena was so pissed she couldn't sleep. She laid in her comfy, cozy queen-sized bed filled with rage and staring at the ceiling, hoping that her stare would burn a hole through the ceiling as well as the upstairs occupants. Her anger subsided, and she slowly started to drift off to sleep. She had almost reached the booth to board the boat to La-La Land when she heard a loud raspy whisper. "Bitch!" Her eyes popped open, and she looked around the room. She was very close to being in a complete panic. She couldn't tell where the whisper came from. She stared up at the ceiling thinking that the argument that had concluded moments ago had to have picked back up. But she was scared because the whisper seemed to have come from inside the room. Everything was quiet upstairs. Her fear grew because there was something familiar about the voice of the whisperer. It sounded like her own voice! Was it possible that she mumbled or talked in her sleep? Her fear was still present and strong, but she started to rationalize what had happened. She was probably still stewing over the argument from above while drifting off and the profanity came out as a result. That had to be it...after all she had been known to giggle in her sleep. If she could emote while happy it made sense that she could lash out while angry. That made sense: her pounding heart started to slow down, and her breathing returned to normal. It was 3:17am. She could still get in 3 hours of good sleep. She slowly started to drift off again. She made it past the booth and onto the boat to La-La Land where she dreamed peacefully for about an hour. That's when the upstairs neighbor's regular routine started up again. Dena was too tired to be mad. She waited it out and made plans to get some earplugs. She fell back to sleep at about 5am and repeatedly hit the snooze button until 6:30.

When Dena got home that evening, she was exhausted. She heated up some leftovers and went straight to bed. She messaged her friends and family during work to let them know she was calling it an early night. She was in the bed by 8pm and was in a deep slumber when she heard a door slam. She sat up and listened. Her apartment was quiet but from above she heard a woman scream, "Why did you shut the door and lock me out?" The man mumbled something and then they were quiet again. Maybe it was a half-hearted joke, but it was probably in poor taste after the fight they had the night before. Dena drifted off to sleep again when the banging started. It sounded like they were moving furniture. No... they couldn't be moving at 11pm on a Thursday night! Yes, yes, they were moving on a Thursday night. Dena reached for the earplugs she had purchased earlier and put them in. It felt like she had cotton in her ears, and she could hear her heart beating over the noise coming from upstairs. She closed her eyes and went to sleep. She drifted off happily thinking that she would get at least a month of peace and quiet once they had moved out. That thought made her blissful.

TGIF and it couldn't have come soon enough for Dena. The work week had been intensely busy, and the lack of sleep had made her weary. She was happy to get home and just lay out on the couch and watch TV. It would probably be an early night. As usual, she put her pajamas on within five minutes of coming through the door. She made a small salad and a tuna sandwich to go with it. She had some fresh tea chilling in the fridge to go with her meal. Once she finished eating, she lay back on the couch and dozed off to sleep with the TV still on. Thwack! Dena sat up and looked around. The sound had come from the kitchen. It was quiet then. She shook off the last of her nap and went to the kitchen to investigate. A large plastic spoon that she didn't remember using was laying in the middle of the kitchen floor. Dena was very confused - where had it come from? Maybe she had used it to stir the tea...no, the tea was made the night before. Uggghhh...who knows. She was so tired that she convinced herself she pulled it out again and just forgot. She held the spoon in her hand and tried to force the memory of her using it to come back. She had no luck, so she put the spoon in the sink and went back to the couch.

Dena was surprised to see that the TV had changed channels to one of the music stations. There was a song playing that she didn't recognize, and she found herself listening to try to figure out if maybe she did know it. But, after a few moments her tired mind and body just wanted sleep. She figured that she had rolled over on the remote and that's what changed the channel. Even though she could see the remote was untouched and laying on the coffee table. Maybe one of her neighbor's remotes was on the same frequency. Trying to figure it out made her more tired.

She laid back down on the couch. She managed to get back to sleep but was awakened again by the neighbors moving around. She went into the bedroom and closed the door which cut down on the noise. Her phone read 10:15pm and she happily hit the sheets. She drifted off thinking she could work out in the morning and go visit her sister. She slept well.

CHAPTER 6

Larry and Annette

A nnette had also been bothered by the arguing from the couple next door. They had been quiet for the most part, but lately they seemed to have fallen into a not-so-routine spell of bickering. It was very familiar to her. Why were they arguing? Annette couldn't make out the reasons. Larry never heard them, he slept like the dead. Annette unfortunately would wake up at the slightest noise. She would go and sleep in the spare bedroom/office on the nights that they didn't quiet down after a while.

One morning, while getting ready for work, Larry asked her why she was leaving their marital bed in the middle of the night. He was a little worried that she was angry with him or maybe that she was hiding something. He had no basis for these thoughts, but it wasn't so long ago that they were at each other's throats.

"My goodness, Larry, you can sleep through everything. The next-door neighbors have been arguing off and on for the past week or so. They were keeping me up, so I went to the spare room to sleep." Annette noticed that Larry looked a little shame faced but she could feel relief radiating from him. "Honey, did you think I was mad? Of course, not," she said, and she kissed his face and smiled up at him. "Anyway, sounds like they are moving out. There was a lot of moving around going on last night." Annette looked at the clock on the microwave, "Babe, we both better go now, or we will be late!"

"TGIF", Larry exclaimed as he rushed to finish dressing. He had plans to surprise Annette with a weekend getaway. Bags were already packed and in his car. He smiled to himself as he grabbed his computer bag. "Larry, what are you up to?" asked Annette sweetly. She knew that Cheshire grin. Larry ran down the stairs and bolted out the door. His legs were so long and spindly as he ran down the stairs that Annette burst into a fit of laughter. She had to use the counter to steady herself. She left soon after Larry, laughing at the thought of him running down the stairs and wondering what he was up to. God help her she loved that man!

CHAPTER 7

Valarie, Elise and Jack

Valarie had not been sleeping very well the past few nights. She kept hearing what sounded like neighbors bickering.

And then there was scraping and scratching coming from the upper unit to her right. The walls were pretty thin there. She made up her mind to start looking for a house immediately. Elise could use some more space as could she. Jack desperately needed a yard - he seemed to be a very emotional dog. He really loved staying in the crate and that just wasn't normal. They had gotten him as a puppy, and he had been a very active dog. And finally, things were starting to become strange around the place.

A couple of nights ago, well more like in the wee hours of the morning, Jack let out one of the few ferocious barks he had in him. Elise woke in a daze and let out a yelp of her own because of Jack's bark. Valarie woke too and knew it was Jack. She got up to see what the trouble was. Did Jack sense danger of "the ex-husband" nature close by? She had barely raised her head when she heard a door slam. It was coming from the unit where the couple had been recently arguing. Jack somehow must have sensed it. Valarie got up to make sure that was all it was. She found Elise in her bedroom staring at something in the room in a peculiar way and for good reason.

Elise had fallen asleep while listening to a music app on her headphones. She didn't hear Jack moving around exactly, but she felt a shift in the room, then she heard him bark. She opened her eyes and saw that Jack was out of the crate. She was relieved at first because Jack's attachment to the crate was so unlike his normal behavior. Elise thought that Jack was getting used to the apartment until she saw what he was doing.

Valarie saw the look on her daughter's face and turned to see what she was looking at; she could just make out Jack from the light coming in from the hallway. She watched Jack, who was normally free to roam the house at night but chose to stay in his crate for the most part, had pulled his blanket and toys out of the crate. It was amazing because all his belongings were in a specific order. He was staring at the crate teeth bared, fur on end and growling viciously. He had never behaved this way before. Valarie looked at the crate and she could have sworn she saw something moving in there; maybe a mouse or lizard had gotten in the house. But the shadow was bigger than a field mouse or lizard. Suddenly there was a loud scratching noise coming from inside the crate. Valarie and Elise jumped. Valarie turned on the light and rushed to the crate to look inside but there was nothing there. Well, except for a long-jagged scratch at the back of the crate wall. Valarie and Elise spent the next two hours looking for the culprit - a big squirrel, a rat, a raccoon, a possum, but they found nothing. Valarie decided to put some food out to see if the unwanted guest would take the bait. Elise and Jack slept with her the rest of the night. They could hear banging from the neighbors, but it was very faint. The rest of the night was peaceful.

In the morning, Elise noticed that her headphones were completely dead, even though she had turned them off before getting out of bed. She plugged them into the charger after she looked in and around the crate carefully. Everything seemed fine so she went on with her normal morning routine.

CHAPTER 8

All

Things remained peaceful for the next few weeks. August raced toward September. Dena, Annette, Larry, Valarie, Elise and Jack took full advantage of the peace. There was some commotion up on the hill, but all was calm in their worlds. Temperatures had finally cooled down. People were finally able to enjoy their patios and balconies without the stifling heat. But one couple up on the hill seemed to have horrible arguments every few days. Annette and Larry gave each other that knowing look of understanding when one of the couples' raging fights broke out. Dena thought to herself, "Don't they know we can hear them? Why are they letting everyone know their personal business?"

All was quiet upstairs since the neighbors had moved. Dena caught up on some reading and writing; she had a few dates with a couple of guys. Nothing special - but she was determined to have a boyfriend soon. She spent more than a few nights with her girlfriends and her sister at some of the well-known, tastier restaurants located all over town. She shopped cautiously, remembering that her closet situation was quite dire. But she managed to squeeze a few outfits, bags, and shoes in. Thank goodness she had kept her footlocker to keep excess bedding in. New shops were moving into the more upscale malls and the stores were much busier than they were a few months ago. Dena was just happy that the traffic hadn't gotten out of control in her area.

Larry surprised Annette with wonderful news. The house was moving ahead of schedule. They would be able to move in by the end of October! They spent many weekends at the site envisioning the future, furniture placement, and entertainment plans for friends and family. Gallatin was one of the new up and coming neighborhoods surrounding Nashville. In fact, they no longer had to be worried about being one of the few families in their subdivision because construction had started on either side of their new home as well as across the street. It was a good thing they decided to buy when they did, as housing prices had skyrocketed. It was now a seller's market and woe unto the buyer. But high-priced housing hadn't seemed to stop people from migrating to the area. It was clear that the population was on the rise.

Valarie, Elise and Jack hardly noticed anything different than their norm. Elise had so many after school activities to keep her busy and Valarie was just as determined to get them moved into their house. By the time they both got home and got Jack situated, they were beat. Valarie decided to have Jack go to a doggy day care of sorts to ensure his mental health was ok. He seemed much better, friendlier, playful, and spent most of his time outside the crate when they were home now. Valarie had gone to see several listings and was close to deciding. She had already encouraged Elise to start packing. Elise was crestfallen. She had just made friends; her grades were top notch and she loved being a part of the softball team. Valarie assured Elise that they were staying in the area and that there was no need to change schools. She would even be close enough to visit the friends she had made in the complex. Elise was much happier once she heard that, but she wasn't thrilled about packing again.

CHAPTER 9

Dena and the New Neighbor

D ena was heading out to meet her girlfriends on a Saturday night when she noticed the lights were on in the unit next to hers. She peeked in the window and saw that furniture had already been moved in. The new renter had wonderful taste. She noted the rich, deep chocolate leather sofa and loveseat and the artwork that was already hanging. She continued walking down the path. She was pretty dolled up in a hot pink dress with multi-color wedge sandals that had bits of hot pink in them. The pink was a wonderful accent to her chocolate skin and the bag from Harrods sent to her by her best friend Donna made the outfit chic, summery and fun! Her path was blocked suddenly by an enormous dog who wanted very much to make Dena his new friend. Luckily the owners, a middle-aged couple, pulled the dog away from her. "I promise buddy, I will play with you later! Just not in this dress!" laughed Dena. The couple laughed and introduced themselves. Dena had never seen them before, but she knew they lived in the end unit on the 2nd floor. She figured they traveled a lot. Then the man complimented Dena on how great she smelled. She thanked him and waited till she was safely in the car before she mumbled "what the heck was that comment about?" Oh well, time to meet the girls and gallivant!

When Dena returned later that night, after a wonderful evening of communing, eating, and drinking with her sister-friends, she noticed that more furniture had been moved into the unit she had been spying on. She started to wonder if the apartment complex was going to use this apartment as a model, it was being put together so well. This unit had three bedrooms and the two guest rooms were visible from the parking lot along the path that Dena walked to get to her apartment. Both were fully furnished by the time Dena got home. The blinds were open, so she could clearly see the summer bedspreads with matching artwork. High quality, classic furnishings were in each room. The only minus was that the smaller bedroom had a terribly old-fashioned TV. The rooms didn't look like they were decorated for children at all. She wondered what the master bedroom looked like. This was the only room not visible from the front windows.

A few days later Dena met her neighbor. His name was Kelly and he worked as a pilot for a private company. He was tall, probably in his early 40's, and single. Dena made sure to get his stats in case any of her single girlfriends might be interested. He was good looking, white, with a decent build and church going. He said that he traveled quite a bit and would only be home a few nights a week. He had a home, but his wife had passed away and now that his kids were grown, he decided to downsize and try apartment living. Dena noted that it was just him in the apartment. She couldn't have asked for a more perfect neighbor – God-fearing, quiet, home a few nights a week, no unruly kids or animals running around. Kelly told her to stop by anytime and let him know if she needed anything. Dena complimented him on his decorating skills and told him to let her know if he needed anything. Kelly smiled and said, "Could you keep an eye on the place while I'm out of town?" Dena assured him that she would. They parted ways and continued with their Thursday evenings.

Early Friday morning, thunder struck hard and loud, so forceful that Dena's bedroom windows shook. It bought her out of a deep sleep. A storm was heading in strong and fast, the skies were gray, and the clouds were full to the bursting with rain. Dena was glad today was Friday. The weatherman was forecasting rain all weekend. Fall was here no matter what the calendar said, and she intended to read all weekend. She got up and started her morning ritual. She was toweling off from her shower when she first heard the rain. She heard the wind blowing and felt cool air come in through the open bathroom door. She was in the middle of brushing her teeth when she couldn't remember if she had left the windows in the living room open. Rain tended to get inside and run down the wall when the windows were open, so she raced out of the bathroom still damp holding her towel and was shocked to see her front door wide open. She noticed that the rain was pouring down as she quickly closed the door. Her windows were all closed tight. "How in the world did that happen?" she said out loud. "I am not that forgetful!" Her front door, which was the only way in or out, had two locks, a standard one and a security lock so that maintenance couldn't just walk in while she was home. She could see forgetting to lock one of the locks, but both seemed unlikely. Terror struck as she wondered if there was someone else in the apartment. She quietly walked to the kitchen and grabbed the biggest knife she had, still naked and holding her towel. She searched the rest of her place and found nothing. She even checked the shower even though she had just come from the bathroom. She rechecked the door to make sure it was locked and shrugged in disbelief. She quickly started getting ready for work. The rain had let up a bit and she wanted to have a sporting chance of getting to the car.

Dena was spooked by the incident with the door all during her workday. She kept trying to remember if she had left the door unlocked. She kept thinking, "Maybe one lock, but both? No way!" The whole thing reminded her of the spoon that she hadn't pulled out but somehow managed to make its way to the floor. She talked to her sister that evening and Liz said to pray or burn some sage. Dena thought it was a little too early for that, if things got any stranger, she would put both plans into effect. Liz was worried. They had grown up in Detroit, Michigan and knew better than to leave doors unlocked unwittingly. "Do you think someone was in there?" Liz asked. "No, I don't think so. Maybe I'm getting forgetful," replied Dena. And they both worried in silence. Liz dropped off a bible that weekend.

The worry faded for a while. The following Wednesday morning, Dena was again in the bathroom going through her morning ritual when she heard what sounded like a glass being put down hard on one of the tables in the living room. She froze; again, she was helpless with just a towel wrapped around her. She thought, "Why do these things happen when I'm naked?" She tried to convince herself that something had fallen over and gathered up her courage to go check it out. Not only was the coffee table clean and clear, but so were the two accent tables. Nothing was out of place. She checked the windows and the cabinet where the TV sat to be on the safe side. Everything was where it was supposed to be. Dena reached for the bible and started praying. She kept thinking how peculiar all this was, but her faith was strong, and she put her complete trust in God.

The next couple of days were peaceful at home but stressful at work. She had met a guy, but he lived out of state, so there were a lot of early morning and late-night calls. It seemed that no matter how hard Dena tried she just wasn't getting enough rest. Friday night she came home and changed into her pajamas. She hung her clothes in the closet and noticed a plastic hanger lying on the floor. An empty hanger was an anomaly considering how packed her closet was, but she was too tired to think about it. She closed the closet door and hung the hanger on the outside of the door, on the doorknob. She grabbed some dinner, tried to watch TV but kept nodding off. She gave up and went to bed. She turned on the TV in her bedroom so that it would lull her to sleep. It didn't take long at all for her to get to the boat to La-La Land. She was seated and enjoying the ride when a loud noise jerked her out of her sleep. She listened with her eyes closed and instinctively reached for the remote control thinking that the TV was too loud. Once the remote was in hand, she shut off the TV, but something was still making noise. SOMETHING was moving in the room.

The sound was coming from the closet; it was a steady, scraping noise. She quickly started to rationalize with her eyes still closed. Something must have shifted, after all the closet was packed. She opened her eyes and saw that the hanger she had placed on the door was swinging back and forth. "Oh my God! Is there someone in the closet?" she thought. She slowly got up from the bed and went to the kitchen to get a knife. She opened the refrigerator door to confuse her intruder and to cover up the noise of her getting the knife out of the drawer. It was a huge knife and she moved carefully with it. She didn't want to hurt herself. She went back to the bedroom and the hanger had just stopped moving. She placed her hand on the doorknob and was ready to open the door when she thought, "You know, the smart thing to do would be to leave or call the police. This is normally where the white girl gets killed in the story." Too late now, time to face the dragon, she opened the door slowly with the knife held out in front of her. She turned on the light switch just outside the door, muscles tense and ready to strike. She had the knife positioned at her middle, determined to hit major organs if need be. She looked in the closet, behind the clothes, expecting to see another pair of eyes. There was nothing there. She looked on the floor to see if maybe the intruder had crouched down. Still nothing there. In fact, all her clothes were in place and her shoes were nowhere near the door.

There was nothing that would have jarred the door and disturb the hanger. She checked the entire apartment and found nothing. "Maybe I have a new animal friend," she thought. Well, that would be easy to discover; she went to the cabinet and pulled out a few crackers then she reached into the refrigerator and pulled out some apple slices. She placed the food on the floor all over the apartment. She went back to bed exhausted. She noticed that the TV in the bedroom had been changed to a music station. The same music station that it had been on in the living room a while ago. The music was soothing so she left the TV on to comfort her. She went back to sleep after an hour.

After a day, Dana put away the crackers and apples because there were no signs of a rodent disturbing the food. The last thing she wanted was other uninvited pests.

Dena talked to Liz again and told her what happened with her possible new visitor. Liz came over that weekend to hang out. They ate, drank, talked, watched movies - nothing happened. Their biggest concern was if it was a furry friend - how did it get in the apartment? They checked the windows for breaks in the screens, they looked in corners to see if there were any spaces, they checked the cabinets for nests or shavings. They checked under the sinks to see if something was able to slip in from the plumbing. They found nothing. Everything was sealed.

Liz flopped back on the couch. "Well, looks like it's another mystery. Next time I'm bringing sage over!" Dena didn't shy away from the idea. "At this point, I'll try it. Either I'm losing my marbles or there is an entity here." Dena pinched her sister's cheeks lovingly. She thought, "I'm so glad she's here, even if she might think I'm crazy." Liz smacked Dena's hand and said, "I don't think you're crazy, but I am really starting to worry." Dena stared at Liz and marveled at the way they could sometimes read each other's thoughts. They laughed off the moment and went back to watching a movie.

The sun was starting to set when Liz said, "I better get on the road before it gets too dark." Dena made Liz a plate to take home with her. "So, do you have a hot date with Jon tonight? Hee hee!" Liz blushed and smiled. She had been dating Jon for over a year and she still blushed whenever Dena teased her. "Well, I guess that's a YES!" said Dena. "Let me walk you to your car. Man, can you believe it's fall already?" The sisters chatted away as they walked down the path to Liz's car. Liz unlocked the doors, so they could start piling in food and blankets. Liz always brought her favorite blankets with her. After everything was packed away, Liz remembered that she had a book for Dena. She opened the trunk to pull it out. Dena stood next to her and began surveying their surroundings. It was an old Detroit habit, checking your surroundings, making sure no one sneaks up on you. She glanced across the road and saw a light coming in from the trees. Liz closed the trunk and noticed her staring into the woods. "What? Did you see a bear?" Dena smirked, "Ha! Very funny! Look at that light. Do you see it?" Liz looked, and she noticed that there was light coming in through the trees in a way that was clearly not possible. Liz checked the sky and noted the position of the sun - it was to the west and the thick band of trees was to the east. They looked at each other and slowly walked across the road to the trees.

There was a path just at the edge of the road. They looked at each other. "Oh, well, it's time for an adventure Dena!" And with no hesitation Liz stepped onto the path. The trees had started to turn gold on the outer band but as they looked down the path and further into the woods, the trees were green, and they seemed to get darker the further in that they looked. But even stranger was the gold light shining from somewhere in the dark.

"Ok...but let's make this a short adventure. I know how you hate driving near the mall when it's dark and heavy with traffic." Liz nodded as Dena joined her on the path. They walked toward the dark, thick trees. It was cooler and calmer once they were truly on the path and that seemed strange to Dena. She wasn't a country girl by any means, but she was sure there should have been some birds or bugs making some kind of noise. It was still too warm for them to have gone in for hibernation. They walked in about a quarter of a mile and the light seemed no closer; in fact, it was dark all around them. The trees seemed to lean in toward them and there was an eerie creaking noise that seemed to surround them. They saw the evidence of others on the path...empty soda bottles, napkins, food wrappers and 2 golf carts much like the maintenance team in the apartment complex used to get around. Both carts were turned on their sides, abandoned, dirty with leaves caught in the seat crevices. They were still no closer to the light. "Dena, do you think it's a house?"

Dena focused on the light to see if she could see a structure surrounding it. And suddenly the light moved! The light moved, and it wasn't in a Sci-Fi sphere kind of movement way, it was more like someone picked up an object and put it somewhere else. Liz and Dena took off running toward the car. They literally ran from the darkness into the light. They stopped once they hit the road; no sense in getting hit by a car after being scared nearly to death. The sun was still a heavy presence in the sky, but in the woods, it seemed like the sun had already set. "Liz, houses don't move. I don't know what that was. New rule – no chasing strange lights into the forest."

"I agree Captain!" Liz faced her sister and hugged her tightly. She was even more worried after their journey in the forest. Dena hugged her back and sensed that her little sister was worried. She kissed her on the cheek and said, "Don't worry about me. If it truly gets too scary or crazy, I will move out. I don't think what's happening is a coincidence and I don't want to figure it out. I will be fine." She kissed her sister on the other check. "Now go home! You don't want to be late for your date!"

The weekend ended, and a new work week began. The leaves on the trees seemed to be turning colors in earnest now. Dena was having a stressful time at work, and she had just met a new prospective boyfriend the week before. She wasn't crazy about the long-distance part of the relationship, but he seemed nice enough.

One day, after a particularly grueling and tiresome day at work, while driving home, Dena's phone rang. She quickly answered it as it was her current beau calling to ask about her day, talk about his day, and making plans to meet. Dena felt her spirit lighten as she drove through the security gates and down the road heading to her apartment. She noticed the sun was setting and that the odd light that came from the forest during her and Liz's adventure had returned.

She dismissed it and focused on flirting with her new beau. She drove past two boys who were skateboarding in the parking lot, and she dismissed the dangers of that as well.

She was thankful she had a hands-free device, so she could maneuver easily down the road while talking on the phone. She parked her car and sat and talked and flirted for a good twenty minutes. She blocked everything else out. She didn't see the two boys get off the road, pick up their skateboards and walk into the woods down the path and out of sight into the darkness.

Dena left her car after the phone call and walked with a bounce to her apartment without a care. She didn't notice the trees making the familiar odd creaking noise as they had when she and her sister had been in the woods. The two boys came out of the woods a while later. They were dirty, sweaty, cold, and scared. They didn't run out, they walked as if they had been lost for days and had finally found their way back home. Their clothes were torn and ragged and they had cuts and bruises from where the branches and twigs had torn at their skin. One had lost his skateboard completely; the other's board was split in half; it was dangerously jagged with splinters. They were brothers and when they returned home, they were scolded and told never to go into the woods again. Their story about strange lights, sounds and shadows was not believed. They were punished and were grateful to be told they could not leave the area without having a parent with them until further notice. No need to worry about their skateboards as that activity had been banned until further notice as well.

CHAPTER 10

Elise

Elise was at home packing mid-morning Saturday. Her mom was out running errands and was going to meet some friends for a quick bite. Jack was at the groomer's; he had gotten caught in some brambles that were quite sticky. Elise and her mom tried to get them out, but the thorns and bits of twig were stuck deep in his fur. They gave up and sent him in to be professionally cleaned and pampered. So, Elise was at home alone with nothing to do but organize and pack.

She figured she would start with her spring and summer clothes since the weather was cool. Shorts in one pile, tank tops in another, summer dresses in a third and swimsuits and pool towels in a 4th pile. She did not want to pack her flip flops yet even though she had been wearing socks for the past few days. She was still holding on to the last remnants of summer. She moved about folding and unfolding clothes, wondering if she should pack accessories, labeling and packing boxes. Sealing and unsealing the boxes as she found other items that needed to be put in them. She became hungry after a time and went to the kitchen to grab a sandwich. She grabbed a pot and put some water in it to boil some eggs. She sat the pot on the stove and went to grab eggs out of the refrigerator. She was about to reach into the fridge when she saw that her mom had already made tuna salad; sometimes it freaked her out that her mom knew her so well. She grabbed the bowl; her mom's tuna salad was the best. She made a sandwich and grabbed some chips. She emptied the water out of the pot and ate quickly. She grabbed a fruit drink to take with her back to the bedroom; she was falling behind schedule and wanted to be done by 4pm so she could go to a movie with friends. She closed the bedroom door behind her out of habit and put her headphones on, so she could concentrate. She went through her drawers and closet taking out light t-shirts, shorts, and pants. She took out all summer dress tops and dress skirts. She marveled at herself - when did she start dressing like an adult? Well, that was a question for another day; back to folding, packing, taping, and labeling. She moved several boxes into the hallway as the space was getting tighter and tighter in her room. She went into the closet and started working on her shoes.

A song that she liked came on and she turned up the volume on her headphones. The next song was one of her favorites as well, so she kept the volume up high. She danced and moved rhythmically around the room and back into the closet as she packed.

Out in the kitchen, the pot on the stove started to boil even though Elise had poured all but a few drops of water out of it. The eye on the stove was on high. It didn't take long for the eye to glow orange and for the pot to become bone dry and turn orange as well. Gray and black smoke quickly billowed from the stove to the ceiling tickling at the smoke detector which refused to blare a warning. The hard plastic handle on the pot began to melt and drip onto the stove. The hot liquid fell onto the eye making a series of loud popping sounds.

Elise was still in her closet with her headphones on unaware of what was happening the next room over. She thought she heard a noise and took her headphones off to listen. "Mom!? Are you back?" There was no answer; so, she put her headphones back on and went back to work singing and dancing to yet another one of her favorite songs. She worried over which shoes to pack. The fall formal was coming up and she had a lovely pair of orchid-colored sandals she wanted to wear to it.

The fire engulfed the rest of the eyes on the stove and started creeping up the wall behind the stove, embracing the microwave. The smoke detector held firm and would not sound. The orange flames, bright and blistering, were almost at the ceiling, having passed over the melted and mutilated microwave. Smoke billowed like a factory chimney into the kitchen, the hallway and master bedroom. It skulked slowly toward Elise's bedroom as if it wanted to trap her until she had absolutely no escape. Gradually, tendrils of smoke drifted underneath Elise's door. It was at this moment that she decided to take a break and get a quick drink from the bottle she had bought with her into the room a short while ago. She stepped out of the closet and felt immediately that something was wrong. She reached for the bottle on her dresser and took the top off to take a drink. She took a sip and smelled a strange electrical smell. She gulped and then coughed and turned to face the door. She took off her headphones, as she saw the smoke drifting under the door. The smoke detector finally decided to sing out. She walked toward the door and touched to see if it was hot. Luckily, the door was cool. She took a moment and gathered herself, so she would be ready to run. She opened the door slowly and saw that the fire was coming from the kitchen. Smoke was pouring into the living room. She hesitated for a moment and ran to the kitchen where she saw that the stove and wall were on fire. She saw the drywall melting under the heat and she abandoned the thought of grabbing the fire extinguisher and ran at full speed out the front door. Thankfully, her phone was in her back pocket, so she called the Fire Department and then her mom. She remained calm and told her mom what happened. She was positive that she never turned the stove on; she didn't know how the fire started. She sat on the grass and cried after she hung up with her mom. She could hear the fire trucks coming down the main road and neighbors started coming out to see what was going on.

Dena heard the fire alarm but figured that someone had burned their lunch. It wasn't until she smelled the smoke that she became worried. She ran outside and saw smoke billowing out of the unit next to her. She saw Elise sitting on the ground across from the apartment at the base of the hill trying to compose herself. Dena went back into the apartment and grabbed a bottle of water and headed back out to comfort Elise. She could hear the fire trucks coming so she felt a bit of relief.

Dena put a hand on Elise's shoulder and said, "Hiya, I'm Dena. Are you okay? Here, have some water."

Elise looked up at the smiling, friendly face of Dena and said, "Hi, I'm Elise. I think I accidentally set the apartment on fire." Then she burst out in tears.

Dena took Elise's hand and said, "Well, good job! But next time you're practicing fire safety make sure it's in a more controlled environment." Elise doubled over in laughter and Dena laughed with her. Dena sat on the ground with Elise. They could hear the firemen coming to see what was going on. No words were needed as the smoke continued to flow out of the apartment. Two firemen ran in, and Elise burst into tears again. Dena hugged her and told her everything would be okay. "It was an accident. It could have happened to anyone. Don't worry. You're okay, that's all that matters." Elise got herself under control and saw that more neighbors were coming around to see what happened. Everyone was friendly and gave words of encouragement or shared similar stories of near misses.

A fireman finally came to question Elise. Elise held on to Dena's hand tightly as she explained what happened. Dena smiled and looked at Elise with all the care that she would give a little sister. Dena kept thinking, "Poor baby, a few more seconds and she might not have made it out." Dena heard someone running and turned to see a woman who had to be Elise's mother running at top speed with worry and terror on her face. The woman grabbed Elise and held her tight. "Baby, are you okay?"

"Yes, Mama. I don't know what happened. I didn't turn the stove on, at least I don't remember doing it. I'm sorry Mama," and then Elise burst into tears again. "It's okay, Baby. I'm just glad you're okay."

The fire was out, Elise was in good hands, so Dena decided to go back to her apartment. "Ma'am? Ma'am?" Dena turned toward Valarie and moved toward her. "Thank you for staying with my baby. I'm sure she was terrified."

"Oh, she handled it like a champ! Apparently, a few of the other neighbors have had some close calls with the stoves. I'm Dena and very pleased to meet you both."

Elise hugged Dena and said, "Thanks for making me laugh, it really helped me a lot." Dena hugged her back and said, "No big deal - just be careful. "

"Mrs. Alvarez, your daughter didn't leave the stove on." Dena could only assume that this was the head fireman on the scene. "The knob was clearly in the off position, and I don't think your daughter was calm or crazy enough to go back and put it in "OFF" while that fire was going." He winked at Elise. "Looks like the unit was faulty in some way; we are still investigating it." Elise had let go of Dena. Dena looked at Elise and Valarie in complete puzzlement. "Well, there have been some strange things happening here. Probably a ghost," Dena said and then she giggled nervously. "Well, Elise - you and your mom take care. I will come and check on you in a day or two. Please come by if you need anything."

CHAPTER 11

Larry and Annette

L arry and Annette were at their new home when the fire broke out in the unit beneath them. The house was nearly complete inside and out. All that was left to do was carpeting, painting, and landscaping. They walked around the four- bedroom house and made furniture and decorating plans. The master bedroom was large enough to put a couch in. There was also a fireplace and garden tub with jets in the master suite. They surveyed all the rooms and came to the bedroom closest to their room. "Well, we already have an office and places for us both to hang out separately," said Annette. "What shall we do with this room?" Larry looked at the room and said, "Well it's too small to be another guest room and too close to our room for that as well." Larry walked around the room thinking in earnest while Annette watched and smiled. She let out a giggle and Larry turned to her. "What's so funny?"

Annette beamed, "I'm pregnant!" And with that the couple christened the house in true style.

CHAPTER 12

Valarie and Elise

Valarie and Elise went into the apartment and opened every window to try to get all the smoke out. They packed an overnight bag and decided to stay at a hotel for a night or two. Valarie had her own reasons behind spending a couple of nights away. She wondered if the fire wasn't an accident. What if her husband or his sister had something to do with it? She made a call to her brother while Elise put Jack in the car with his crate. "Are you sure he hasn't made any contact with his sister?" "No, Valarie," sighed Benjamin, "Nick has actually been in solitary confinement for the past few weeks. He got into a fight with a guard and took a big chunk out of the guard's arm with his teeth. I don't think he had anything to do with this. As for his sister, let me do some digging. I will call you later. Love you, Sis, and stay safe."

"Love you too, Ben." She put the burner phone in her back pocket and made a note to throw it away on the way to the hotel. She didn't know if she should be relieved or worried. Was the fire a legitimate accident or was someone behind it? She hoped that for once it was just a freak accident.

As it turned out, Ben was right. There was nothing connecting Valarie's ex-husband or his sister to the fire. In fact, it appeared that the ex-sister-in-law had given up on stalking Valarie and Elise altogether. She received word from her sister that Elena had left the states and was living with a tribe in the West Indies. Elena had been gone for months. Valarie was relieved; she began to relax. She was happy to focus on moving again.

The fire department, leasing office and insurance agencies were all puzzled. No one could pinpoint how the fire started. The only thing they knew for sure was that Elise had not turned the stove on. Repairs were nearly complete. The apartment smelled like fresh paint finally. Elise and Valarie had done everything to get the horrible electrical burning smell out of the kitchen. All the other rooms were back to normal after a couple of days, except for the kitchen. The fire had also charred the side of the refrigerator which was replaced quickly along with the microwave and oven.

Elise didn't want to touch the new stove. She was terrified that it might explode. "How do we know that this one doesn't have a glitch, Mom? I'm just saying, better safe than sorry. I can live off cold sandwiches until we move."

Valarie smiled at the thought of not having to cook for a while, "Honey, what are the odds? It was a freak accident. We will be fine. I'm going to make pancakes for dinner just to prove it to you."

And they had pancakes, and everything was fine.

CHAPTER 13

Dena

As the days went by Dena saw the stove and microwave that had been completely singed were placed outside of Valarie and Elise's unit. The charred remains sent chills up Dena's spine. Elise was lucky to have made it out. As promised, Dena went over to check on them but, they were not at home. She left a note and plate of brownies. She hoped that Elise had recovered from the scare.

October came, and the weather turned cool in earnest. Dena pulled out her fall weather clothes and boots. She loved this time of year. She changed the bedding on her bed to heavy comforters and pulled her thick blankets off the shelving in the laundry room. The heat was turned on and she was happy to find that it worked better than the air conditioning. That first whiff of heat was familiar and comforting. She was still exhausted from work and took every opportunity to sleep. Her long-distance romance fizzled out and she was taking a break from dating. She was still getting a few hits online but nothing very interesting yet.

CHAPTER 14

Annette and Larry

The next few weeks were filled with packing and cleaning. They gave most of their furniture away as they were getting new things. They had heard about the fire and were even more anxious to move. The smoke from the fire had invaded their living space. They had to air their apartment out for a few days to get the smell out. Annette used so much lemon cleaner to get the place clean that Larry almost missed the smell of smoke. They couldn't wait to be in their own home, away from pesky accidental fires started by neighbors, loud music and arguing. And they had a baby on the way. Life was wonderful, and they could hardly wait to start this new chapter.

Surprisingly, their closing was a breeze, and they were able to move in during the middle of October. It was a crisp, cool Friday morning when the moving truck arrived, well, more like a moving van. They mostly had electronics and a few keepsakes to put in it. Both sets of parents came out to help them move and get settled in. Larry and his dad wrestled one of the 3 big screen TVs into the van while Annette and her parents packed up the rest of the kitchen items. Larry's mom swept and cleaned the rooms that had been packed up. Really there was nothing to sweep, Annette had swept and scrubbed all the floors very thoroughly. She didn't want to impose too much on her parents or in-laws.

Annette looked out the kitchen window for the last time and she felt happiness and for some reason relief. The stay in the apartment had nearly ruined her marriage and for what? There was no real explanation to be had. Suddenly, all she wanted to do was finish packing and get to the new house. She hadn't told her parents about the baby yet and she figured she could wait another week or two. She liked having this secret with only her, Larry, and the baby in on it.

"Ewwww! Annette! Did you know that there is a ton of cat hair on the hall closet floor? Whew - and boy does it stink!" her mother-in-law called out.

Annette froze. The cat was never allowed in that area of the apartment. In fact, now that she recalled, the cat steered clear of that closet. Then she thought, "How is that possible? I just cleaned that closet two days ago!" Annette walked quickly toward the closet, certain that her mother-in-law was playing a joke on her. But how would she know about the cat hair argument?

"Constance? Let me see! I can't believe - ", Annette opened the closet door and to her horror the floor was indeed covered with what looked to be cat hair except the hair was all black. She turned on the closet light to make sure and she smelled something awful. She ran to the guest bathroom and hurled. Constance ran to the kitchen to get a cloth for her. While Constance was in the kitchen Annette's mom came to comfort her in the bathroom. "Honey? Are you okay? Here, let me give you some water." Annette's mom offered her a cup of water she brought with her from her journey from the kitchen. It was like she instinctively knew what to do, as moms do sometimes. Annette rinsed out her mouth in the sink and took small sips of water. Constance returned with a wet towel for Annette and sensed that the two women needed a private moment, so she went back to the kitchen to help finish cleaning up there.

"Mom!" Annette sobbed. "Something has been in the apartment." She nodded toward the closet. Their cat's hair was grey and black. Annette's mother looked at her daughter, worried, brow furrowed, and tried to make sense of what she was saying. She pressed the towel to Annette's forehead and then to her neck. "Stay here dear, I will take a look."

Grace went to the closet and stood in front of it for a moment. The door was closed but she felt like something might leap out at her if she opened the door. She was puzzled by this feeling. She called out to Constance, "Hey Connie! Can you bring me a broom and the mop bucket from the kitchen?" Grace opened the door and the smell hit her immediately. She took a step back and coughed. She took the bandana from her back pocket and placed it over her nose and mouth. Constance arrived just at that moment with the broom, mop, and bucket. "I will go check on Annette," said Connie as she brushed past Grace and headed to the bathroom Annette was in.

Grace opened the closet door again and the smell was much easier to bear with the bandana covering her face. She swept the closet twice to make sure she got every hair up. Annette was right, the hair on the floor didn't match the hair on the cat at all. Did some animal come in here and shed all this hair? It would have had to have been more than one animal. That just didn't seem possible. Grace exhausted all the possibilities of how this might have happened while she thoroughly mopped the floor with a disinfectant cleaner. She heard someone moving behind her and realized it was Annette.

"Honey, stay back. This cleaner is pretty strong." She stole a look at Annette. "We don't want anything to make you or the baby sick," she whispered. Grace turned and winked at Annette. Annette smiled and put her finger to her lips in a shushing motion. Mother and daughter stood there looking like copies of each other. They said nothing more about the closet. The three women finished packing and cleaning just as the men drove up for the final load. And in a few moments Annette and Larry were officially moved out.

CHAPTER 15

Dena

Dena made plans with Liz to have their annual Halloween Scare Fest, which consisted of two days and one night of scary movies, gaming, food, drinks, and festive desserts. This year they were spending it at Liz's place. Dena grabbed her bag which she had packed a couple of days before. She grabbed a jacket and would check to make sure she had a blanket in the car. She opened her front door and saw that Elise had returned the brownie plate. There was a card wrapped in a bow on the plate. Dena beamed and placed the plate in the kitchen. She put the card in her bag, locked up, double checked the lock (doesn't hurt to be too careful) and headed to her car.

She ran into Kelly and had a brief conversation with him. He was going to be home for the next few weeks. He had to have back surgery and would be out of commission for a while. Dena asked if he needed anything and he said "No, I have a lady friend that will be staying with me, and my daughter is a nurse. She will be coming to check on me too." "Okay, but if anything fails just bang on the wall and I will come running," Dena giggled. Kelly laughed and told her to have a great weekend.

And she did. Scary movies, cupcakes shaped like ghosts and bats. Lots of conversation with her sister. A few drinks and some much-needed rest. She came home early Sunday morning to a quiet apartment. She put her bag down and pulled out her phone charger. She came across the envelope from Elise. She had completely forgotten about it. The card said that they were moving this weekend and to please come by on Saturday to say goodbye. Dena was crestfallen. She had missed them completely. Luckily, Elise left her cell phone number and Dena texted her immediately to apologize. Elise replied and said that she would invite Dena over as soon as they were settled in. Dena told her to be sure to come by for Halloween if she and her mom were in the area. Elise was going to a party in the complex, so she would be sure to stop by. They said their farewells and continued with their days.

For Dena, that meant more scary movies and decorations for Halloween in her apartment. She missed her sister; it was a lot less lonely when they lived together. Dena pushed the sadness away and got into the spirit of the season. She watched movies and checked her online dating accounts. She responded to some messages and saw some interesting prospects. Liz called, and they talked on the phone for an hour even though they had just seen each other that morning. She asked Liz to come over next Saturday, the day before Halloween. "You can help me scare up the joint," giggled Dena. Liz agreed to come. "I have a date, but I can come in the morning and leave about 3pm." They continued talking for a few more minutes and eventually said farewell and continued with their day. It was still early, and Dena was able to watch a few more scary movies and play some video games. She continued to send messages to perspective beaus during movie and gaming breaks. She eventually sunk into the cool Sunday afternoon, had leftovers from Saturday that she bought from Liz's house and went to bed.

Dena's week was quiet. Work stayed steady in that it was mostly chaotic and she had to keep her firefighting skills honed. She was able to sleep well, the apartment above her was still vacant. She did meet a man who lived close by. They had gone from talking online to texting in as little as a few days. He seemed nice. She hoped he would ask her on a date soon. She still had a couple of other suitors she messaged with online. Friday had arrived, and she went to bed early in anticipation of Liz's arrival.

Saturday went by quickly. Liz and Dena spent the day hanging paper pumpkins and decorating the windows with cotton cobwebs and glow-in-the-dark stickers. Dena had bought a plastic cauldron to hold candy. The girls laughed and talked and decorated. Soon it was time for Liz to head back home. Dena felt sad as soon as she got back to the apartment from walking Liz to her car. She wondered if this was normal. She used to like being alone from time to time when she and Liz lived together. She wondered if the apartment was causing her to feel so depressed. She flopped on the couch and her phone alerted her. She thought it might be Liz; maybe she forgot something. No, it was Chris, her new beau. He asked if she was free to talk. She happily messaged back that she was available. Seconds later her phone rang, and she had a great conversation with him. At the end of the call Chris asked if they could meet in person next Saturday and Dena said, "Yes."

Dena was so content. She felt really calm. She watched another movie and hoped that she would get a bunch of trick or treaters on Halloween. She went to bed about midnight and quickly drifted to sleep. A little while later she awoke to a knock at the door. It was 1:30 in the morning! Dena slipped out of bed and over to the bedroom window. She slowly, quietly, and carefully lifted the blind to see who was at the front door. She stared for a few seconds in shock. It was a man in shorts staring at her front door. It was someone she recognized! He turned to look up the hill and she got a quick glimpse of his face. It was Kelly! Dena went to the door to let him in, but he was gone. She looked down the path in both directions, but it was like he disappeared into thin air. She grabbed some shoes and walked over to his apartment where she found his front door wide open. The lights were on, and his apartment looked as cozy as ever. She called out to him, "Kelly! Kelly! Hey Kelly!? Are you okay?" She listened and she could hear the faint sounds of music playing. The music appeared to be coming from the master bedroom. The one room she couldn't see from the front door. The music seemed to be playing loud. She wondered if Kelly couldn't hear her calling for him with the music up so loud and with the door closed.

She remembered Kelly saying that he was going to have back surgery. She remembered him saying that someone would be staying with him. The apartment seemed to be empty. Dena walked the length of the path to see if anyone was inside. The blinds were open and the light from the living room reached into the guest bedrooms enough so she see that Kelly wasn't in either of them. Everything else was dark.

Dena walked around the path to the front side of the unit where Kelly's bedroom was located. The blinds to the bedroom window were open and the lights were on. Dena could hear the music faintly, but she saw no signs of Kelly; even the master bathroom light was on. Kelly was nowhere to be found. The apartment was empty. Dena had already noted that his truck was still parked in his normal parking space as she walked up the path to the side where his bedroom was visible.

She thought maybe he was heavily medicated and sleepwalking. She thanked God that he hadn't tried to drive in what appeared to be a complete medically induced stupor. She jogged back to his apartment entrance. The door was still open. She shivered as she reached for the doorknob. She called out one last time, "Kelly?!" No response. So, she closed the door and got back on the path leading to her apartment.

She walked slowly listening for any sound or sign of Kelly. She looked down the path as far as she could, but there was no one there. It was dead quiet. She walked past Elise and Valarie's apartment, which was still vacant. She looked in every corner and around every bush and tree thinking he might have collapsed from the drugs. After about fifteen minutes she headed back to her house. She checked Kelly's apartment one last time hoping that he had wandered back home on his own, but he had not. She walked back to her apartment and unlocked the door. She kept looking all around, looking for any sign of her neighbor.

Once inside she pondered what to do. Call the police? Was this an emergency? What if he's drunk and just doing "white boy" things? She didn't want him to get into trouble. She took off her shoes, so she could think better. His truck is here, he couldn't have walked too far. The area is safe; so, I don't think anyone would hurt him. But what if he wandered into the woods? He could fall and hurt himself. She looked at her front door and knew instantly that she was not going into the woods. She looked at her shoes and confirmed with her heart and mind that she was not going into the woods. She walked into her bedroom to grab a jacket convincing herself that she was a smart woman and that there was no reason for her to go into the woods. She decided she would call the non-emergency police if... suddenly, she heard a noise outside. She ran to the bedroom window and peeked outside. It was Kelly! He was barefoot and walking with a strange gait and an uneven pace back to his apartment. Dena ran to the front door just in time to see Kelly walk into his apartment and close the door behind him. His face was completely blank. She had her answer. He was safe. Time for bed. As she climbed into bed, she heard a hard cold rain start to fall. Thank goodness Kelly came home. She would have been wandering around looking for him in the haunted woods in the cold rain. Great way to spend Halloween.

When Dena awoke, it was raining even harder. She got dressed and grabbed an umbrella and a Halloween goodie bag. She walked down the path to Kelly's apartment to make sure he was okay. She knocked nervously, she still had not adjusted to southern ways. In the north, you minded your business, and in the gritty city whatever happened, happened, and it was no one else's concern. She heard someone stirring inside. She could hear slow and heavy footsteps heading to the door. It took at least two minutes for Kelly to make it to the door and open it. Dena noticed a blanket on the couch as he opened the door. She looked up at Kelly and he looked dog tired. He smiled at Dena, "Hey Dena! You alright?"

"I'm alright! I was just worried about you. I think you were sleepwalking last night, and you knocked on my door. I just came to check on you and give you some Halloween treats."

Kelly looked absolutely puzzled. He shook his head and winced in pain. "I didn't leave the house last night. I fell asleep on the couch and my back is killing me."

It was Dena's turn to be puzzled. She started again slowly and softly, "Kelly, I went to my door and answered it, but you were gone. I walked over here, and your door was wide open. You weren't here, so I closed the door and looked for you around the path."

"Darlin', you sure you're feeling, okay? I've been asleep on the couch since about 6pm yesterday." But he didn't seem quite sure of himself.

Dena shrugged, "Well, maybe it was someone else. Or maybe it was a Halloween prank. Anyway, are you in a lot of pain? Is there anything you need?" She watched as he stumbled to shift his weight. Out of instinct she reached out and grabbed him gently around his waist to keep him from banging into the door. He leaned on her as she walked him back to the couch. She gently sat him down. She put the bag on the table. "Are you even supposed to be up?"

Kelly winked. "Probably not but I can't sit still forever." He was looking through the bag of candy and smiling. "Could you get me a glass of milk to go with this candy feast?" They both laughed. "Now that, I can do."

Dena spent the rest of Halloween on her couch watching horror movies and Halloween specials. She got a call from Chris, and they talked for some time. She received a message from Elise saying that the Halloween party had been canceled because of the rain and that she would stay in touch. Liz called too. Her Halloween was a bust as far as trick or treaters.

Dena's was as well. "I guess the kids only go to houses down here," said Dena. "I'm going to have to take all this candy to work tomorrow. Oh, my goodness, Liz I forgot to tell you what happened with my neighbor last night! I can't believe I forgot!" The girls laughed and talked for hours while the cold rain continued to fall. Dena suddenly realized that they missed each other equally. The conversation was winding down when Liz said, "Just beware of neighbors wandering about at night."

"I just don't get what that was about. I mean, I know I didn't imagine it. He must have been under some serious medication," said Dena.

"Well, he's never done anything creepy like that before, right? It probably was just the drugs, "said Liz.

Dena hesitated, and Liz could tell something was on her mind. "Dena, did something else happen?"

"Yes, but it was weeks ago and perfectly explainable. Remember that day I stayed home because I was feeling sick? Well, I heard Kelly leave early that morning to go to work – heard him start up his truck and take off." Liz listened quietly, and Dena continued. "A couple of hours later, I heard weird music blasting just out of nowhere. I was in my bed, and it came booming through the walls on Kelly's side. I mean it startled me so that I jumped up." Dena stopped because she knew the next part might be kind of hard to believe. "So, I waited a few minutes thinking that maybe Kelly came home for lunch, but the music kept on blaring. I didn't have a choice but to call Kelly, I didn't want him to get in trouble with the property management company. He had given me his cell number in case anything happened. Luckily, he had landed about 30 minutes before and had a couple of hours of down time before his next flight. He said it would take him about 20 minutes to get home. The music was so loud, I didn't hear his truck or him opening the door. I did hear a kind of a thud which I assumed was Kelly fumbling his way around the apartment to turn off the music." Dena stopped talking and Liz could tell she was thinking. Liz waited patiently for Dena to find her words. "Liz, the music didn't stop after the thud. I guess Kelly was held up in traffic because he didn't arrive until 15 minutes after I heard the thud. I only knew he was home because that's when the music shut off. I waited, and I heard Kelly moving around and he let out a sound that sounded like he was puzzled. I thought he might come over and say something, but he left. I figured he was on a tight schedule." Dena paused again. "I've been thinking that maybe something fell over because of the vibration of the music, but I never heard Kelly shift back in place anything while he was there. But what's strange is that Kelly never plays his music that loudly, and it was the same song playing repeatedly. And I remember the song, but it was from when we were kids. In fact, I remember the first and only time I heard it was at the church in Dickson on a scorching hot Sunday. It said something about the light or there's a light...I can't remember." Now it was Liz's turn to be silent and gather her thoughts and words. "Liz? Are you there?"

Liz let out a deep sigh. "You're talking about 'There's a Light'. The song is called, 'There's a Light'. It goes, 'There's a light in my life shining over me, there's a light in my life shining over me'. That's all I can remember. It was sung at a funeral we went to in Dickson. I can't remember who died but it was a relative and whoever it was, was far too young to be dead. It wasn't from natural causes."

"How do you remember this? You had to have been a toddler when this happened." Dena was beyond confused.

"I remember because Mama didn't want me to go in the church. She didn't want me to see a dead body at such a young age. I was so excited, and I wanted to see all the people. I think it was my first time visiting Dickson. I remember hearing the song play, because it was so loud, and I think it was a favorite song of the person who died. We sat under a tree, and it was sweltering hot. It was so still and peaceful and then that song chased all the quiet away. Dena, that is either weird or a huge coincidence. I don't remember ever hearing that song since that day."

"This is just too strange Liz. I can't believe you remembered something from so long ago. Is this more than a coincidence?" Liz and Dena thought in silence. After a few moments, Dena sighed and said, "Well, I guess I need to start looking for a house. I can't keep living in weirdness and fear."

"Yeah, and whatever you do, don't tell Mama. You don't want to worry her. I will help you look, but are you sure you want a house?"

Dena thought for a moment and said, "I think so, maybe we could move back in together. You don't have to decide now, but just maybe. Well, I guess I better get some sage and start burning it. Oh shoot, will that set off the smoke detectors?"

The girls laughed and talked for a while longer before hanging up, both a little shaken and worried. Dena talked to Chris later that night and the conversation made her feel better. Their first date was scheduled for next Saturday. They were both really excited about it. It was strange, but it almost seemed like the happier she was, the less weird things were around the apartment. Dena began to wonder if there was a direct relationship between how she felt and the things happening in the apartment. Could that be all that it was? Did she just need to be happy? Interesting thought. And with her happy feelings about her family, friends, and a new man in her life, she went to bed and slept peacefully. She was quite the hero at work the next day with her huge bowl of candy. Not to mention it was the good candy.

Dena spent the rest of the week taking down the Halloween decorations. She wondered if she should get a Christmas tree. But where would she put it? Her place was small but very cozy. She also spent time trying to figure out the perfect outfit to wear for her date with Chris. Not to mention, she needed to start packing for her trip home to Detroit for Thanksgiving. She was happy and excited about it all. Work was still a downer but at least it was steady. She had so much to look forward to that she had forgotten about all the strange events that had been happening. Even her TV had gotten back on the Dena train and had stopped changing channels on its own in the middle of the night.

Saturday was here before she knew it. She selected some blue jeans, a black turtleneck, and black calf-high boots to wear on her date. They decided to meet at one of those chain restaurants that you see on TV where everyone is smiling and happy. She looked at herself in the mirror. She put on very little make-up and put her hair up in a bun. She put on her favorite black winter jacket with a belt, grabbed her purse and was on her way. She was still really excited about the date. She met Chris and he was sweet, funny, and smart. They talked for hours and then they went to his apartment and watched a movie. Dena couldn't believe she was going to his apartment so soon, but she felt comfortable and happy. They kissed and had a great time. It was past midnight when Dena left. Chris walked her to her car and told her to call him once she got home. They kissed again and Dena started home. She listened to her favorite songs on her music app and sang along to the music. She felt happy. She thought about all the good things in her life. How well her friends and family were doing. She felt like she was floating on a cloud. She entered the gate to the complex and drove to her usual parking spot. She couldn't stop smiling and she felt so thankful. She parked, got out of the car, and walked down the path. Everything was dark and still. She probably would have felt nervous any other time, but she was so happy that she barely noticed the quiet. In fact, she was grateful for the silence. There had been far too much negative energy -- or was it evil? - going on. She didn't want to use the word "evil"- there hadn't been any demon manifestations or deaths. Just a lot of weird, unexplainable things. She locked her door and went to the apartment phone to call Chris and let him know she got home safely. The phone rang before she could pick it up. It was Chris! "Hey! Just wanted to make sure you got home okay. It was getting pretty late, and I hadn't heard from you." Dena beamed and floated even higher. "Yes, I'm fine. I really had a great time." Dena and Chris talked for thirty minutes more and made plans to go out the following Saturday.

CHAPTER 16
Kelly

Kelly was still healing from his surgery. He slept a lot and took meds to stave off the pain. He didn't like taking pain pills, he knew how easy it was to become dependent on them. He had seen more than a few pilots let their drinking and abuse of pain meds get out of control. He saw how it could destroy careers and families and promised himself he would never let any substance ruin his life. He loved flying and couldn't imagine what his life would be like if he couldn't work.

The pain was unreal; he hated to admit it, but the pain meds were a blessing. He had to take them on the hour, every few hours or else the pain would come back lightning hot and in full force. To make matters worse there was no one to watch out for him. He and his lady friend were on the outs and his daughter was called out of town due to a shortage of nurses at another hospital. She would be back in a few days, and she called to check on him daily, but she was worried about him being by himself for too long.

Kelly laid down and tried to get comfortable. He could feel the meds taking over. He cut his dosage down to fight off addiction as well as the strange dreams he had been having. At least he thought they were dreams. Some seemed too real at times. He closed his eyes and tried to play back what he thought had happened over the past two weeks. His memory was scattered and full of holes. He thought he was dreaming most of the time until his next-door neighbor came by and said she saw him sleepwalking. He had never walked in his sleep in his life, or he just wasn't ready to admit to it. Dena's claim scared him. He tried not to let on, but it explained some things that had happened that night. Well, if he was honest with himself, it wasn't just that night.

Kelly reminded himself that his neighbor Dena was sweet and kind to put up with all the noise that had been going on in his apartment. Things had a habit of turning themselves on and off. Arguments that sprang up out of nowhere between him and his lady, Beth. The last one was so bad that she told him it was a good thing his daughter was coming to take care of him because she was done. His daughter had even said that he didn't seem himself lately and that was before the surgery. He figured it was nerves and stress. Being a pilot is wonderful but there is a certain amount of stress to it - even though it hadn't really bothered him before now. Then there was the stress of moving and getting used to a new place. But he knew deep down he was fooling himself. Things had been off since the first night of him moving in.

He remembered that first night. He remembered how great the place looked for the most part. Beth, his lady friend, had done all the decorating. She had gotten most of the furniture and decorations at a huge discount or at cost. He would have spent double or triple if Beth hadn't helped him. He had just finished putting his clothes away in the master bedroom; the second batch of movers had left about 20 minutes earlier. He walked from the bedroom, turning off the lights, stopped in the living room and turned off all the lights in the kitchen as well. He left one small lamp on in the living room so he would be able to see when he got back. He wanted to grab something to eat and make sure he locked up his old house and put the keys in the lockbox for the realtor. As he was closing the door he thought, "I wonder if I should close the blinds? Naaah, nobody can see anything with just the lamp on. Plus, I'll only be gone 20 minutes at most." He locked the door and walked down the path. He investigated the windows of his unit from the outside and smiled. "Nope, can't see a thing except a shadow of the furniture here and there." He heard a dog up ahead and saw a woman sidestepping the huge beast., The dog seemed friendly enough, but it was huge. Kelly hated dogs, had hated them since he was bitten as a kid. He waited a moment to see if he was going to have to rush in and save the woman in the bright pink dress. But she held her own, and the owners were close by. Next thing he knew, the woman in the dress was in her car backing out. That was the first time that Kelly had lost track of time, it was like he was lost in a daydream for a moment. He shook it off and walked down the path. He got in his truck and drove to his old home. He went in and turned on the lights to see if he had missed anything. He still had a couple of days before he had to turn the place over to the realtor. The new family was slated to move in three weeks later even though the closing was scheduled for the upcoming week. He wandered from room to room – the place was completely empty and clean. He shut off all the lights except for the one on the porch which was solar powered. He put his keys in the lockbox that hung just above the doorbell. He checked the door one last time to make sure the place was locked up tight and walked to his truck.

Kelly was hungry. It was just him tonight as Beth was out of town working on a remodeling project for a wealthy client. She still had her own place, which worked out great because they both travelled so much. Kelly started pondering all the restaurants in the area. He wanted a burger, just not a fast food one. He stopped at one of the chain steakhouse places on the main road heading back to the apartment and went inside. He eyed the menu for a few minutes and the waitress behind the bar took his order. The place was busy; it was a Friday night, and the game was on. He sat at the bar and ordered a beer to sip on while he waited for his steak burger. He had drunk nearly all of it when the waitress returned with a smile and his piping hot burger and fries in a to-go bag. "Thank you, darlin'! You have a great evening." He winked at her like he winked at all pretty girls and went on his way. He was home about five minutes later.

He grabbed his food and hopped out of his truck. He headed down the trail, looked up and stopped dead in his tracks. The lights were on in his apartment. He walked faster; maybe Beth had come back from her trip early. She was the only other person that had a key. But, if she had gotten back early, where was her car? Kelly headed toward the front door and was stopped in his tracks a second time because the door was wide open. He hesitated for a moment and then walked inside. He put the food down on the table in the living room and looked all around to see if anyone else was there. "Beth! Beth, honey? Are you here?" He checked the bedrooms, no one else was there. He went back to the living room, closed the front door, and locked it. He pulled at the door to make sure that it held. The door held steady, and Kelly was completely stunned. Maybe the previous tenant had come back. He was too tired to really think about it. He would talk to the management office in the morning.

Kelly ate while watching the last of the game. He threw his containers away, turned off all the lights again and went into the master bedroom to take a shower and head to bed. He closed the door behind him out of habit. His kids had moved out of the house he had just sold some years ago. His wife had died a few years before that. His wife and he made a habit of closing their bedroom door after the kids got old enough to understand the rules of privacy. He closed the blinds to the picture window that led out to a kind of porch. He suddenly remembered there was a door off the kitchen that led onto the porch. He ran out the bedroom and hooked around to the right to go into the kitchen. The kitchen door was closed and locked. Kelly, still bothered by the earlier front door incident, turned around and walked through the darkness back to his softly lit bedroom. He closed the door and turned on the TV for background noise. He took a long hot shower and got into bed. He was asleep within ten minutes. He tossed and turned a bit while he slept. He heard a noise, like something had fallen, and he woke up with a start. The TV and lamp were still on, and everything was still. The TV was showing static, which was strange. Maybe the cable had gone out, but normally when that happens, there is just a blank screen showing. He checked his phone, and it was 2:18am. He got up and went to the bedroom door. He thought, "Something in one of the other rooms must have fallen over." He opened the door and let out a yelp. Every single light and lamp had been turned on. "Am I sleepwalking, what is going on?" Beth wouldn't have come over this late without calling first. He immediately went to the front door, which was still locked. He checked the windows, then the closets, he looked under the beds. By then, he was exhausted. If someone was in the apartment, they could murder him at this point as long as he got a few minutes of sleep. He went back to the bedroom, left the door open and got in the bed. He turned off the lamp and the TV and was asleep within 5 minutes. He was so tired that he didn't notice that the cable was back on and playing music.

Kelly woke up to the sound of his phone ringing. It was Beth. He reached over and answered, "Hey Babe! How's everything going?" He took a quick look at the phone and noted that it was after 10am. He was usually up and dressed by 7am on the weekends. He tried to sound like he was awake but failed. Beth knew immediately. "Yeah, I guess all that moving wore me out." Beth chatted away about her new client and how he was very particular and that the job was going to take a few days longer. Kelly listened and responded in the right spaces in the conversation. Beth had to go. She had to find some rare fabric print at some shop that was a 3-hour drive away from where she was working. "Aww Babe! I hate to hear that you have to work on a Saturday and that you will have to stay longer. Man, my next flight isn't until Tuesday, I was hoping to see you before then. I understand. Don't work too hard this weekend." Beth lamented about not being able to come home sooner. She told Kelly to rest up and that she would see him in a few more days. The call ended.

Kelly rolled over and looked at the ceiling. He closed his eyes for a moment and woke up to a dull pain in his lower back. He looked at the clock and it read 11:15am. "I better get up! I have never slept like this before."

Kelly slowly rolled over to get out of bed. The more he moved the more his back hurt. He convinced himself that the pain was from moving all the furniture and heavy boxes around; even though it didn't feel like a normal muscle ache. He made his way to the kitchen slowly and got a glass of water and some aspirin. Aspirin was the strongest pain killer he had in the house. He looked in the refrigerator and remembered he hadn't gone grocery shopping yet. He grabbed some milk, a bowl and some Cheerios and sat down at the dining room table for a quick breakfast. He was almost sitting when he realized he needed a spoon. The box of silverware was clearly labeled and sitting on the counter. He opened it and grabbed a handful of wrapped up spoons. He took one out and rinsed it off and headed back to the table. He attempted to sit down again. The pain was dull and nagging in his back, but he knew the aspirin would kick in shortly. He sat or rather flopped into the chair, and the dull pain became a bit sharper once his back hit the chair support. He groaned and winced in pain. He grabbed the box and poured himself some cereal. He reached for the milk and the pain became even sharper. His arm trembled and he almost dropped the milk. He steadied himself, opened the milk and poured some in the bowl. He took a few bites of the cereal and wished he had grabbed some juice. But he didn't want to risk flaring up the pain anymore. The aspirin finally took hold, and the pain became noticeably less. It was down to a dull squeak of a pain once he had his fifth bite of cereal.

Kelly zoned out for a moment, or at least what he thought was a moment. When he came out of it, he was still holding his spoon full of soggy cereal halfway to his mouth. The bowl was almost empty. There was a nearly empty glass of orange juice on the table. Kelly checked his surroundings. Everything was quiet and in place. He glanced over at the microwave clock which read 12:35. He had lost almost an hour. The pain in his lower back had returned. Not as bad as before but it was not shying away. He got up slowly and went to take some more aspirin. He reached in the refrigerator and pulled out a couple of beers. This was not normal behavior for Kelly, and he knew it, but something was off, and he needed to find a way to balance it out. He sat on the couch, turned on a movie and started on the first beer. He laid down on the couch and figured a beer nap would bring him back to normal. He should be up and ready to get some unpacking done by 2pm. He finished off the first beer and closed his eyes. He woke up about fifteen minutes later and started on the second beer. Things were getting back to normal already. He started on the 2nd beer and watched TV. Another movie had come on. It looked like one of movies that are normally shown on the women's channel. The ones his daughter would call murder porn movies. He finished off the 2nd beer and laid back down. He let the sound of the movie lull him to sleep. It was a dark and dreamless sleep although dreamless is not quite right. He felt like something was moving in the darkness of his dreams, but he couldn't quite figure out what it was. Whatever it was seemed to be toying with him, like a cat playing with a ball of string. The cat or thing in the darkness seemed to be getting closer to him. Kelly started to run in his dream. He heard a ringing sound and he started to run toward it. He could feel the thing in the darkness chasing him and he could hear the ringing getting louder.

He woke up in that instant and realized the ringing he was hearing was his phone, which was still in the bedroom. He sat up and tried to get his bearings. The TV was still on and there was a hard rock music video playing. The volume was down pretty low; Kelly figured he had rolled over on the remote and changed the station. He then noted that the remote was safely in place on the coffee table.

The pain in his back was gone. He got up and ran to the bedroom to answer the phone. It had just stopped ringing as he reached the bedroom door. He made his way to the nightstand where the phone was laying and picked it up. He had missed eight calls - all from his daughter and Beth. The time on his phone read 7:25pm. "What the hell?" He sat on the bed, shocked that he had slept for so long. He looked at the phone again and called his daughter Madeleine first. "Daddy, where have you been? Me and Beth were close to calling the police!" Kelly sighed and smiled to himself; my how the tables had turned. "Baby, I'm fine. I must have overdone it last night when I was moving. I fell asleep on the couch hours ago. Sorry, didn't mean to scare you! My phone was in the bedroom, so I didn't hear it ringing. I am ok. Just a little tired and sore." He stayed on the phone with his daughter and made sure she was at ease. "Daddy, I will be back in town in a couple of weeks. Can't wait to see what your new place looks like."

"Honey, you make sure you stay with me when you come. Give you a break from your five roommates in that house y'all are sharing." Maddy laughed at his old joke. "Sure thing Daddy! Talk to you soon. You better call Beth before she calls the law on ya!" They spoke a few seconds more and ended the call.

Kelly called Beth and received the same amount of worry and fear that he got from his daughter. "Baby, I am mad at myself! The day is gone, and I haven't hardly unpacked anything. I ain't never been so tired." He didn't tell her about the back pain, he was sure it was stress and physical strain causing the pain. "Honey, you might as well grab something to eat and go back to bed. That move probably did take a lot out of you." Beth paused, "I'm just glad you're ok. I will be home on Wednesday. I can help you unpack then."

Kelly hung up the phone and looked around the bedroom. It was already dark outside. "Dang it! I slept the whole dang day!" He got up and went back into the living room to clean up the beer bottles and figure out what to eat for dinner. He turned on the lamp and almost tripped over a beer bottle that had rolled across the floor. "How did you get over here?" He picked up the bottle and went to the table to pick up the other one when he was overcome by shock and a little bit of fear. There were four beer bottles on the table and another six on the floor. Counting the empty one he had in his hand made a total of eleven. He didn't remember getting any more beer out of the fridge. In fact, he didn't have that much beer in the fridge to begin with! Where did all these bottles come from? He went to the fridge and saw that the six-pack container that he had pulled the first two beers from was still on the shelf, but it was empty.

He went back to the couch and looked for the other beer holder as well as the last stray beer. He looked under the couch, in the couch, under the table and all over the floor. He didn't find anything. He started picking up the empties, thinking while he cleaned. "Where did the extra beer come from? Where is the last empty beer bottle? Did I have company? Welcome Wagon? No, welcome wagons normally come with a basket, not just beer. Is it possible that I left the door open, and someone came in?" Kelly stopped what he was doing and went to check the doors. Everything was still locked up tight. He tried to push away a creeping final thought that would explain everything away but instinctively went to look for his truck keys. They weren't on the kitchen counter. He was positive that's where he put them last night. "No way. I still have on just my shorts. No way I left the house undressed." Kelly went back to the bedroom and looked around. Maybe he put the keys on one of the nightstands. He went over to check the stand on the opposite side of the bed next to the closet and saw the jeans he had on last night crumpled on the floor. He paused for a moment, still trying to push back that final solution to explain all of this. He picked up the jeans and his keys fell out of one of the pockets.

Kelly dropped the jeans; he collapsed on the bed. He was truly afraid. He knew he had put the jeans in the hamper the night before. That was his routine, after being married for years and years, that was what you learned to do. He couldn't fight the thought anymore. He had to seriously consider that he may have been sleepwalking. "Sleepwalking," he thought. "I've never done that before. Why now? Did I actually leave the house? I had to have left to get the beer. I drove to a store and don't remember it? How could that be possible? It's not!" Kelly argued with himself for a few more minutes. He got up, grabbed the jeans, and put them back in the hamper. He went to take a shower and figure out what to eat for dinner. "Too much aspirin and beer! But what about last night? I was completely sober! No, that had to be it! Or maybe it's PTSD!"

Kelly was so confused that he hadn't noticed that the TV had been on the whole time and had changed over to a music station. While he was in the shower, the TV switched back to the movie channel he had been watching.

CHAPTER 17

Dena

Time had flown by for Dena. She was getting ready to fly home to be with her parents for Thanksgiving. Her sister would be on the same flight. She couldn't wait to see her family! She couldn't believe she had waited so long to pack. Normally, her suitcase would be packed and by the door a week in advance. She had been so busy with dating, work, reading, spending time with her friends and keeping up with her local family that time had literally gotten away from her.

Things were going wonderful with Chris; they had a standing date for Saturday night every week. Chris worked long hours during the week, but he texted her often during the day. He really was a great guy. They had a lot in common but there were enough differences to keep things interesting. Chris surprised Dena and took her to a museum with classic European automobiles for their second date. They had a blast learning about different vehicles from the 1940's and 1950's. After the museum, they went for a drive on Natchez Trace to look at the fall leaves. It was beautiful. Dena had only seen fall leaves this colorful back home in Detroit. They grabbed a bite to eat at a restaurant off the Trace which was famous for their fried chicken and biscuits. The next two dates were just as wonderful.

Dena was still not liking work too much and she decided to make a change. She knew she needed something more challenging to keep her from being bored and burned out. She brushed up her resume and started looking for other positions within the company that might be more interesting to her. She really liked her company and hoped something would open up soon for her. She wasn't going full throttle on the job search as her boss was recovering from cancer and she was extremely loyal to him. He was a kind man and understood that she wasn't happy. He offered his support and guidance; Dena was eternally grateful for his assistance.

Things had been quiet at her apartment. No more loud neighbors, weird noises, or happenings. She really believed that since she was happy things were turning in her favor. She had to admit that Kelly scared her with his late-night walk. She wondered if he was sleepwalking and didn't want to admit to it. She could sense that he was trying to hide something the last time they spoke. She gave him a wide berth for the time being even though she felt bad about it. She knew he was healing from surgery, and it didn't seem like anyone was really taking care of him. She shook that thought away and continued packing. She had plans to meet with Chris tonight since she wouldn't see him until after the holiday. She was living on the edge - dating on a Tuesday night. It would need to be an early date since she would be spending the night with her sister and heading to the airport with Liz in the morning.

She closed her suitcase and put it near the door. She went around the apartment to make sure she hadn't forgotten anything. Nope, the place was as clean and as cute as ever. She grabbed her bags and headed out the door. As she was locking up, she heard loud voices up on the hill. She decided to ignore them and headed down the path. She looked up and saw Kelly standing in the middle of the path with a woman. The woman was about Kelly's height, and slender. She was dressed very stylishly. Her shoes matched her bag and her scarf. And the scarf was a thing of beauty. It was pink and brown with gold tones and a hint of red in a wonderful design. Dena couldn't contain herself, "I love that scarf!"

"Thank you! Kelly was just saying that he hoped we would run into you. You must be Dena! So, glad to meet you!" Dena looked at Kelly and winked. "Been talking me up, huh? Nice to meet you too!" Dena had no clue who the woman was, sister, girlfriend, cousin, aunt – she played along. "Dena, this is my lady, Beth. I told her how you loved the apartment. Beth did the decorating." Kelly was blushing a bit. "Ohhh, you did that? It is amazing! I love the artwork hanging in the living room! The warm colors really make it cozy!" At this, Beth whipped out her business card and told Dena to call her. "I can get you anything you want at cost and maybe even less than that!"

"Kelly, she is a keeper! How's your back doing? You look like you are getting around much better now!"

"Well, it's doing much better now that I - "Just then, the voices that were background noise became the center of attention. Dena, Kelly, and Beth turned to look up the hill at the unit where the yelling was coming from.

"YOU JUST DON'T UNDERSTAND! YOU NEVER WILL!"

"I am trying to understand, please give me a chance and explain it to me so I can understand," said the woman. Her voice was trembling, and it sounded like she was on the verge of tears. The man's voice came booming in over the women. "NO!! IT'S IMPOSSIBLE FOR

YOU TO GET IT! YOU AREN'T EVEN TRYING...ALL YOU DO IS LOOK DOWN ON ME AND MY FAMILY! AND NOW I KNOW YOUR TRUE FEELINGS AND MOTIVES!"

The voices were coming from an open door on one of the balconies. Dena had noticed that this couple tended to leave the door open when one of them came out to smoke on the balcony. "Well, it wouldn't be Thanksgiving without a good ole family squabble," said Dena. They all laughed nervously because it sounded like things were escalating past a "good ole squabble." Another voice could be heard from the unit. It was barely a whisper, but it seemed to calm the couple down or at least got them to speaking to each other in civilized tones. "Well, I better get going! I'm off to Detroit for Thanksgiving. Kelly, call me if my apartment decides to be haunted while I'm out." Kelly and Dena laughed while Beth looked puzzled. Kelly looked at Beth and said, "Babe, I will fill you in on the details over dinner. I will keep an eye out Ms. Dena, and you have a wonderful Thanksgiving and be safe up there in the big city." "You do the same," and off Dena went to meet Chris.

Dena thought to herself, "I guess the madness has moved up on the hill. Hope it doesn't stay around too long." She was glad she ran into Kelly and Beth. He seemed normal after all and that was a relief. Then she thought to herself, "How strange that Kelly and I seem to be doing okay right now and the weirdness is going on up the hill." She decided she would talk to Liz about it on the plane trip in the morning. But she never did talk to her sister about it. They got so involved in talking about all the fun things they would do once they got home, and Dena didn't want to spoil it with questions about haunts and weirdness. So, she let it go.

CHAPTER 18

The Couple on the Hill

Malcolm and Bonnie had been living together for seven years. Neither of them wanted to get married because they had both had terrible first marriages. Malcolm had two nearly grown children from his first wife. Bonnie had one son who was also nearly grown and a young daughter Katie, who was 11. All the kids were coming home for Thanksgiving and Bonnie had been looking forward to it until Malcolm started throwing temper tantrums that Tuesday evening. Katie was still living in California with her dad. She would be home for Thanksgiving to check out Nashville and to see if she wanted to move there permanently in January.

Bonnie and Malcolm moved in at the beginning of October from California. The weather had just turned cool, and it was the perfect day to move. Bonnie had been excited about the move; she was looking forward to her new job and meeting new people. She had hoped that Malcolm would become as excited. He had a new job lined up as well. He took a bit of a pay cut, but with rent being much cheaper than the homes in L.A. it was a win-win. Bonnie couldn't get over how inexpensive everything was. The savings on the apartment, groceries and gas would allow them to pay off some of their long-term debt in no time. Bonnie had even managed to forgive Malcolm for not selling the house in California. She had urged him many times to do so, saying that it would give them a nice nest egg, but in the end, she understood that the house meant a lot to him and the kids. So, she let it go. She sat in the bedroom and got back to making her lists for Thanksgiving. So much to consider, groceries, place settings, games. She was glad that all the kids would be under the same roof. If only Malcolm would cheer up.

Malcolm had his doubts about the move. He was a West Coast dude. He grew up in Culver City and moved to Ladera Heights for the kids during his marriage. His wife left him and the kids before they were high school age. She just left -no note, no phone call, no email. She had done this before, but she always came back home. Sometimes it was drug related, sometimes it would be a man, a few times it was a woman. This time, she didn't return and this time he didn't try to track her down. This time she eventually sent farewell letters to him and the kids. This time he let her go.

He and the kids had suffered enough. And the truth is, you can't make someone love you. It was time to move on and he hoped that maybe she would come back on her own someday, but until then, he had to make sure that his kids, Micah and Janae, would have stability, love, and strength without her. They made a pact to not let the actions of their mother affect them. It was out of their control and in God's hands. The three of them shed a lot of tears but eventually, they were able to move forward and find peace without their mom. They knew she was safe and that was all that they would ask to know.

The more Malcolm thought about it, the more he was unhappy with the move. He felt like he had been taken advantage of by Bonnie.

Bonnie could be very forceful, unbearable, and downright devious when she didn't get her way. Forceful to the point of putting his house up for sale behind his back to finance a move out of state. Why did he forgive her for doing that? He had told her repeatedly that he wanted to stay in California. He didn't want to leave his home. Malcolm did not like to argue, but there were more than a few shouting matches over what Bonnie had tried to do. He realized that maybe she felt threatened by the memory of his very much alive wife, but that would be crazy. Did Bonnie feel like she was competing with his wife? Was it a woman thing? A jealousy thing? A racial thing? He slowed these thoughts down because they always made him very tired. He focused on the upcoming holiday and the fact that his kids were coming to visit. He missed them dearly and he missed home. In the end, he was just glad that he was able to rent out the home in Ladera Heights to his nephew and not sell it outright. He wished he had stayed in Cali. He looked at his caramel-colored hands, rubbed his knees back and forth nervously and placed his forehead in his hands. He tried to silence all the thoughts and emotions running through him. The noise inside his head finally quieted.

"KILL HER!"

Malcolm whipped his head back and around. He thought for a moment that he had nodded off and had a nightmare. In some sort of way, he had to have nodded off. He was still sitting in the chair in the living room, but one of the large knives from the kitchen was now on the table next to his seat. He knew it wasn't there before he sat down. He shook his head and stood up. He put the knife back in the kitchen.

"I'm going out for a drive. I will be back." He grabbed his keys, opened the front door, and left. Bonnie barely heard what he said, and he was gone by the time she came out of the bedroom. She felt sad and she knew her sadness was partly her fault. But she had to get Malcolm out of California before his wife made actual contact with him, so she lied, cried, and pried so she could have him to herself. Malcolm's wife had been out of the picture for at least seven years, or so she believed. Bonnie had started to question everything, and it was her own fault that she had to question anything to begin with.

It was on a warm spring day that it happened. Bonnie was working from home or rather from Malcolm's home. She was enjoying the peace and quiet when she heard the FedEx truck pull up. She thought to herself, "Malcolm must have purchased something for the house or yard again," as she went to the door to retrieve the package. The street was quiet as all the neighbors were either at work or school. When she looked down, she saw that there were three packages. "Wow, Malcolm must have a really big project he's working on." She picked the packages up and bought them inside. She carried them to the dining room table which was a common area in the house and spread them out on the table. She saw that there was a package for Malcolm, one for Micah and one for Janae. She was a little hurt that there was not a package for her. She looked at the return label and saw that they were from someone in the family. A woman that had the same last name as Malcolm. The first name was familiar, but she couldn't quite place it.

"Donita," she said the name out loud hoping that it would help her remember. It took her a few seconds to remember that Donita was Malcolm's wife, Dawn. Or was it, Don? Or was she even his ex-wife? Malcolm had always been non-committal about the status of their relationship. When she would press him, he would only say that the marriage was over, but Bonnie could sense that Malcolm still had some emotional investment in the relationship. She had known this since they first got together, but she trusted him when he said it was over. She felt that he trusted her, but she couldn't be sure at times, and she really couldn't blame him. She had done some dubious things to keep their relationship going, but it was all for love. Or at least that's what she tried to convince herself of.

On the package addressed to Malcolm there was an envelope attached. She sat at the dining room table trying to figure out what to do next. Maybe there were divorce papers in the letter; no, divorce papers normally come from an attorney's office. Or they are served by someone in a horrible suit. She really didn't have any knowledge on how divorce papers were sent, she was pulling all her knowledge from TV shows and movies. With her divorce, everything was out in the open; at least everything about the divorce was out in the open. There were no complications, the marriage was over. Bring on the paperwork and let's get it done. The complications within the marriage, well they were not so easy to sign away in the divorce decree, but Bonnie would bide her time with that.

Bonnie stared at the letter, willing her mind to see the contents of it. When that didn't work, she examined the package to see if she could remove the letter, so no one would detect that anything was missing. She swept her long blonde hair from her face and picked up the package. She shook it gently and turned it over a few times trying to figure out what it could be. Her blue-green eyes were furrowed and intent. She looked at the clock - she had a few hours before she had to decide on her next plan of action. She pulled out one of the dining room chairs and sat down slowly. She sat there for a few very long minutes with her hands placed in her lap, gazing at the boxes. She wasn't so concerned about the ones for the kids. She spent most of this time focused on the one for Malcolm.

She knew he preferred to be called Malcolm, but she called him Mac to distance herself from the memory of his wife. It was probably silly and more than a little bit insecure, but she had genuine reason to feel that way. She had planned on being with Malcolm - Mac - even if it meant breaking up his marriage. Luckily, his wife left him before her desperation drove her to it. She knew she was making the same mistakes as she had in her first marriage, but she couldn't look back now. She had the man she wanted, and she was going to drive this train, white knuckled and with no regrets to the end of the line.

It was that final thought that made her spring from her chair and grab the scissors from a drawer of an end table. The end table, sitting in the corner, rich mahogany, tasteful and expensive and she hated it. Every piece of furniture in the house was picked out by Malcolm and Donita and it enraged her from time to time, but especially right now. She picked up the table by the legs and threw it against the floor with all her might. The table withstood her act of rage and came away with a small chip on the back that could be easily hidden by putting it back in its original position in the corner. Bonnie sat the table upright and removed the scissors from the drawer. She placed the table back in the corner and it seemed to be laughing at her, mocking her. The table seemed to say, "You don't belong here. You never did."

She glared at the table and her frustration and anger doubled over. She turned to the box addressed to Malcolm- MAC- and tore the letter from it. She was so angry that she stood there with the letter crumpled in her hand. There was no way she could cover up the fact that she had touched it, so she opened it. Hands trembling, she tore the letter out of the envelope. "Who writes letters anyway? How stupid!" Her contempt for Donita grew and grew, she was blind with rage and couldn't make sense of the letter. So, she slammed it on the table and walked away from it.

She went to the kitchen and got something to drink. The microwave clock read 11:20 am, she still had time to figure this out. Her mind teemed with questions. The biggest one was, "Why now? Everything was perfect, well not really, but it was getting there. Who does she think she is? She abandoned her family and now she wants what? To come back. To visit? What could she possibly want?"

Bonnie guzzled water from a bottle she pulled from the refrigerator. The water dripped down her chin and throat. She drank half the bottle without coming up for air. She started coughing when some of the water went down the wrong way. She threw the half full bottle into the sink and stomped back to the dining room, wiping cold water from her chin and throat. She threw herself into a dining room chair and stared at the crumpled letter on the table. "No looking back now." She snatched the letter off the table and tried to smooth the creases out. Her breathing which had been short and labored slowed to a steady rhythm. She gently placed the letter on the table and smoothed it out some more. It still looked like a crumpled mess. Nothing left to do but read it again.

She picked it up slowly and gingerly, with all the care one would have as if they were deactivating a bomb. And in all fairness, that's what it was. It was a bomb. The hard part was finding out whether the bomb was a dud or a megaton. Turns out it was somewhere in between. Bonnie read the letter; well, it was more like a note, 4 times. Then she sat and thought about what to do next.

First, she needed to get rid of the evidence. She gathered up all three boxes and put them in the trunk of her car which was in the garage. This was a piece of good luck for her. There were no nosey neighbors who might pry and ask about the contents. She would find a place away from the house and open them later.

Next, she would need to get Malcolm out of town for an extended amount of time. She knew he wouldn't go for an extended vacation. Or worse he would suggest going to their family's beach house. A place she loathed. Any memory or place that included Don- Dawn or Doni - was out of the question. That's when she decided - it would have to be a permanent move.

Again! What luck! She had recently been made aware of a position in her field that she was a shoe in for. Initially, she had turned it down because it was so far away and really who wanted to move to Nashville? She spent most of the afternoon researching the position and the city of Nashville. She then had to work on how to sell the move to Malcolm.

In her excitement, she called a couple of realtors to pin down an asking price for Malcolm's house. This was a move that would come back to haunt her.

She moved about the house making dinner and practicing her "pitch" to Malcolm on selling the house. She needed to see if his job would transfer him. "No", she thought to herself "that seems too invasive." But she did do a few job searches to see if anything was available in his field. And as luck would have it, Nashville was booming, jobwise. He would take a slight cut in pay overall, but he would have much better luck moving up the corporate ladder. She just needed to convince him that it would be worth it.

Her last-feat would be figuring out how to stall Donita. She had to make sure that Donita didn't just show up or send more letters and packages. Or worse an email. Or horror of horrors, what if she showed up at Malcolm's job. She thought and thought as she chopped up the salad and put on the steaks. She would have to put this plan on a fast track. And she knew the best way to get Malcolm to see things her way.

She bought the matter up subtly over dinner by starting a huge argument where she accused Malcolm of still having feelings for his wife. She claimed that she never fit in here and that the house and everything in it was a shrine to a woman who had abandoned him and his kids. She cried and screamed - played the martyr. And it worked. Malcolm agreed to seriously consider the move. He tried to ask why they had to move so far away, and Bonnie replied that the only way she would get a fair shake is if they started over on even ground. That meant moving to a place where neither one of them had any attachments.

All was going well with her scheme until a realtor reached out to Malcolm regarding the asking price of the house. She was able to tap dance her way out of it, but she knew that Malcolm still didn't fully trust her because of it. She had gotten her way and felt it was worth it but, she wasn't quite sure.

She put those thoughts behind her where they needed to stay, sat on the couch, and closed her eyes. She felt like she needed to cry. She waited but nothing happened. She put her hands down on the cushions to stand up when she felt a sharp pain. She snapped her eyes open and looked at her right hand. She was bleeding, her hand had been cut from a knife lying on the couch.

"Was it there when I sat down? I don't think so. Did Malcolm leave it there?" She knew that Malcolm was not that careless. She ran to the kitchen to wash out the wound. It was a small, deep cut and it stopped bleeding fast. She went back to the couch, grabbed the knife gingerly by the handle and put it in the sink.

Malcolm did not come home for a couple of hours and her mind and insecurity got the better of her. Maybe he was cheating, maybe Donita had tracked them down or maybe he just didn't want to be around her anymore. She knew she had done a lot of things to throw the relationship off track, but she still felt like everything she had done was justified. Or was it? The self-doubt was not only creeping in, it washed over her like a cold wave. With every passing minute that Malcolm was gone a darkness began to take over Bonnie. It was like a foul bile that was building up in her stomach slowly but intensely. By the time Malcolm arrived home she was beyond enraged. "Where the hell have you been? You could have called!! Oh, so is that how things will be now that we are in a new place? Are you going to replace me? I can't believe this is how you treat me after all I sacrificed for you!"

Malcolm looked at Bonnie and watched her shrieking and carrying on and thoughtfully, calmly decided on his next move. He waited for Bonnie to take a break from the screaming, dropped the bag of takeout on the counter and softly said, "Did you check your text messages?" He watched as she picked up her phone from the living room table. He waited to see if she would calm down or if she would turn the argument sideways. He watched to see if her shoulders would relax or tense up. As soon as he saw her back stiffen and her shoulders become rigid, he made his decision.

She turned around with her brow furrowed and her mouth in a grimace. He looked at her and let out a long, loud sigh, and walked back out the door. He got in his car and drove over to the local steak restaurant. He sat at the bar, watched the game, and sipped on a beer. Malcolm half listened to the game and casually surveyed the restaurant and its patrons. His eyes rested on a fellow bar stooler for some reason. Some guy with an easy smile and laid-back demeanor caught his eye. They locked eyes for a moment and the easygoing bar stooler nodded his head and went back to watching the game.

Malcolm could not look away for some reason. He became angry and not because of Bonnie, but because of this total stranger. He felt anger and envy all at once. What right did this guy have to be happy and smiling? Why was his life so easy? Malcolm felt his fist balling up and it felt like a dark madness was starting to creep into him. His head started swimming and so he closed his eyes and took a deep breath. It seemed to ease the anger building inside him. He didn't understand why he was so angry and with a stranger who had only given him a friendly nod. Perhaps, it was time to go home. Malcolm nursed his beer some more and picked at his now cold appetizer. He let his thoughts take him away for a few seconds and when he snapped back into reality, he felt at ease. He looked up in time to hear his fellow easy-going bar stooler say, "Thank you, Darlin'," as he winked and got up from the bar to leave with a takeout order.

Malcolm sighed and thought to himself, "This guy must not be married or in a long-term relationship." Malcolm couldn't stop thinking. He kept playing over every step he had taken in the last month to try to figure out how he had gotten here. Each time he tried, he felt like he was travelling down a road in which there were turns in the road where signs had been misplaced or removed altogether. What's worse is that it felt like the missing piece was just out of his reach. Each time he reached further out to grasp it and each time the answer slipped inches away from his hands.

Malcolm gave up and paid his bill. It was getting late, and he needed to go home and face the beast. He hoped that she had taken a sleeping pill and had already gone to bed.

When he got home, he looked into the dark bedroom. He saw that she went to sleep while listening to a podcast. She was always listening to something dealing with self-help and it seemed to calm her down. Malcolm listened closely to make sure she was sleeping and not waiting to ambush him with part two of their argument. He heard music coming from the headphones. At first, he thought it was a commercial, but the melody sounded familiar to him and played longer than a thirty-second promo would.

He felt like a creeper watching Bonnie, so he backed out of the room slowly and quietly and shut the door softly.

He went to the kitchen and found a note on the counter with an apology. He went to the fridge to grab a water and saw that Bonnie had left him a piece of chocolate cake on a plate with a glass of milk beside it. He sighed and took out the plate and glass. He took a couple of bites of the cake and drank half of the milk. This was an old trick that Bonnie would use to make peace and Malcolm would concede when it was used. Thinking about it now, he realized that this was a manipulation of some sort. He just couldn't figure out how. All he knew was that he felt like he was being used or made a fool of in some way.

Malcolm looked at the plate; the cake was heavy with rich, thick icing. It was so overdone that it looked disgusting. Bonnie must've gone out and bought a slice from someplace close by. Malcolm thought to himself, "Either she doesn't know me, or she doesn't care." He blamed himself for letting this old makeup game go so far. Truth was his favorite cake was German chocolate and it had to be homemade. He liked chocolate cake, but it had to be homemade or close to it. And although this cake was pretty, it was not homemade. It reminded him of Bonnie, pretty but not genuine. Not the real thing. He had had these thoughts before and always brushed them away. He started thinking about all the "sacrifices' Bonnie had made for them, and he really couldn't say they were genuine losses to her. In fact, they seemed like genuine gains, and he seemed to be losing the most. Malcolm sighed for the five hundredth time that night and dumped the cake in the sink. He poured the milk down after it. He turned on the water and hit the switch for the garbage disposal. Without warning, the same unruly kitchen knife from earlier came flying out of the sink. Malcolm ducked just in time. The force was so strong that the knife tore through the air and struck the wall directly behind him, where it stayed. The tip was embedded in the wall, the handle jutted out and shook from the force. The poor knife seemed to be shivering in fear and saying, "How did I get here?" Malcolm shut off the disposal and took a deep breath. He was in shock. He pulled the knife out of the wall, washed it, and put it in the dish rack. It was the same knife that he found while sitting on the couch. Malcolm picked up the knife and looked at it for a few moments. "Any more trouble out of you and I'm gonna have to get rid of you!" There was no reasoning behind any of it and to Malcolm the knife still looked terrified.

Malcolm left the kitchen and went out to the balcony for a cigarette. He calmed himself down and made a mental note to buy some plaster for the wall to cover up the damage from the knife. He could start picking up some groceries for Thanksgiving too. Plan in place and with everything sorted out as much as it could be, he decided to go to bed. He hoped that Bonnie was still asleep. He was too tired to deal with an interrogation right now. And on this night, luck was on his side.

Things remained quiet as the Thanksgiving holiday approached but the air in Malcolm and Bonnie's apartment remained stale and unappetizing. Both hoped that the mood would change once the kids came to visit.

CHAPTER 19

Kelly

———⟨∞ ∞⟩———

Kelly's plans for Thanksgiving were a bust. Beth was called away on a special project by some rich fella up north who was "jonesing" for some new taupe draperies or some silliness such as that. She got the call late Tuesday night and she left after they argued early Wednesday morning.

His daughter, Maddy, the nurse, had come by for a few days to check on him. His pain management was in a decent place, and he was getting around well. He would be back to normal in no time.

Unfortunately, Maddy had to leave the day before Thanksgiving as well, to tend to an emergency in North Carolina. This is the life of a travelling nurse. Thankfully, she would be back early next week, and the assignment wasn't very dangerous. He often worried about her being called away to treat some horrific illness, like a deadly infectious disease or some awful natural disaster like an earthquake.

Kelly's son was serving in the Air Force in England. He hadn't seen him in about eight months. Joey had called to check in on his old man regularly. Kelly nearly went into a laughter-induced stroke when Joey asked him, "Fancy a pint, Da?" The Irish, English and Southern drawl was quite the combination. Joey couldn't make it home for Thanksgiving, but maybe he could come for Christmas.

Kelly felt suddenly renewed while thinking of his loved ones. He would call Beth and apologize. He didn't know what came over him. He all but accused her of carrying on with a stranger for no reason. He had to make this right. Maybe a belated Thanksgiving celebration was the answer. He was off work for at least another two weeks. Beth and Maddy had a four-day weekend after Thanksgiving.

Kelly leapt off the couch to grab a pen and pad so he could start planning a feast. He was bound and determined to shake this loneliness and evil to get his life and family back on track.

First things first, he needed to apologize to Beth. Kelly made notes on what to say. He wanted it to come from the heart and to be sincere, but he felt in this case that his thoughts would be better expressed if he wrote them out first. There was not much to say. He had behaved like a jealous schoolboy; he didn't know what had come over him. Maybe it was the medication, but that's no excuse. He decided to keep it simple. "Darlin', I was a jerk. No excuses for my behavior. I'm sorry, please forgive me and let me make it up to you."

Kelly got lost in his thoughts for a moment. He felt like he was being watched and he zoned out as he had on a few occasions. It was different this time; it didn't seem as cold and ominous as usual. The moment of darkness passed quickly for him.

He said a short, heartfelt prayer. He was so nervous his hands were shaking. "Please Lord, let her forgive me." This was their first major fight, so he felt his chances for making up were strong. Plus, it was the holidays and Beth was like family to the kids and him at that point. You can't be without your loved ones during the holidays. Kelly would call her as soon as she had settled in after her morning flight.

CHAPTER 20

Dena's Place

Things were not so quiet at Dena's apartment. The couple on the hill had calmed down from the fireworks that took place on Thanksgiving, but tempers still flared between Malcolm and Bonnie. The unit on the opposite side of Dena was still empty and the unit above her was still empty.

Kelly could hear strange noises coming through the wall that connected his and Dena's apartment, but he didn't think anything of it. Well, it was more like he didn't want to think anything of it. He was happy and wanted to stay happy. He could hear a steady creaking, like a piece of wood being bent or a door hinge that needed oil constantly crying out. He heard other sounds that he couldn't explain and dismissed them as the building settling.

Kelly did a great job of convincing himself that what was going on was normal. It was not. In his heart of hearts or ear of ears he knew that he had heard sheets flapping and soft music playing. He tried to dismiss it as the TV or that it was just in his mind. But again, he knew this was not the case deep down. He was just happy that whatever was happening was taking place while Ms. Dena was out of town.

But things inside of Dena's apartment were pretty much terrifying.

Inside Dena's apartment, the heat was at 130 degrees. The oven was on full blast with the door open, as was the microwave. The inside of the microwave glowed a bright orange color and the circular tray was moving around at 15 miles an hour. It was all impossible, but it was happening.

The comforter on her bed was crumpled up and on the floor. The matching burgundy bed sheet hung in the air on its own, flat, and waving back and forth, causing loud flapping and snapping noises. The cream-colored pillows with burgundy trim were sitting at the head of the bed lengthwise and bowing in unison to the flapping. There were deep red stains in the pillows and if you just happened to be standing in the doorway, you would think they looked like red eyes crying tears of thick blood.

If you turned away from the doorway, you would see that Dena's TV was on. It was on a music station playing jazz- infused gospel music. A somewhat familiar song was playing. "I see the light. I see the light." But the melody was off-key, and the singing was ominous and dark. The song changed its tune and words, "I see the dark, I see the dark. The cold, cold dark is where I belong. It is my home. Where he will come and take me away deeper into the dark. I see the dark."

In the kitchen, all the cabinet doors swung open and closed to the beat of the song playing. The eyes on top of the stove burned bright orange and the heat intensified within the apartment. The temperature shot up another two degrees.

The wax around the sprinkler head didn't budge and the smoke detectors didn't blare because there was no smoke. Nothing was burning in the apartment. Which by all accounts was inconceivable because everything should have been burning.

Behind the closed door in the laundry room, heavy thick strands of oily jet-black fur that stank to high heaven fell from the white ceiling like long wisps of black snow. The smell was powerful and seeped into Kelly's apartment. Kelly noticed the smell but thought a neighbor was cooking cabbage or kimchi.

Back in the bedroom, where the sheet was still waving, there appeared to be with every wave something just out of eyesight, something dark and tall. Something that appeared to have its arms outstretched and moving rhythmically. Like a conductor!

The heat from the stove and microwave caused more waves in the air. Waves of heat on which the music started to conduct itself. The music became louder, but not so loud that it would disturb anyone outside of the apartment.

The butcher knife that had been put safely in the drawer was now on the counter with the sharp-ended tip embedded into the counter. The knife spun slowly in a circle on the counter. It was soon joined by a matching carving fork that copied its movements. They danced a disjointed waltz in the heat and utter bizarreness.

The "party" continued off and on throughout the weekend.

Loud at times, even lively if not dark – but on it went.

CHAPTER 21
Bonnie and Malcolm

The kids would start to arrive soon. Malcolm knew they would do their best to soften the mood and blend together to soothe their parents as always.

His kids and Bonnie's kids had not spent a lot of time together, so a certain amount of initial awkwardness was expected. He hoped the kids wouldn't feel awkward for long. It made him feel even worse that the kids couldn't relax and enjoy themselves because of the tension between him and Bonnie. Bonnie spent a lot of time trying to lash out at Micah and Janae, especially Janae.

Michael and Katie were not spared either. Katie had already mentioned to her older brother a few days earlier, that she wished she could stay at home with their dad. Michael tried to comfort her and let her know that it was only a few days and that it would be fun to see Micah and Janae again. He couldn't explain his mother's moodiness over the years. He thought that maybe she was on prescription meds, but he didn't find anything when he looked in the bathroom cabinet. He had to admit his mom had always been a drama queen.

It was like she was in one of those drippy romance novels he used to see at the grocery store as a kid. His mom always said those books were trash. But Michael was a curious child and would pick one up and read the back cover occasionally; he tried to do it while his mom was not looking. Every so often he would get caught and his mom would tell him to put that "trash" down.

Often, the descriptions of the heroines on the backs of the books reminded him of his mom. Only to a certain degree. He had seen his mom play the victim many times and then once she had gotten her way the dramatics were done for the moment and placed on a shelf until use for the next time.

Michael ignored most of what his mom said and did. He was a boy, and it was easy for him to go off with his friends or shut himself in his room. His sister Katie was not so lucky. Michael felt like his mom needed to have another version of herself in Katie. But Katie was much too smart and free willed to fall for any of their mom's emotional episodes. She could tell that most of it was contrived, and she had little patience for it. Often, it seemed like Katie was the adult and Bonnie was the child.

Michael had been dreading this trip for a while too. So much so, that he figured out an early exit plan. He would arrive a few days early while his mom had to be at work during the day and leave early Sunday morning so he wouldn't have to spend too much time with her "bonding."

He was looking forward to seeing his "step-siblings", they seemed cool but the way his mom behaved when they were all together made everyone uncomfortable. It was like they were being forced to get along and accept each other when the truth was that everyone understood the situation and his mom's interference was not needed.

What was there not to understand? His parent's marriage wasn't working, his mom seemed to be the reason for it. She denied it. The adults wanted out, they got out and moved on. The only issue that Michael had with the divorce of his parents was how much mom used him and Katie as ammunition for getting what she wanted and then in the end she gave up the fight or whatever it was and let them go live with their dad. This really hurt him and made him see his mom in a different way. He felt like he wasn't her son but an object that she could use to get what she wanted. Something only to be used when it suited her.

He saw a connection between the way she treated him and the way she behaved toward his dad. The whole separation/ divorce came about suddenly. Like a light switch that had been turned on by his mom. Literally, one day, she was happy and the next she loathed everything about his dad, the house, the cars, and their life. Michael guessed that sometimes marriages just fall apart like that at times. Michael could tell that she resented him too at times; he mostly thought it was because he looked like his dad. But at times, he couldn't tell if there was something else, she disliked about him.

Michael loved his dad of course. They were very much alike; they even looked alike. With the same dark brown hair, hazel eyes, and dimples. His dad was very laid back and Michael tried to be. He had seen how not being in control of your emotions could wreck a home and lives. He had seen and learned enough to know two things: he didn't know if he wanted to be married or have a family, but he didn't want to push everyone that loved him away. He did not want to be friendless or lonely. This is how he saw his mom. He also did not want to be a drama queen or king.

Maybe his mom had calmed down and she was more at peace now that she was in another city with a whole new life. Maybe he would have a great time and they really would bond as a family. He really liked Malcolm, Micah and, well, Janae.

He really, really liked Janae. She was beautiful. She was so smart and funny, and he could really open to her. It seemed weird to have a crush on a girl that was practically his stepsister but, Michael couldn't help himself. He tried not to think about her but there was nothing he could do since he would have to have contact with her during this trip. Every time he closed his eyes, he thought about her smile, her voice, her big brown eyes. The way she looked at him when they talked. She really listened to him. Not like the girls he went to school with who seemed to be so shallow and short sighted. Being with Janae was a fantasy, Michael would never cross that line if their parents were together — it was just too weird. Plus, he had no idea if Janae felt the same.

All Michael's hopes and fears came to a head not long after he arrived in Nashville.

As predicted, his mom was at work and Malcolm picked him up from the airport. He texted his mom to let her know he landed safely, and that Malcolm had picked him up. He knew she would be in a meeting and was surprised when she answered his text. "Okay, see you soon."

He felt dread immediately and tried to calm himself down.

It was about a 30-minute drive to the apartment and Malcolm and Michael happily chatted away. They caught up on the Lakers and the Rams. Malcolm had the obligatory "school and grades" conversation with him. No worries there. Michael's grades were great! Michael had the obligatory "work and fitting in" conversation with Malcolm.

"Well, are you making new friends? You have to be open to meeting new people, you know!" They were at a stop light and looked at each other. Laughter erupted from both, and it was genuine and pure. They laughed and talked the rest of the way home about any number of subjects.

"So, how are the kids?" Michael asked with a smile that turned into a chortle. Malcolm shook his head at Michael and filled him in on Micah and Janae.

Malcolm liked Michael and Katie. They were great kids. He could see they had figured out a way to deal with their mom's moods and he admired them for it. He wished he could figure out how they did it. He wanted to ask at times but asking a child how to deal with their mother seemed so inappropriate.

Malcolm could tell that Michael had a crush on Janae and that Janae seemed to like Michael. He knew that it was an awkward situation in which neither child wanted to cross the line. Malcolm thought they made a great couple, and he understood their reasons for not dating and he never talked to either of them about it.

"Listen, I've thought of a few activities outside of the house, so you kids aren't cooped up with me and your mom the whole time. Both you and Micah have your licenses, so I'm fine with you driving the car if you stay close to the house. If not, you can use a ride-share app. One rule - you need to stay together. I don't think that will be a problem as you seem to be a responsible young adult." Malcolm looked sternly at Michael as he said this. His smile relaxed into a wink and a smile.

Michael laughed and said, "I promise to be on my best behavior."

They were pulling into the gates of the apartment complex and Michael felt uneasy. He was sure it was due to him seeing his mom. He had been dreading this for some time. He was so happy that Malcolm could sense this and had given not just him but all the kids a means to escape if things got too intense. At that moment, Michael felt very close to Malcolm. It was very much like a feeling he would have for his own dad.

Malcolm pulled the car in front of a garage door and waited for it to open. He looked over at Michael, who had a very serious expression on his face. "I know, it's pretty swanky here. Just be on your best behavior and the complex police won't bother you."

Michael looked at Malcolm and said, "I will, and thank you. This place looks huge! How many bedrooms do you have?"

Malcolm gave Michael a tour of the apartment and showed him where he and Micah would be sleeping. "Now, I will let you and Micah fight it out. You can take the couch which pulls out or the smaller guest bedroom. The girls will have the larger guest bedroom with the full-size bed."

Michael nodded. He looked at the couch and it looked comfortable enough. He noted the size of the flat screen TV and thought it would be perfect for streaming movies and games. He and Micah would have no problems figuring it out. He left his bag in the smaller bedroom for now so it would be out of the way. The apartment was nice! He could tell where Malcolm had introduced some of his style into certain areas. Those were the warmest parts of the apartment.

"So, are you hungry? There's a decent sushi place nearby, or whatever you want is pretty close."

"Sushi? In Nashville? Is it fried or barbequed?" Michael joked, "I have got to try this! Let's go!"

Michael had to eat his words along with the amazing sushi. The place was in a strip mall, and he knew as soon as they turned in that this restaurant would be the real deal. The best local eateries were normally off the beaten path. There were some fried options on the menu, however most of the items listed were authentic. Michael and Malcolm caught up some more.

"Micah and Janae's plane will come in early tomorrow. I will drive you around so you can get used to where everything is. Sometimes the map apps are not as accurate around here. There is so much new construction going on right now - pretty hard for apps to keep up."

They headed back to the apartment about 1pm. Michael put the leftovers in the refrigerator. They barely fit. He could see that Malcolm was ready to prepare a Thanksgiving feast! He was glad that Malcolm was cooking.

His mom was not the best cook. Well really, she only pulled out all the stops when it was time to impress someone or to gain favor. Malcolm seemed to love to cook and would always make something special when the whole "family" was together.

Michael went into the living room and sat on the couch, while Malcolm checked his phone.

"Hey, I've got to answer some emails for work. Your mom should be home in an hour or so. Make yourself at home. I will be in the office nook. Welp - looks like the emails have turned into a conference call. Hopefully, it won't take too long."

Michael saw the intensity in Malcolm's face and nodded. He went to the spare bedroom so he would be out of the way. He texted his dad and Katie to let them know he was safe. They both responded immediately. His dad texted that he would call him later. Katie said, "See you tonight."

Michael texted some friends and tried to lose himself in a game on his phone, but he felt restless. He was sure it was due to his mom's impending arrival. The good thing was that they would have to go pick up Katie not too long after his mom got home. More cushion between him and his mother. He was thankful for it.

But, even still, his anxiety grew as every minute passed. He felt like the walls were closing in. He had to get out and get some air. Maybe a walk around the complex would soothe him. He checked his phone to make sure that it was charged and went to see if Malcolm was still on his call.

Malcolm was just wrapping up the call. "Yeah Chris, I have your notes. Nothing like a last-minute change to keep you sharp right? Yeah, thanks man. If I don't talk to you, have a great Thanksgiving. I will get these changes out before 4pm." Malcolm ended the call.

Michael waited a moment and said, "Hey, do you mind if I walk around the complex? I'm feeling a bit closed in back there."

"Sure man. It's hard to get lost. Clubhouse is up front where we came in. There's a pool up there and workout room you can check out. It's nice and spacious. Just be back in 20 minutes. Your mom should be home by then."

Michael nodded and promised he would be back soon. He thought the tension he was feeling would ease up but at the thought of his mom coming made it worse.

Michael walked up the side path toward the clubhouse. The weather was mild. Much like California. He had on a light jacket and that kept him warm. He made it to the clubhouse in about eight minutes. Malcolm had given him the gate card so he could get in and out of the clubhouse.

Michael went in the back way where the pool was. It was a decent size. It was closed for the season and the gate around it was secured. There were two large grills and patio furniture. He had to admit the pool area would make for a great party area.

He checked out the gym. The equipment was new and there were a lot of different machines. He wandered around the room for a moment and then he left.

There was a separate room with tanning beds. There was also a business center with computers, printers, and a fax machine. "People still use fax machines?"

He went into the main area of the clubhouse and saw that it had already been decorated for Christmas. There were four grand

Christmas trees, decorated and lit in each corner. There were multiple couches and chairs for lounging. The area was well lit. There was a coffee bar with gourmet coffees that you could make yourself. It was all great looking but eerie. There was Christmas music playing over the speakers. Something was missing. Warmth was missing.

The building seemed to be empty. The music playing over the speakers made the clubhouse seem even more eerie. It was somewhat loud, kind of a jazz hybrid version of a popular Christmas song. He could also hear someone talking on the phone and assumed it was a leasing agent. He decided it was time to go back to the apartment and wait for his mom. But instead, he sat on the couch and zoned out. He tuned into the music and a sudden feeling of loneliness took over him.

He tried to shake it off after a few moments, but it felt better to sit on the couch and let the solitude wash over him. Just a few minutes had gone by, but it felt much longer. He fought the feeling to stay on the couch and got up hastily. He didn't check his phone, yet he knew he was dangerously close to, if not already, late for meeting his mom.

He lost his bearings trying to leave the building for a minute and finally found his way out of a back door of the clubhouse. He found his way back to the path leading to the apartment. He walked quickly, long legs pumping as he noticed that the sun was just starting to set. He went to the front door which he had left unlocked when he left. He took a deep breath at the bottom of the stairs and had barely closed the door when he heard the beginnings of an argument.

"You let him go by himself? He could be anywhere?!" Bonnie had felt particularly charged and wanted to have a good fight before picking up Katie. She had been bored at work and needed an outlet. It seemed trite when she really thought about it, to start an argument over where her very responsible 17-year-old son was at this moment. It's not like he had been missing for hours. They were hardly in danger of missing the pick-up time for Katie and yet, starting this argument felt right, so she went with it.

"Hold on, I will call him, he probably just lost track of time. He's only five minutes late." Malcolm grabbed his cell phone.

"Only five minutes late? He could be smoking dope at some weirdo's house for all we know! Or worse he's cuddled up with some inbred tramp in the woods. I knew I should have taken the day off! I knew I shouldn't have trusted you!"

Michael stood at the bottom of the stairs, silent and listening. He slowly opened the door and slammed it shut as loudly as he could without trying to take if off the hinges. He hoped that would stop the argument. He ran up the stairs, saying, "Hey, I don't know how time got away from me! The clubhouse is cool! Is it time to go get Katie? Do I have time to use the bathroom?" Michael sidestepped his mom and dashed to the bathroom to give them a few moments to collect themselves. But of course, Bonnie could not collect herself.

She hissed at Malcolm, "You can't let him go wandering around on his own! It's dangerous out there. Just because you let your kids wander around the neighborhood at all hours of the night like wild, rabid wolves!"

Malcolm could feel the rage building inside him once Bonnie compared his children to animals. He tried to get his temper under control, but he couldn't. "Wolves? Did you just say wolves?" He laughed to try to get himself under control, but it was another failed attempt. He gave in to the anger he had been holding in.

"Don't ever compare my children to wild animals, ever again. Speaking of which, my children want to be with me! Your kids don't want to have anything to do with you!" He stopped there, realizing he was about to go too far.

"Malcolm, I didn't mean it like that! It was just a figure of speech." Bonnie sensed she had crossed some cultural line, but she had decided that there was no such thing as a cultural line if they were truly a couple. He would need to get over it.

Malcolm turned and looked at her and saw that she was relishing the moment.

"YOU JUST DON'T UNDERSTAND! YOU NEVER WILL!"

Bonnie backed away. "I am trying to understand, please give me a chance and explain it to me so I can understand." She forced her voice to tremble and worked up some tears for good measure.

Malcolm could see right through her act and his anger doubled and exploded. "NO!! IT'S IMPOSSIBLE FOR YOU TO GET IT! YOU AREN'T EVEN TRYING...ALL YOU DO IS LOOK DOWN ON ME AND MY FAMILY! AND NOW I KNOW YOUR TRUE FEELINGS AND MOTIVES!"

Michael had come out of the bathroom at this point. He took note of what Malcolm said and thought, "Good for you, my dude! You're much too good for her anyway." Michael stepped in between Bonnie and Malcolm, and said, "Hey, it's not that serious. It was totally my fault, I promised to be back on time, and I lost track of time. Honest mistake. It won't happen again, I promise." He continued slowly and in a soothing tone. "Besides, shouldn't we get ready to go and pick up Katie? We don't want to be late." He turned sideways and headed to the stairwell. He winked at Malcolm so his mom couldn't see. "I don't think I locked the front door, let me check it before we leave."

Malcolm turned away from Bonnie and saw that the balcony door was open. He closed it with an incredulous smile on his face. He looked out the window for a moment and saw a woman getting into her car. He also heard a door close from across the bottom of the hill. His heart sank. Had the neighbors heard this argument? Did he look like the angry black man that couldn't control his temper? Had the police been called? He locked the balcony door and grabbed his phone and jacket. He headed toward the garage exit.

Bonnie stood there dumbfounded. She was trying to figure out how she lost control of this argument. Not only had she lost control of the argument; it had been completely diffused. How?

"Mom, you coming? We don't want to be late. Or do you want to stay here and rest while we're out?" Michael chose his words carefully; he didn't want to restart the storm. "This will probably be your last chance to be alone before your home is invaded with all of us unruly kids, you know?"

Bonnie nodded, "Yes, you're right. I think I will stay and take a long bath. See you when you get back." She went over to Michael and kissed him on the cheek while giving him a squeeze. It was as if she remembered that she was a mother who hadn't seen her son in more than a month.

Michael grabbed his jacket and headed down to the car. He smiled at himself. "Looks like I'm finally learning to play the game." He hopped in the car, "Mom decided to stay here and take a bath."

"Did she? Or was she persuaded?" Malcolm looked at Michael with more than a hint of suspicion. "Kid, you really know how to do some damage control! Where'd you learn that?"

"Aww, you know how it is. Years of being on the end of that, you learn how to deflect and gain control."

"So, uh, you pretty much blew smoke and got lucky then, huh?" countered Malcolm.

Michael laughed, "Yeah, that's it really! I was just hoping she would calm down! What was that about anyway?"

"Man, I don't know. She does it a lot now and I never know when it's coming. But enough of that. Let's go get Katie and figure out dinner. I'm sure your mom is too tired to think about that after the dramatics."

Michael laughed and silently patted himself on the back for the good deed he had performed. He settled into his seat as Malcolm drove toward the gate. He hoped that this was the only blow up that would happen this weekend. But he knew more was to come. He was glad that Micah and Janae would arrive tomorrow. Mom would want to put on a show for them, so hopefully nothing like what almost happened tonight would happen again.

Malcolm enjoyed the peace with Michael in the car as they went to get Katie. Every so often, he would look at Michael and could tell the boy was really riding high on his victory this evening. Malcolm smiled to himself and could feel his bond with Michael becoming stronger.

They had spent a fair amount of time together over the years and yet he felt like he had missed out on Michael growing up, but he knew that Michael and his real dad were close. He made up his mind that he would make a better effort to build on their relationship.

Katie waited outside of the terminal for her brother and Malcolm. Her flight had arrived on time, and she was quite independent and industrious.

She hadn't checked a bag, so she followed the signs to the baggage claim area and waited for a moment before she became bored.

Katie knew she was in a strange city and that she should stay inside where it was safe, but she was filled with anxiety. She wasn't ready to see her mom and she wasn't sure she wanted to stay for the holiday.

She didn't want to abandon her brother, but she just wanted to be at peace at home or somewhere else.

She pondered about going outside and wandered around the baggage claim area for a while. Then without a second thought, she stepped outside into the night air.

It was cool, cooler than California and there were a lot of people milling around waiting to be picked up. She felt like she could get lost in the crowd. She found a concrete bench and sat down on the cold surface. She got lost in her thoughts and her anxiety levels crept higher and higher. She pulled herself out of her thoughts and looked around. There was still a good-sized crowd of people, although some of the faces had changed. It was one of the busiest days of the year for air travel.

Katie had a thought, "What's to stop me from going back into the airport and calling Dad? What's to stop me from asking to return home now instead of Sunday? What's to stop me from spending Thanksgiving in the home that I know?"

She knew that she had to decide on whether she would agree to live with her mom after this trip. The truth was that she had already made her decision and she knew her mom would see that as soon as her eyes fell upon her. Katie knew that her mom would be filled with rage and would conceal it behind dramatics and false kindness.

Katie looked around and then down at the ground. She couldn't abandon Michael, Janae, and Micah. Or maybe she could. There would be enough people in the house for her mom to concentrate on. Maybe Katie would not be missed at all. She nodded her head and made up her mind.

She stood up and headed back toward the doors when her phone rang. She pulled the phone out of her pocket and saw that it was her brother calling. "Hello? Yes, I am downstairs sitting outside of the terminal. Okay, I will keep a lookout for a white car - 4 doors. Got it."

Well, her escape plan had just fallen through. She slumped back on the concrete bench and waited.

Michael could hear the strangeness in his sister's voice. He knew that she, just like he, was not thrilled about coming here. "Just travel jitters," he thought. He felt confident that he would be able to cheer her up once they picked her up.

The evening air was a bit chillier than the afternoon. Malcolm and Michael pulled up into the busy terminal. It was brightly lit, and they saw Katie sitting on a bench, brow furrowed, completely lost in her thoughts.

"Katie! Katie! C'mon," Michael yelled as he hung out the window.

Katie snapped back into reality and jumped up, grabbing her bag. She walked to the car, slowly.

Michael jumped out and opened the trunk for her bag. He opened the back door, so she could climb in. Then he thought, "She probably needs to ride up front, so she can see the city." He wrapped her up in a big hug and kissed her on her forehead, knowing she hated that. Katie yelped and swatted at her brother. He took her bag and held the front passenger side car door open for her, "Milady, if you please." He bowed deeply.

Katie giggled and curtsied, "Thank you kind sir." She gingerly sat in the car and Michael closed the door after she was safely inside.

He tossed her bag in the trunk and got in the backseat.

Malcolm watched and grinned from ear to ear. Chuckling to himself at what he had just witnessed.

"I know, I mean who curtsies anymore? That's pretty high brow!"

Katie turned and looked at her brother sternly, "Peasant!"

Malcolm and Michael burst into laughter as Malcolm pulled away from the curb.

Katie felt relieved that her mom was not in the car. The I40 entrance to the highway was directly off the airport exit. They headed west. She looked out the window as Michael and Malcolm talked about all the things they had done that day. They pulled onto Briley Parkway, still chatting away.

Michael saw the sign for Opryland Mall and had a wonderful idea.

"Malcolm, do you think we can grab something to eat at the mall? You know, sit down and regroup before going home?"

Katie knew this was too good to be true. Something must have happened with Mom already.

"Regroup? What happened?"

Michael could sense the fear in her voice and was a little shocked. Katie was always better at handling Mom than he was.

"Nothing too bad. Your mom just got into one of her moods," Malcolm answered. "But your brother handled it like a pro. The situation was diffused." Malcolm cleared his throat, not quite believing that the situation was done yet he hoped for the best.

"I think we should go to the mall to eat. There's a great new Mexican place I've been dying to try. They make the tortillas and guacamole in front of you." Malcolm looked at the shocked faces of Michael and Katie.

"Sir, are you making an executive decision to not include our dear mother in tonight's dinner plans?" asked Michael.

"Well, I uh...YES! I am! Let's eat in peace!" Malcolm was tired of being hen-pecked, if that was the proper term for what this was. He just knew that lately, he felt as if he had been "handled" and it was not a feeling he liked or wanted to continue.

"I will call your mom and tell her. We will bring her something to go." He got onto the exit at Briley Parkway and followed the signs to the mall.

He found a parking space close by. He was shocked since it was 6pm and prime dinner time. However, he took it as a sign that he and the kids were not supposed to go home just yet.

He sent Michael and Katie into the restaurant to get a table while he called Bonnie. He leaned against the car as the phone rang. He calmly waited as the phone rang and to his surprise, voicemail picked up.

"Hey Bonnie, I'm taking the kids to that new Mexican place at the mall. Text me and let me know if you want anything. See you later." He hesitated and then hung up the phone. "I wonder if she's out buying more chocolate cake," he thought. He looked at the phone, sighed, put it in his back pocket and went inside to join the kids. They had an amazing meal and caught up some more.

Bonnie was not out buying cake. She was most definitely at home. Or maybe the appropriate term is that "she was in the space that Michael and Malcolm had left her."

She waited until she was completely alone to let down her guard.

She kept replaying the argument repeatedly in her mind. She kept trying to figure out how she had lost control. Then she moved on to how to get control back over everything.

She paced the floor, walking from the kitchen to the balcony doors. After a few laps, her pace quickened; she kept going, walking in her bare feet with an unlit cigarette between her fingers.

She was lost, completely gone. Her body walked the floor faster and faster. She dropped the cigarette at one point and started wringing her hands as she paced back and forth, back and forth, back and forth, endlessly.

While Bonnie was pacing, the lamps in the living room suddenly turned off. She was oblivious to it. She continued to pace in the darkness, faster and faster. Not once did she bump into a wall or a piece of furniture. She inched closer and closer to the glass balcony door with each lap although she never hit it. A single thought played in her head, "I must get it back. I must get it back. I must get it back." The thought kept playing in her head, faster and faster and to the rhythm at which she paced. Almost like a song.

While she paced, her cell phone flashed showing that she was getting a call. She didn't hear or see anything for some time.

Malcolm decided to show the kids around the mall a bit, after dinner. The decorations were bright and merry. Trees adorned the hallways and wreaths were on nearly every store front. The trees and wreaths were lit in almost every color imaginable.

The stores were pretty standard. Just then Katie saw her favorite sneaker store, and all bets were off. She spent 20 minutes looking at shoes. Malcolm and Michael took note of the ones she stared at or held for a long time. She held a pair of leather powder blue low tops for quite some time and even tried them on at Michael's urging. He took a picture of the box and size without Katie seeing it.

They visited other stores. Clothing and toy stores. They stepped into the cinnamon roll store just to smell the buttery, sugary, cinnamon goodness of it all. They stopped for smoothies.

Malcolm noted that he still had not heard from Bonnie and he decided to let her stew in her own anger juice by herself. He just hoped that the rest of the evening would be quiet.

The trio walked slowly through the mall and Katie's eyes lit up when she saw an aquarium-themed restaurant.

"How come you didn't bring us here to eat?' she asked Malcolm.

"Well, I want the whole fam - I mean I wanted us all to come as a group." Malcolm answered. He didn't know why he kept getting hung up on calling them a family. He knew he loved Katie and Michael; he just couldn't get past some unknown barrier.

Katie barely heard him. She shrieked when she saw the entrance to a wax museum. An actual wax museum. She had been to the one in Hollywood a few times, yet she was far more excited about this one as it was done by the much better-known competitive brand.

"Can we go here once Micah and Janae arrive? I really would like for us all to go together." Well, really, she meant everyone except for her mom.

"We absolutely can," said Malcolm. "Or better yet, why don't you guys go and me and your mom will stay at home."

Katie's face lit up again.

Malcolm could see the stress lines relaxing in her face. "She's just a kid, far too young to have age lines. All this because she doesn't want to be around her mother?" he thought.

Malcolm turned away a bit hurt and looked at Michael. He was surprised to see that Michael had the same disappointed look on his face. He slapped Michael on the back and pushed the group forward to see the next big surprise around the corner. He knew this one would interest Michael.

Michael, who was turning into a regular comedian, clasped his hands together and widened his eyes. He was doing a great job of mimicking a small child on Christmas Day.

"Could it be? All my life I have dreamed about this and here it is! Right here!" Michael then proceeded to skip to the entrance of a large video game arcade/sports bar/restaurant/ bowling alley created by one of the largest chains in the country. So large, that Michael had frequented two of them in the Los Angeles area on many occasions.

Malcolm covered his face and tried to distance himself from this seventeen-year-old boy skipping in a public place. He put his hand on Katie's shoulder to guide her away from the scene.

Katie watched her brother in absolute shock and burst into a fit of laughter. "That's some gait you have there! Have you thought about skipping professionally?"

Michael was almost at the entrance when he stopped in full skip and turned to look at Katie. "What's this? I'm the funny one here." He walked back over to her and said quite earnestly, "Don't steal my moment." He then turned back around and resumed skipping into the arcade.

It took a few minutes for Malcolm and Katie to regain control of themselves from the sheer bout of cackling they were experiencing. Once they were able to compose themselves, they headed for the entrance.

They found Michael surveying the games and he seemed to be thinking quite intently. They walked up to him, and he said, "Yes, I think that we can probably check out a few games and have lunch. Maybe play a few rounds of bowling. Yes, I think this could make for a wonderful afternoon."

Malcolm looked at Michael, smiled and shook his head. "Well, the only thing left to see at this end is the movie theater. But there is something cool that's close by that you would probably like. Let's head back to the car."

Back at home, Bonnie had stopped pacing. She was no longer in the living room. She had moved to the bathroom and was in the middle of taking a bath. The idea of her taking a bath was not her own, especially since what was going on in the bathroom was nothing that she would ever have imagined.

The bathroom was dark except for two red candles that were lit and positioned on either side of the tub. The candles gave off very little light, so essentially, she was in a very dark room. She sat in the tub, which was filled with water. Her eyes were closed, and she seemed to be in the same trance that had taken her over while she was in the living room. The water she sat in was tepid and dark. There was music playing softly in the background. It sounded like an oldies station.

She continued to sit in the tub, eyes closed, limbs unmoving. Slowly, she began to come out of the trance. Her eyes remained closed, her body felt cold and wet. She could sense movement in the room, but she couldn't open her eyes to see what was happening. She tried to move; her body was completely limp as if she was paralyzed. She thought that maybe she was stuck in a bad dream. She tried to relax so she could figure out what to do. Relaxing was hard; she was so used to being in control that she couldn't focus on one thing at a time when she really needed to.

"Start with something small. I can hear so maybe I can hear if someone is home."

So, she listened, she heard the music playing softly, old big band, swing music. Not anything to her liking, plus it seemed to be coming straight from an old record player. She could hear the soft scratches in the music as if the needle needed to be changed. It seemed to be coming from all around her, from above, the sides and even resonating in the water. She knew this was not something that Malcolm or Michael would listen to and neither one of them would invade her space while she was in the tub.

She focused on listening to hear anything else. There was nothing. No movement in the apartment, no voices.

"What if I'm not in the apartment? Nothing feels as it should." She felt herself beginning to panic and managed to get back in control. "This is crazy. I'm at home. I fell asleep in the tub after some sort of manic episode. I've been in the tub so long that the water is cold. Everyone is still out of the house."

She wasn't concerned with her easy use of the word "manic" or the fact that she couldn't explain the music. She would deal with that at another time.

She tried to open her eyes. She could feel her eyelids flutter a bit before they gave out. She focused on what she could see through her closed lids. She saw movement - candlelight. It was dim and moving above her on the ceiling, she thought. The candles must be throwing shadows on the ceiling. She surprised herself when she let out an actual sigh of relief.

She could tell she was regaining control of her body again. She decided to rest a moment so she could gather more strength. Then she would try to open her eyes again. She heard a strange tapping coming from the doorway. She couldn't tell if the sound was coming from inside the bathroom or just outside. She didn't know if the bathroom door was open. Fear started to build inside her - what if someone was in the apartment? Maybe they had drugged her and put her in the tub. Maybe they were waiting for her to wake-up so they could torture and kill her.

She went back to calming herself down. Even if someone was in the apartment, she would have to remain calm and think of a plan.

She tried to gauge her surroundings and the position of her body in the tub. She could tell that her face was facing toward the wall. She shook off that thought and realized that she could probably open her eyes without being seen, in case someone was watching.

She waited a few minutes to see if the tapping would stop and it had. She had no clue as to when it had stopped but it had. She waited a while longer to try to sense any movement in the bathroom. She listened for breathing or any other sounds of life beyond her own in the bathroom.

She heard nothing.

She decided to open her eyes. She knew she had the strength to do more than that, but she wanted to start slow.

Her eyes focused on the white bathroom wall; the familiar subway tile that she had fallen in love with was a relief to see. She waited and listened to make sure she was alone, then she slowly turned her head toward the light and what she saw drew her back into the blank, black sea of darkness she had just emerged from. The last thing she remembered was a man. A very tall man, wearing some sort of hat with horns. Horns so long and curly, and yet they touched the ceiling. His chest was bare, and his skin was gray and...and? She couldn't think of the words. Scaly wasn't right and while her mind was trying to grasp at that she noticed that there were two candles floating in a circle, close to the ceiling and in time with the music. Wrapped in his left arm was a large black cat with huge, glowing orange eyes, quietly hissing at her.

What broke her from what she assumed was not reality were two things.

First, his hands, they weren't hands at all, they were.... claws.

That was the closest she could get to describing them.

He wasn't looking at her at first but staring straight ahead. It seemed as if he sensed that she had awakened, and he or it looked down at her.

And second, its eyes were bright red and glowing, with large black pupils. By the time she had gotten to the pupils she had slipped back into the blackness.

Malcolm tried calling Bonnie again. She still was not answering. He thought that he was going to be in for a long night of arguing in hushed voices. Maybe he could sleep on the couch to avoid it.

"Well, your mom's not answering. Let's go over to the hotel and look at the lights." He tried to hide his concern. Then he thought, "This is probably her way of trying to make us worry so we will rush home."

"I will send her a text to see if we should pick something up for her on the way home, after we look at the lights. You know she tends to take super long baths. Or maybe she went to bed early," said Michael. He could see the look of worry on Malcolm's face. He honestly didn't want to go back to the apartment; it was more than just his mom's strange behavior; he just felt the place was off. He convinced himself that he was just nervous being in a new place and that there wasn't anything strange going on. Yet he couldn't convince himself of that completely.

"Okay, let's see those lights!" Malcolm and the kids got in the car and headed around to the hotel entrance. It was still early even though it was completely dark outside. He would have the kids home no later than 7:30pm. He figured he would call Bonnie one last time if she didn't respond to Michael's text.

Bonnie woke up, still sitting in the tub. The water was freezing and gray and it stunk! The candles were still lit and sitting on the edge of the tub. Wax was running into the tub from the candles that she didn't recognize. The bathroom door was closed and there was no music playing.

She grabbed the sides of the tub to stand up and her hand grazed against something on the side of the tub.

She got out first and turned on the lights. She blew out the candles and pulled the stopper out of the tub. She had to turn her face away from the water because it smelled so bad.

She started cleaning up the mess and when she reached to start cleaning up the wax, she noticed the cat hair on her arm from where she had brushed it against the tub. The cat hair was horribly pungent, and she turned and grabbed the sink to steady herself while she dry-heaved.

After a moment, she went back to cleaning. She pulled the cat hair off her hand and threw it in the trash can. The tub had drained and the bottom of it was covered in the black cat hair. It still reeked even though it had been sitting in water for some time.

She looked down at herself and saw that she was covered in the hair too.

She ran to the kitchen and grabbed some paper towels to clean the hair out of the tub. She sprayed the tub down with bleach and cleaned it three times. The tub was sparkling by the time she was done. She was worried that the red wax might have bled into the surface of the tub, but it must not have set long enough to do so. She threw away the candles.

Then she took the paper towels and tried to wipe as much of the hair off her body as possible.

She then turned the shower on and scrubbed herself down until her skin was pink. There was still hair on the bottom of the tub once she was done. She got more paper towels and wiped up most of it and then scrubbed the tub with bleach again.

She turned on the fan in the bathroom to get the heavy smell of the bleach out.

She reached for the robe hanging on the back of the door and slid into it. It was the first time that she felt like her normal self in what? Hours?

What time was it? She went to the living room to find her phone and stopped dead in her tracks!

Both lamps were on but one was laying on its side. The balcony door was open. The pillows on the couches were either out of place or on the floor. Her carefully picked out decorative throws were unfolded and laying over the tables.

A slight breeze blew in through the balcony door and feathers floated up from the floor. Bonnie could see that one of her carefully picked out throw pillows had been completely gutted.

Bonnie could feel the panic rise in her again. She ran over and closed the balcony door and locked it. She turned around to survey the room for any more damages. As she surveyed the room over she thought, "What if someone was in the apartment? What if they are still in here?"

She grabbed her cell phone off the kitchen counter and saw that she had missed three calls from Malcolm and a text from Michael. She started to call the police and thought if someone were in the apartment, they most likely would have made themselves known by now.

She read the text from Michael and answered it with shaking hands. She put the phone in her bathrobe pocket and went to the bedroom. She went to the bench at the edge of the bed and opened it. She reached down past the comforters and the packages that Malcolm's wife had sent to the house when they were in California and found the holster with the gun in it.

She unsheathed the gun and turned the safety off. She searched the entire apartment twice, quickly, and quietly. She checked each closet and cabinet. No one was there. She put the gun back in the holster and returned it to the deepest part of the bench. She made a mental note to get rid of the packages the ex had sent.

She ran back to the living room and started cleaning up the feathers. She grabbed the nearly full trash can from the bathroom and put the remnants of the pillow in it. She put the pillows back in place on the couch and folded up the throws and placed them over the backs of the couches. She doubted that Malcolm or Michael would notice that a pillow was missing.

She vacuumed the floor and saw the discarded unlit cigarette laying on the floor. It was soaking wet and covered in cat hair. She picked it up gingerly and threw it in the trash. She could smell something coming from it and she crinkled up her nose. She quickly finished vacuuming and checked the apartment from top to bottom several more times.

Once she was done, she tossed her robe in the washing machine. She went to the bedroom and put on a fresh set of pajamas. She then went to the kitchen and poured herself a glass of wine. She checked her phone and saw that Michael had responded to her dinner request. She sat on the couch and replayed the evening.

What happened? She remembered being in the living room and being angry that her drama bomb for the evening had been diffused. She remembered walking to the window and thinking about how it happened. She remembered turning and walking back to the kitchen and then her memory went blank.

How did she get in the tub? Where were her clothes? She ran to the bedroom and checked the hamper. She checked the bathroom, but she knew they weren't there because she had cleaned it several times. She checked the entire apartment again and saw no sign of her clothes. She looked under the beds and the furniture in all the rooms and...nothing. She went back to her seat in the living room.

The water - why was it so disgusting and gray? Had she had an accident in the tub? Even if she had, where had all the cat hair come from? The hair was real. She could see strands of it pressed against the inside of the plastic bag that was still on the floor in the kitchen.

What about the man she saw? Or was it something else? Was someone in the apartment? Did they drug her? The cat that was in his or its arms. That would explain the cat hair. "No, that was not real!"

If someone were in the apartment, how did they get in? They didn't climb in through the balcony. Bonnie jumped again and checked the garage entrance door. It was unlocked as always, and the garage door was down.

She came back inside and checked the front door at the bottom of the stairs. Not only was it locked, but the privacy lock was also in place too.

So, she had an extremely vivid nightmare, where smelly cat hair fell from the ceiling, or someone had been in the apartment through some unknown entrance.

The truth had to be somewhere in between. But what was the truth?

Bonnie finished her wine and turned off one of the lamps in the living room. She put the wine glass in the sink. She looked around the living room and saw the plastic bag from the bathroom again. She grabbed the bag, grabbed her keys, and drove it to the dumpster just inside of the gates that led out of the apartment complex.

Her head started throbbing as she headed back into the apartment. She checked all the doors again. She left the garage entrance door to the kitchen open so Malcolm and the kids could get in once they returned. She checked the apartment one last time for any clues or items that needed to be discarded and found nothing. She went into the bedroom and closed the door. She was very close to locking it then thought against it. If something was coming into the apartment, it didn't need a key.

She shivered and got in the bed. She turned on the TV for noise mainly and laid down. Her head still hurt so she grabbed some aspirin from the nightstand and swallowed them dry.

She couldn't stop her mind from wondering so she tried her best to clear her thoughts. But every few seconds something random would pop into her mind. Like, what about the music? Where was it coming from? "There was no music," she countered herself.

"What was it staring at? It looked like it was staring through the wall. Could it see through walls? Is that how it knew she was alone?"

"Okay, so now you are going full on crazy, huh?"

Exasperated with herself, she rolled over on her stomach and put her hand under the pillow as was her normal sleeping position. Then she recoiled in terror. She turned on the lamp on the nightstand and stared at the pillow. She reached for it and flipped it over finding another mound of long black cat hair. She jumped up and grabbed the hair with her hands and ran to the balcony. She threw the hair out of the sliding glass door, closed it, locked it, and went back into the bedroom.

There was no time to wash the sheets, so she grabbed some linen spray and used it on the entire bed. Malcolm and the kids wouldn't be home for another hour or so. That should give the smell of the spray enough time to weaken. She turned off the lamp and laid back down, her headache was gone yet she was wide awake.

Then Bonnie did something she rarely ever did.

She cried. The tears came fast and hot. She buried her head in her pillow and let the fear and sadness take her over. The room was dark except for the light coming from the TV. While her head was buried in the pillow a pair of eyes bright red with huge black pupils watched her from the opposite corner. And if she hadn't been crying so loudly, she would have heard the not so soft purrs of a cat.

Bonnie drifted into an uneasy sleep at about ten minutes to seven. She felt herself falling deeper and deeper into a terrifying chasm. She tried unsuccessfully to slow her descent. It seemed to be unending.

Malcolm and the kids pulled back into the garage just after 7pm.

"Hey! We had a great time tonight. I want us to continue to enjoy the rest of the holiday week and not make your mom the "bad guy." Malcolm continued slowly, "I don't know what's going on with her but let's try to make sure that she feels secure in her relationships with all of us. Maybe she's nervous about us being together in a new place for the holiday."

He sighed, "Anyway, let's give her a break and try to be patient and a bit more understanding."

Malcolm walked up the stairs leading to the garage entry door. He turned around and looked at Katie and Michael and saw that they were listening and genuinely taking in what he was saying. Malcolm felt proud, "Okay, Janae and Micah will be here in the morning. Who wants to go with me to the airport to pick them up?"

He overlooked the fact that they were still standing just outside the car door. "Guys, it's gonna be okay. If it wasn't, we would have known by now. Remember, patience and understanding."

Michael and Katie looked at each other and sighed. They made their way to the stairs and climbed them slowly but steadily.

Michael had already opened the unlocked door and surveyed the area for any "land mines." He looked back at the kids, "All clear. Wait in the living room and I will check to see if your mom is still up." He took the bag of still warm food from the same steak restaurant he had been to a few weeks before and set the it on the counter, braced himself and headed toward the bedroom.

He stepped lightly as he entered the hall and saw that the door to the bedroom he shared with Bonnie was closed. He could hear that the TV was on, he noted that there was no light coming out to the hallway from under the door.

He gently opened the bedroom door, "Bon, we are back," he said gently.

The room was indeed dark. He could see the shape of Bonnie lying in the bed. Covers pulled up to her forehead. Nest of hair sprawled out on the pillow. "She must have been really tired; she didn't put her hair in a ponytail like she normally does."

"Bonnie, are you hungry?" Malcolm waited for a moment and when there was no response, he gently closed the door and headed back to the living room.

If he had stepped in the room, he would have seen that Bonnie was not exactly sleeping. Her eyes were wide open, and she was staring at something in the corner across from where she lay in the bed.

The bright red-orange eyes were still there, seemingly hanging in mid-air and staring deep into Bonnie's. Bonnie didn't move or speak. Tears streamed down her face making her pillow wet and cold. She could feel herself sinking into a horrid, dark nothingness and there was nothing she could do to stop it.

By now, Malcolm was out in the living room putting away the food they had gotten for Bonnie.

Michael gave Katie the tour of the apartment and showed her where she and Micah would be sleeping. Katie saw that her mom's bedroom was across the hall from hers. She wondered if she should go in and say, "Hi." She edged closer to the closed bedroom door, she put her hand on the doorknob when everything inside of her said not to go in. So, she didn't.

Katie took off her low tops and jacket and put them away. She went to the guest bathroom and washed her hands. Then she joined Michael and Malcolm in the living room where they sat and watched TV.

Malcolm figured the siblings wanted some time to catch up, so he left them about 9:30pm and headed to bed. He locked the garage door and checked to make sure his keys were hanging on the hook next to the refrigerator.

He turned off all the lights and checked the door at the bottom of the stairs that was the front entrance to the apartment. He hugged Katie and gave Michael a fist bump and went to the bedroom.

Bonnie was still "sleeping."

Malcolm went to the bathroom, turned on the lights and closed the door. He undressed and brushed his teeth. He caught a slight whiff of bleach and figured Bonnie had decided to do some cleaning to blow off steam. As he brushed his teeth the bleach smell became overwhelming, and he noticed that the bathroom looked extremely bright and white – much more so than normal.

"She must have really been mad. No wonder she's out cold," thought Malcolm.

Malcolm grabbed the remote which was laying in the middle of the bed, turned on the last of the news and set the TV timer for 90 minutes. He made it as far as the sports highlights before falling asleep. He hardly noticed that Bonnie hadn't moved. Nor did he see the orange eyes in the corner or the cat hair that fell from the corner out of thin air.

Thanksgiving Eve was here, and Malcolm was excited. He woke up ready to work a few hours and then start his Thanksgiving meal prep. It was going to be an amazing feast.

Not surprisingly, he woke up before his alarm went off at 6:30am. He knew that Bonnie was already up which was highly unusual.

She would stay in bed and hit the snooze button until 7:15am, then she would jump up, shower and be ready for work in 20 minutes flat complete with accessories and make-up. He didn't know how she did it.

Malcolm got up after he realized Bonnie wasn't in the bathroom. He figured she went to go see the kids since they didn't spend any time together the day before. He headed to the bathroom to start his morning routine. He thought to himself, "I am really excited about spending time with the family."

Malcolm stopped brushing his teeth and realized that he had used the word "family" for the first time regarding his relationship with Bonnie and the kids.

What does that mean? He saw the kids clearly as a part of his life, his own as well as Michael and Katie. He still could not fit Bonnie into the picture.

Malcolm hated following this path of reason because it meant that a life-altering decision was coming. If he couldn't see Bonnie as a true lifelong partner in California or here, then what was he holding on to? "Well, no going back now. It's out in the open. Time to start working on an exit strategy," he thought.

He looked at himself in the mirror. His face seemed more relaxed, and he knew it had to do with Michael and Katie.

Michael and Katie!! What would a break-up mean for them? He really did love them both. He would never want to hurt either of them.

He also remembered that this trip would decide if Katie wanted to live here in Nashville with Bonnie and him. He could sense that she really didn't want to move in with them. He didn't need to hear it from her. Malcolm ending this relationship would certainly take the pressure off Katie having to choose between her mom and dad.

He knew that Michael would be fine, this was his senior year, and he would be off to college soon. They would be able to stay in touch no matter what.

Malcolm thought some more while finishing his morning ritual.

He knew that Micah and Janae had only been tolerating Bonnie. Both kids had tried hard to make a connection with Bonnie, but her behavior at times made it very hard to get close to her.

Micah had just turned 20 and was into his second year at Frederickson Engineering and Science University. He was doing very well and spent most of his time on campus studying and hanging out with his friends in his spare time.

There wouldn't be much of a change for Micah; he would probably be relieved.

Janae would be even more relieved than Micah.

THE OAKS ON THE GLEN

Janae had entered college early at the age of 16 and was studying drama and arts. She was very beautiful and could be an actress if she wanted or even a model. But she chose to work behind the scenes as a writer, editor or set manager. She could do anything she wanted, she was incredibly smart and determined.

By now, Malcolm was in the bedroom getting dressed. The rest of the apartment was quiet. The kids must still be sleeping.

He glanced at the clock on his nightstand. It read 6:50am.

He continued with his "break-up thought process/plan."

Yes, Janae would be very relieved. Both kids had remained respectful and kind toward Bonnie. But Malcolm could see that Janae was on the edge of rebelling whenever her jaw tensed up and it took a lot for her jaw to tense up.

Usually, someone would diffuse the situation and things would stay calm. But it was tiresome because Bonnie never knew when to draw the line and behave like an adult.

On the plus side, he knew that Janae and Michael liked each other, and they would be more likely to pursue a relationship if he and Bonnie were not together.

Is this becoming a win-win situation for everyone?

Well, except for Bonnie. But Bonnie had to know that everyone was unhappy. He doubted that she was happy either. But she would carry on as if everything was fine.

Malcolm left the bedroom and went to check on the kids.

They were still asleep in their beds.

There was no sign of Bonnie in the kitchen. He pulled out milk, eggs, bacon, and sausage from the refrigerator to make breakfast for the kids. He felt a breeze coming from behind him while he was standing at the sink.

He turned and saw that the balcony door was open even though he had closed it and locked it last night. He figured Bonnie must have had a cigarette late last night or early this morning. He went out and stood on the balcony and took in the view.

It was quiet. The air was cool and brisk. He could smell wood burning which was comforting on a fall day. He turned around to go back inside when something caught his eye.

There was something in one of the chairs.

At first, he thought it was a blanket or a jacket. When he got closer, he realized that it was clothing. In fact, it was the clothing that Bonnie had on yesterday. Her shirt, pants and sweater were thrown over the chair.

Malcolm was taken aback. He picked up the clothes, which were freezing, and knew they had been in the chair for some time. As he gathered the clothes, Bonnie's panties and bra fell from the pile onto the floor. He quickly picked them up and headed inside to put them in the hamper.

He grabbed his cell and hesitated in calling Bonnie. He felt like he would be poking an angry bear.

Where was she? Did she go into work?

He went back to the fridge to give himself a moment to think. He saw that the food they had brought for Bonnie last night was gone.

He called her. The call went to voicemail. So, he texted her. "Hey! R u okay? Where r u? Did u have 2 go in 2 work? Call me, I am worried."

He checked the garage and her car was gone. "She had to have gone to work," he thought.

He started prepping for the Thanksgiving dinner. He went back to the fridge, he pulled out celery, onions, tomatoes, and peppers.

He then pulled out ham, turkey, greens, and buttermilk.

He set to work on making breakfast. Bacon, sausage, eggs, and pancakes to rouse the sleeping children. He laughed at himself. He cut up scallions to put into the eggs. He prepped the bacon and sausage for the oven and started working on the pancake batter.

He glanced at the phone every so often to see if his text message would be answered.

He moved around the kitchen getting vanilla, nutmeg, cinnamon, and sugar. He debated on what kind of fruit and nuts to add to the pancakes. He decided on bananas and walnuts. He crushed up the bananas and walnuts and added them to the batter.

He took in the irresistible smell of the bacon and sausage cooking in the oven.

He put on a pot of blueberry-flavored coffee purchased from a local coffee place called, "We've Got Beans!"

His phone remained quiet. He was caught between worry and relief. Then he remembered, if something had happened to Bonnie, he would be the number one suspect.

He picked up the phone and called her again. Voicemail again.

He could hear Michael and Katie stirring from their beds.

The bacon had gotten to them.

He went back to cooking the eggs and started on the pancakes.

He melted butter in a pan and went to pull the syrup, potatoes, and cocoa powder from the pantry.

Katie popped into the kitchen first and sat in one of the bar stools so she could watch Malcolm in action.

"How did you sleep K?"

"I slept pretty well and then the smell of bacon and coffee woke me up!"

"You drink coffee?'

"No, but I would like to try some if you don't mind. It smells wonderful."

Katie had bedhead hair and was wearing powder blue and white pajamas. She twirled around in the bar stool chair. "Man, I miss being a kid. Twirling is so 3rd grade."

Malcolm laughed and shook his head. He tried not to show that he was nervous. His hands were shaking slightly but he pushed on. At least he could give the kids a good meal before the police picked him up for suspicion of whatever could happen to a missing woman, particularly a white woman in a relationship with a black man, who had argued heavily during a holiday weekend.

Then of course, he was the last one to see her alive. Then there was the bleach smell in the bathroom and the clothes he retrieved from the balcony with his DNA all over them.

"Yep, they are going to fry me," he thought.

The eggs were going to have to take great strides in possibly being his greatest last home-cooked meal.

Michael finally appeared around the corner with an equally impressive case of bedhead himself. Michael greeted Katie and sat on the stool next to her. He looked across the bar at Malcolm and said, "Wow, we haven't had one of your home-cooked breakfasts in a really long time. Should I pull out my formal breakfast attire? I think I have a cravat in my suitcase, although I left my pipe at home."

"I don't know if a cravat will go with your hair," chided Katie.

Malcolm was so entertained by the kids, that he almost forgot about his missing...Bonnie.

He reached for the phone again to see if she had answered his text and just as his hand touched the surface of it, it started ringing! It was Bonnie!

Malcolm turned the eggs on low and stepped away to answer the call. "Hey Michael, will you keep an eye on the eggs for me?"

"Sure, but I expect a portion of the tip," Michael responded. He hopped off the stool and went in for a closer look at the eggs which were salted and peppered to perfection.

"Hey Bonnie? Where are you? I was worried halfway out of my mind?" He was mostly worried that she was dead, he was going to prison and would never escape her.

"Sorry, I got called into work early this morning to work on some finishing touches on the project. I will be back in a couple of hours." Bonnie paused, "How are the kids?"

"The kids are fine. I'm making them breakfast now."

"I'm more concerned about you. The balcony door was open this morning; I went to check it out and found your clothes lying in one of the chairs. What happened?"

"Oh!" Bonnie quickly thought of a lie. "I was getting ready to put them in the laundry and had a sudden craving for a smoke. I must have laid them down in the chair and forgot. Glad you found them."

Bonnie was shaking by this time, hoping that Malcolm didn't hear the fear in her voice.

"Okay, well I have Michael watching the eggs, so I better relieve him. Do you want to talk to Katie and Michael while I finish up breakfast?"

"No, I've got to run. I'm going into a quick conference call, but I will check back in as soon as I can. Take care and I should be home no later than noon. Hugs and kisses to you and the kids."

"Ok, but -" The line went dead. She had hung up.

Malcolm went back into the kitchen and took over for Michael. He delivered Bonnie's message while he plated the food on the table just across from the kitchen bar.

They say down to eat, and the breakfast was absolutely amazing.

CHAPTER 22

Dena

Dena and Liz were up and preparing breakfast with their parents. It was always a whirling dervish when Liz, Dena and their mom were in the kitchen. Each one had their own dish to prepare.

Dena made hash browns. Liz oversaw the toast which would be cooked in the oven. Their mom made the bacon and sausage.

Dad was on the couch watching his girls and listening to them chat and giggle while making the morning meal.

They had maneuvering around the kitchen down to a science. Dena grabbed the plates from one cabinet while Liz grabbed the juice glasses from another. They headed into the dining room to set the table. Mom grabbed the juice out of the fridge and followed them.

Liz started on the eggs and Dena kept an eye on the hash browns while putting together a fruit bowl. Mom grabbed mugs for anyone that might want tea and Dad had made a pot of coffee before all the cooking had begun.

The delicious food was laid on the table, with the family sitting around. Dad said a prayer while everyone held hands and then they dug in to eat.

They were laughing and talking about memories and things they were going to do as a family during the holiday weekend. The parents asked about their daughter's beau's and jobs.

It was warm and happy.

CHAPTER 23

Kelly

———————— ⦃⧼∞⦄∞⦄⧽ ————————

K elly had just finished writing his apology to Beth. He would have to wait a couple of hours for her to land and get settled in before he could call her.

He decided to make himself a nice breakfast and then head out to fight the holiday crowd and get a Christmas tree as a special surprise for the belated Thanksgiving dinner he was planning.

He went to the kitchen cabinet and grabbed the most sugar-filled cereal he had on hand and filled up a large bowl with it. He had some microwaveable turkey sausage and some fresh squeezed juice, courtesy of Beth.

He poured himself a glass while thinking about the apology he would have to make in a few hours. He was nervous. What if she didn't forgive him? This was their first real fight. She would have to forgive him. He knew she would listen.

The microwave went off. He grabbed the sausage and sat down to have his own breakfast feast.

He said a prayer first. He prayed for Beth to have a safe flight, he prayed for Maddy to make it home safe, and he prayed for his son to be surrounded by friends on his first holiday so far from home. Then he prayed for himself to be a better person and for the darkness to be kept away.

Then he ate. And it was a great meal.

CHAPTER 24

Up on the Hill

Malcolm, Michael, and Katie had finished breakfast and were working on the dishes when there was a knock at the front door.

"I'll get it," Malcolm said with a puzzled look. He glanced at the clock - 8:45am as he jogged out of the kitchen and ran down the stairs to the front door. He had no clue who would be showing up this early in the morning just before the holiday.

He opened the door without thinking about looking through the peephole. To his amazement and surprise, it was Micah and Janae!

"What are you doing here? Your flight isn't due in for two hours!" He grabbed them both into the snug landing at the bottom of the stairs and hugged them tightly. He loosened his grip, so he could get a good look at them and pulled them in for another tight hug.

Micah and Janae barely had time to think before they were pulled into the stairwell. They knew their dad was hugging them and that he was really excited to see them, but that was all they could figure out.

Janae could hear movement upstairs and she was able to see Katie appear at the top of the stairs with messy blonde hair and in her pajamas. She freed a hand and waved at her.

Katie waved back and walked away quietly as this seemed to be a private moment.

When she turned to go back into the kitchen to finish the dishes, she realized that her brother was nowhere to be seen. She heard the water running from the bathroom and went down the hallway to see why he had disappeared. She peeked into the open bathroom door and saw her brother furiously brushing his teeth and his hair at the same time. She put her hand over her mouth and quietly backed away into the living room where she could laugh without him hearing it.

Micah and Janae were making their way up the stairs by then with Malcolm in tow.

"We were able to catch an earlier flight and we didn't want to wake you, so we took a ride share from the airport here."

Janae emerged at the top of the stairs first. She was wearing a black and white, pleated plaid mini-skirt, with a long sleeved, white-collared shirt and a sleeveless vest over it. Her coat was red and unbuttoned and matched the red low top gym shoes she had on with black over the knee socks. She was stunning -flawless, cocoa skin, big dark brown eyes with a wide nose that framed her face perfectly. Her hair was tied up in a knot with a red scarf. Her smile was broad and widened even more when she saw Katie.

Micah emerged next, tall, and lanky like his father. He had the same flawless cocoa skin as his sister. Katie spotted a silver nose piercing in his left nostril. He had the same nose as his sister. They were doppelgangers of the opposite sex. He had on blue jeans with a tan sweater and a deep brown coat with some nice brown leather brogue-style shoes. Katie knew that Michael had been eyeing a pair of them for a while.

"Hi Katie!" Janae walked over and hugged her tightly. She smelled like shea butter and coconut. The smell made Katie hungry again.

"Hi Janae! You look amazing!"

"So do you!" Janae smoothed out Katie's hair. "Where's your mom? Where's Michael?" Janae didn't give a flip about where Bonnie was. She only wanted to make sure that she gave her dad's girlfriend a wide berth this weekend and she figured the best way to do that, was to be in a completely different space than Bonnie.

She was really interested in where Michael was. Janae liked Michael, but she knew that nothing could come of it unless their parents broke up. She knew her dad was unhappy and that this thing between him and Bonnie would probably end sooner than later so she was optimistic about getting closer to Michael.

"Mom had to go into work and Michael is getting dressed," said Katie.

Micah put down the bags he was carrying and came over to hug Katie. "Hey! How's it going? You got the VIP pass to all the hotspots, or no?"

Katie hugged Micah back, "No, not yet. Give me time!"

Michael came jogging around the corner, "Micah! Hey man! How are you?" The two young men greeted and hugged each other. "Man, I'm catching up to you in the height department."

He turned and hugged Janae. "Hey! Glad you to see you both! I thought your flight was coming in later!"

Malcolm noticed how smooth Michael was in not showing too much attention to Janae.

Michael and Katie showed Micah and Janae around the apartment. Micah and Janae put their bags away and came and sat in the living room with Malcolm and Michael afterward.

They caught up while Katie got dressed.

"Are you hungry? We just had breakfast, but I can make you something if you want," said Malcolm.

Janae looked at Micah. "Uh, Dad, we want to try this shake place that we've heard about. It's in downtown Nashville, if you don't mind."

"No, I don't mind at all. Michael knows the lay of the land on this side of town a bit. Take the car and use the GPS, just be careful and take the local streets to get downtown. The folks here drive a lot different than we are used to."

Katie walked into the living room with her hair in a smooth ponytail. She had on jeans, a dark green sweater that accented her eyes and some green gym shoes. "I'm ready! Who wants to go clubbing?"

The group sat and talked for a short time.

CHAPTER 25

Bonnie

B onnie wasn't at work. She hadn't left the complex. She was completely scared and confused.

Somehow, she had wound up in the forest in her bare feet, wearing her pajamas. She had no idea how she had gotten there. She had been in some sort of a trance. It was worse than the night before because she had no clue where she was at first.

She followed the path deeper into the woods without knowing, scratching her feet on the dead wood beneath her. The forest became darker and darker the further she traveled into it. It seemed to become colder too.

Instinctively, she turned around and walked in the opposite direction. The forest sky became lighter, it was still cold but not as bone chillingly cold as it had been. She realized that she had her phone in one hand and her car keys along with a carryout bag of food in another when she came out of her trance. She dropped the mysterious bag of food and headed toward the car. She tried not to run as she got closer to the road.

Her car was sitting in the middle of the road, turned sideways so no one could get around it.

She stood at the edge of the tree line and looked to see if anyone was outside that might see her.

When she realized that no one was in sight, she ran to the car and jumped in. She turned the car on and turned the heat on full blast. She drove to the back of the complex to figure out what to do.

"Maybe everyone is still asleep in the apartment and I can sneak back in without being noticed." Then she looked at her phone and saw all the missed texts and phone calls from Malcolm. He knew she was gone.

She closed her eyes and leaned back against the headrest. She worked on a plan as her body temperature returned to normal. She tried to steady her breathing and started coughing. Her throat was dry and on fire. She reached for the bottle of water she had left in the cup holder overnight.

She unscrewed the top and began to sip the water slowly. She knew if she didn't remain in control, she would most likely choke on the water and make the situation worse.

She continued to sip and thought of what to do. She looked down at herself. Her feet and calves were covered in dirt and scratched from the brambles. Dirt and mud were caked under her toes and fingernails.

"How did I get out there? How long was I out there? Did someone bring me out there? Do I have a crazy stalker?" Each of her questions was more puzzling than the last. She realized that she might be having a complete mental breakdown and pushed that thought way down deep, away from her reality.

"I must have been sleepwalking. That's never happened before."

She took a few more moments and figured she would have to find answers to her questions later. Right now, she had to contact Malcolm and come up with an excuse for leaving the house without any word to anyone.

Once she had the lie in place, she realized she was going to have to find a way to clean herself up and get back into the house. Luckily, she had some dry cleaning in the trunk of the car along with her gym bag. She was certain that there was a shower in the clubhouse she could use. She had her key card to get into the building. Okay - it was time to call Malcolm.

The call went well until Malcolm mentioned the clothes being in the chair, that's when she decided to hastily end the call. "I must have been sleepwalking. I will do a search for causes on the internet once I get a chance. But first, I have to get out of this muddy mess."

She checked her surroundings to make sure that no one would see her. Then she got out of the car and got the dry cleaning out of the trunk. She also grabbed her gym bag which would have extra underwear in it. She laid the dry cleaning across the back seat and placed the gym bag in the front passenger side seat so she could rummage through it easily.

She found everything she needed. Soap, shampoo, deodorant, a brush, and underwear were all accounted for.

She drove to the front of the complex. She took the road on the other side of her apartment so she wouldn't be seen in case Malcolm and the kids were outside. She parked on the side of the building and went in the back gate of the clubhouse.

Luckily, the back of the clubhouse was deserted. She gathered her dry cleaning and gym bag and went into the women's restroom. She stuck her head in first to make sure the coast was clear but then she realized there weren't any showers in the clubhouse.

The showers were in the outside bathhouse near the pool. And they were locked because it was well past swimming pool season.

She couldn't stay in the women's restroom for too long with her legs and hands caked with mud. So, she ducked into a stall and put on her workout outfit and gym shoes. The pants and shoes were uncomfortable on top of the layer of mud on her skin but at least she didn't look like a crazed housewife escaping a horrible monster. She did the only thing she could think of which was to sneak back out to her car and go to her job.

There was a full gym with a shower on site at her office. It should be dead there as everyone was either off or leaving by noon.

She pulled into the parking lot of her office building slowly.

Her suspicions were correct. There were less than ten cars parked in the lot. She parked as close to the door as possible.

The entrance to the gym was just inside the front glass door and to the right. She carefully folded her dry cleaning and put it in her gym bag. She smoothed her hair down and looked in the mirror. She was glad that there was very little mud caked in her hair and face. She would still need to conceal as much of herself as possible.

She searched her backseat and found a purple baseball cap. By sheer luck, it matched her outfit. It must belong to Malcolm. She plopped the hat on her head and pulled it down tight.

She looked around one last time to see if anyone was watching. She grabbed her gym bag and slung it over her shoulder. She got out of the car and closed the door in a smooth motion. She headed to the door, swiping her key card while keeping her head down. She immediately turned right, avoiding the gaze of the security guard at the front desk. She swiped her key card again and entered the gym.

The gym was empty, which was not surprising. Not too many people work out the day before Thanksgiving. She walked quickly and intentionally toward the women's locker room and braced herself as she slowly pulled the door open. The lights in the locker room turned on once they sensed her moving around. She headed for the showers, she grabbed a clean towel from the shelf and set up shop at the shower stall at the end of the row. The tile was gray and bright. She put her bag outside of the door and hung her dry cleaning on one of the hooks. She took off her shoes and clothes. She shook out as much of the mud as she could from the shoes and pants onto the shower floor. She had a thought and laughed at herself. "Why didn't I just tell Malcolm that I went for a run and fell in the mud? Much simpler story and less work for me."

She shook her head and kept on with her train of thought. "I probably could have gotten some sympathy from him that way." She reached into the side pocket of her gym bag to examine her pajamas. She could probably sneak them into the washing machine easily. She suddenly froze at the sight before her.

She waited a few moments and pulled the pajamas completely out of the bag. She did it slowly and carefully.

Her pajamas were covered in the long shiny jet-black cat hair and the smell was even worse than last night. It smelled like rotten eggs and cat urine. She dropped them onto the floor. She gagged and ran to one of the bathroom stalls to throw up.

She was completely naked and vulnerable. The tile floor was cold under her feet and lights now seemed too bright. She made it to the toilet just in time. When she was done, she flushed the toilet and went to the sink to rinse out her mouth.

She headed back to the shower using the cold tile wall to steady herself. Bonnie turned on the water and tried to fight off the dizziness that had taken over her head.

She grabbed her soap and shampoo and walked into the hot water. She put her soap and shampoo on the small shelf inside the shower. She let her body go limp while the water ran over her skin. She watched as the mud ran down her calves and feet into the drain. She let water run through her hair and ran her fingers through her hair to make sure there weren't any brambles or leaves caught anywhere.

She purposely kept her mind blank because she had no way to explain any of the things that had happened. She focused on what she felt was real now. She washed her hair thoroughly. Then she washed her body. She felt scratches on her back and thought they must have come from the dried branches in the woods. She got to her feet and washed her toes and toenails thoroughly. She then cleaned under her fingernails to get the mud out.

She repeated the process again to make sure she didn't miss anything.

When she was done, she stood under the hot water for a few minutes and let the thoughts she had been pushing away enter her mind.

"What happened? How did I wind up in the woods? How long was I out there? How did my clothes end up in the balcony chair? Did I go outside and take my clothes off on the balcony?"

She thought of all the things that happened last night until this morning. Her "rational" side determined that she had to be sleepwalking. That's the only explanation.

Well, that should be easy to fix. "I can just lock the bedroom door - but all the doors to the outside were locked. Malcolm always locks up the apartment at night." The panic worm starting wriggling in her again and she pushed it away. "No, there is a solution to this. I will figure it out."

And with that, she turned off the shower and dried herself off. She put on the bra and underwear that had been packed in her gym bag. She reached for the deodorant and put it on. She then grabbed her shampoo and conditioner from the shelf in the shower and dried them off with her towel. Then she put them all in her gym bag.

Bonnie used the hair dryer in the locker room to dry her hair. She put on the top and dress pants that were in the dry-cleaning bag. She had a standard pair of black pumps that she kept in her trunk.

She slid on her shower shoes and braced herself to complete the hardest task of all.

She pinched her nose and picked up the soiled pajamas covered in cat hair. She put them in the trash and went back to the shower stall to finish packing up. She made sure that there were no cat hair strands on the floor.

Once she was satisfied, she grabbed the damp towel and threw it in the towel bin. She headed toward the door and rehearsed the lie she told Malcolm in her head.

She glanced at her phone and saw that it was 11:15am. She texted Malcolm and let him know that she was on her way home.

She hit the button on her key ring to open the trunk of her car and put her gym bag inside. She would clean the soiled clothes at another time. She stood on one foot and balanced herself as she put on the heels while putting her shower shoes in her bag at the same time. She closed the trunk and got into the car to head home.

She turned the car on and took a moment to regroup. Then she put the car in reverse and headed out of the office building parking lot.

Malcolm was enjoying the lively conversation with the kids when Bonnie's text came through. Michael saw Malcolm wince and brilliantly shifted the subject to the shake restaurant Micah and Janae were dying to try. "It is getting close to lunch time. We should probably head out before it gets too crowded. We'll be back by 3pm, ok?"

Malcolm eyed Michael with a curious look. Was the kid a genius?

Michael grabbed the keys off the hook and hung back a bit. He turned to Malcolm and said, "Hey, I'm sure you and my mom didn't get a chance to finish your disagreement last night. I figured you'd want to do it without us around."

Then Michael said something he hadn't planned on saying, "You are far too good for my mom. Don't lose any sleep or worry over any of us offspring if you want to get out of this relation - well whatever this is. You've given it your best."

Malcolm saw a distressed look cross Michael's face and knew that Michael had not intended to go so far. Malcolm closed the door, grabbed Michael, and hugged him. "I don't know what's going to happen, but I thank you for saying that."

Both Malcolm and Michael's honesty was raw and real. They gave each other a final look of understanding and Michael left to join the group in the garage and get some lunch. He would see if he could bring up the subject of a possible split of the parents over lunch. It's not like it hadn't been discussed between the four of them before.

Katie even brought it up a few years ago at the ripe old age of eight, completely out of earshot of both parents, of course. She saw how horrible her mom had been to Janae and she asked without thinking, "Why does Malcolm stay with Mom? She is absolutely awful." Janae and Micah looked at each other. Michael winced and looked at Katie.

There was a brief uneasy pause when Micah spoke up.

"Your mom is not horrible all the time. I think she just feels uneasy around us. I'm not sure why that is, but she will have to get used to us at some point." Micah paused and looked at Katie, "Well thanks for killing that elephant in the room, what did the poor elephant ever do to you?"

The "siblings" erupted in laughter. Since then, there had been other conversations mainly bought up by Michael and Katie.

Micah and Janae had conversations with just the two of them about their father. They knew he was unhappy. They knew he didn't truly love Bonnie because he would have married her by now. They wanted him to be happy, so they were respectful and never said a bad word against Bonnie in front of her.

Their father knew that they were being mistreated and immediately came to the rescue of his children whenever Bonnie had gotten out of control. She would always apologize, yet Malcolm always felt like she was doing it to placate him and doubted that her admissions of guilt were genuine. Sometimes, he wondered if Bonnie was a sociopath. A person pretending to be normal when, she was a monster.

Micah, Michael, Janae, and Katie headed downtown to the famous "Shake Emporium." They were chatting away and laughing when Michael decided he needed to go ahead and get the ball started.

It was as if Katie was reading his mind, "Michael, what happened yesterday with Malcolm and Mom before you came to get me from the airport? You never really said."

Michael sighed and gripped the steering wheel a bit tighter. Micah and Janae looked at each other. They knew the ride was about to become uncomfortable. They both braced themselves and tried to detach from the conversation. It was hard hearing about the moments where Bonnie was hurting their father, especially when it was witnessed by one of them. They listened to Michael, and the events that played out yesterday were ugly and difficult. Then Michael said, "Look, we all know that Malcolm is a good man and father, we know this. Our mom is a hard nut to crack. I mean we haven't figured it out and we are her own children."

They had made it to the Shake Emporium and Michael pulled in and parked in the lot behind the restaurant.

He looked at Katie and then back at Micah and Janae. "I don't say this lightly, I mean I love you guys, we kinda grew up together. Well, mostly on weekends, I mean not a full-on sibling connection on all fronts but that's not our fault."

Michael stammered, "I just want to let you know that I made a group decision and told your dad, Malcolm..." He trailed off. "This is really hard to say."

Micah and Janae watched Michael's face intently. His brow was furrowed, his eyes were quite serious.

Michael began speaking at top speed, "Guys, I gave your dad permission to break up with our mom! I hope you're okay with that. I mean enough is enough, right? We all deserve to be happy, right? Especially, Malcolm! Well, it's done, I can't take it back."

Michael turned around and waited for the aftermath. There was complete silence. He decided to be patient and wait it out.

Katie looked at her brother from the passenger seat. She was worried. She knew that they, the kids, would be fine. She and

Michael could go back to Dad's. Micah and Janae could go back to school.

It wouldn't be so simple for Malcolm or her mom. Would they both go back to California? She knew Malcolm still had the house there, so he would have a place to stay. And she also knew he had given up his job to come to Nashville; she was sure he could find another job or even go back to his old company. She didn't think about money much, but she knew that all this moving was costly and that they had a lease and new furniture. She knew that Malcolm and her mom weren't broke but still it was a lot to consider after living in a town for only a couple of months.

She pondered all these things while waiting on a reaction from the back seat.

Micah looked at Janae. Janae bowed her head and looked at Micah, "Well, big bro! I think you need to address this. I'm just going to pull up the menu on my phone while we're sitting here and sink as deeply as I can into the seat cushions so I'm invisible."

Micah looked at Janae, "Okay, I got it this time. Next time it's all you J."

Micah took a breath and said, "Look man, that's uh, really noble and all. We love our dad, and we want him to be happy. We LYL and you're right we've been around each other for some time."

Micah paused, "The decision to leave will either be on your mom or on our dad. Now, do I think my dad has had enough? Well, probably. However, we have to respect his decision and choices for the most part as his kids."

Katie had turned around to listen to Micah at this time. She wondered if their parents did break up would she ever see Janae and Micah again. Would she ever see Malcolm again?

"All that said, kudos to you Mike-Mike for letting him know that you won't be hurt if things don't work out. I'm sure that's one of the reasons he is trying to make this work. He doesn't want to hurt anyone, especially us." Micah took his finger, pointed at Katie, and made a circle that included all four of them.

Janae saw the hurt look on Katie's face and said, "And hey, no matter what, we are gonna stay in touch. We've been together too long not to." She reached out and touched Katie's face and saw a tear roll down Katie's face. She had never seen Katie cry before.

Michael was shocked by it too. He tried to lighten the moment, "Well now that that's all settled, let's go eat."

Michael and Micah opened their doors at the exact same time. They both felt awkward seeing Katie cry. It was very unusual.

Katie turned around in her seat and let the tears fall silently. She believed Janae. She knew they would still be in touch, yet she had a strange ominous feeling that she didn't understand.

Janae was out of the car and opening Katie's door. She took Katie's hand and looked at her tear-streaked face. Janae wrapped her arms around Katie and hugged her good and proper. "It's going to be fine, little sister. I will always be no more than a phone, text or face call away. I promise. Now let's go get a shake!"

Katie stopped crying while Janae held her. It was true, she loved Janae as a big sister, and she didn't want to lose Janae or Micah.

They linked arms and walked over to the boys, laughing, and talking, tears gone.

Micah looked down at Katie and gave her a hug. He grabbed Michael and Janae and pulled them in. They clung together for a few moments then let go.

Then they walked into the restaurant and had the best burgers, fries and shakes ever!

Meanwhile, back at the apartment, Malcolm was busy cutting up vegetables while sautéing shrimp and fresh crab for his surprise dish. The knife that had once been a mischief maker was doing a great job of cutting and slicing. It was happy to be of service today. Malcolm continued cutting up onions and celery. He added them to the garlic that was already in the sizzling pan. This was the perfect time to make this dish when no prying eyes were around.

While he cooked and chopped, he thought about what Michael said again. Strange how the kid had confirmed his best plan of action within hours of Malcolm thinking about it himself. Just then the timer went off letting Malcolm know that the oven was pre-heated and ready for the dressing.

He put the dressing in and continued working on his special dish. Once that was ready, he slid it into the oven too.

Janae would make the macaroni and cheese and biscuits. Veggies would be prepped and cooked in the morning. He would get up at 4am and put the bird, which was already dressed and seasoned, in the oven. Fresh cranberries were on deck. He, Janae, and Micah would make the chocolate cake, sweet potato pie and apple pie later today once the kids were back.

Bonnie entered the apartment and was blown away by the amazing aroma. She hadn't eaten since the night before. "Wow, it smells wonderful in here. Need any help?" She picked up a carrot stick from one of the various bowls on the counter and took her shoes off.

"Let me go put my gym clothes in the wash and change out of my work clothes."

She walked down the hall, past their bedroom and straight to the laundry room. She carefully pulled the gym clothes out of her bag, not knowing what to expect. Fortunately, there were no surprises. The load was too small, and she didn't want anyone to be suspicious, so she went to the bathroom in her bedroom and grabbed the large hamper. She did a quick sort and pulled out all the dark colored clothes. She bundled them up in her arms and put them in the wash.

She went back to the bedroom and took her work clothes off. She laid them on the bed. She would come back later and put them in the closet. She grabbed some sweats out of a drawer and put them on before going back into the kitchen.

"Where are the kids? Did Michael and Katie go pick up Micah and Janae?"

Malcolm continued to stir as he listened to Bonnie's questions. "Micah and Janae's flight came in early. So, we didn't have to pick them up from the airport. They all went to that new shake restaurant downtown for lunch. They will probably walk around downtown and do some sightseeing."

Malcolm went to the wine rack and picked out a nice red wine, opened it and poured two glasses out. "You were knocked out when I got home. Did you check in on Katie this morning before you left?"

Bonnie took a drink of wine, swallowed, "Yes, she was fast asleep. I didn't want to wake her, but I did give her a kiss before I left," Bonnie lied. She took another sip of wine and listened to the soft jazz that was playing.

Malcolm normally listened to music when he cooked. His taste depended on the occasion and meal. Today it was jazz, tomorrow it could be neo-soul or ole school hip hop. She didn't really like jazz, but it was better than hip hop.

She watched Malcolm moving around in the kitchen and thought to herself, "I'm a terrible mother. I haven't even seen my daughter and she's been under this roof for hours. It seems that I'm losing my mind while trying to hold on to a man that doesn't want me completely. It's been years and he hasn't even hinted at marriage. And it's my fault, I built this horrible fantasy. I manipulated him and all the kids to get us here. Why?"

Malcolm had finished with his prep for now. He took a sip of wine and turned to talk to Bonnie.

"I'm glad the kids are here. They seem happy and well. It's nice having a house full of laughter."

"Yes," Bonnie replied dryly. She was starting to hear a ringing in her head. Then she vaguely remembered that she hadn't eaten since yesterday at lunch.

She hopped up and went to the fridge.

"You're still hungry? Did you not eat that huge burger and salad we saved you, from last night?" asked Malcolm.

"Oh yeah, I left it in the fridge at work. I didn't realize it until I got home." So that must have been what was in the bag she was holding this morning in the forest.

Bonnie made herself a sandwich, "Hey, I have some work I need to finish up on. Shouldn't take me longer than an hour."

"Ok, the kids said they would be back by 3pm. Don't work too long."

Bonnie grabbed her laptop out of her bag and took it into the bedroom. She set it up on the small desk that she would use while working from home. It sat in the corner, flush with the balcony door that connected to their bedroom.

The ringing in her ears seemed to have almost gone away. She sat down in front of the laptop and started her research on sleepwalking.

She did an internet search and found that the causes varied and most of them did not apply to her. The one cause that stood out the most was stress. Well, she certainly had to be stressed from all the lying, misdirecting and manipulating she had put into action. Then there were the unsettling events that happened last night that she didn't want to consider. All these things could be an after-effect of extreme stress.

Seeing monsters and invisible cats. Leaving her clothes in odd places. She still couldn't believe she did that. Was she actually naked on the balcony? Did she strip there or walk out there with her clothes in hand? She cringed at the thought and hoped that none of the neighbors saw it.

And what was the cure to her nightly strolls? Simple relaxation? Well, bathing would not be a solution. Maybe a glass of wine before bed would help or maybe a mild sleeping pill. She had a low dose sedative on hand in the medicine cabinet. She would try the wine tonight to see if that would work.

She suddenly felt very tired and the ringing in her ear, although much softer now, was still there. She looked at the clock on the nightstand. It read 1:30pm.

It didn't seem like she had been in front of the laptop that long. Had she lost track of time somehow? Did she have some other kind of illness she needed to research?

"I didn't sleep through the night, maybe I am exhausted. Sleep deprivation was another cause of sleep walking; maybe it was a combination of stress and the one night of missed sleep," she tried to convince herself.

She grabbed a throw off another chair in the corner and yelled to Malcolm, "I'm going to take a nap before the kids get back."

"Ok, I might do the same out here."

Bonnie took the clothes lying on the bed and hung them in the closet. She laid down on the bed and was out before her head hit the pillow. She had strange dreams. Dreams of black cats with silky long hair, horns, gray scaly skin, hooves! The hooves were new and very unsettling. Then there was darkness, complete darkness, and it was a cold and slimy darkness. She shivered while she slept and pulled the blanket tighter around her.

Malcolm checked in with work. No emails or messages. He had finished cleaning the kitchen and figured the kids would love a bucket of fried chicken with all the southern fixins' for dinner. He would place an order for delivery once they got back.

He poured himself another glass of wine and sat on the couch.

He hummed along with the tune playing on his music app. He loved Coltrane during the holidays and family events. The song played and he sipped his wine while listening.

Bonnie seemed much calmer than usual. "Calm before the storm", he wondered. He knew that she was lying about the food and about some of the other things they had discussed. Something was off, she didn't even bring up the argument from the day before. She didn't apologize for it or want to continue it and that was not like her at all.

Malcolm didn't want to read too much into it. He felt great! The kids were here. They were happy. He decided it was going to be a great Thanksgiving no matter what happened.

The song ended and he turned off the music app and turned on the TV. There was a cooking show on, and he drifted to sleep while watching it. He slept well, very content in his plans for the evening with the kids and with Bonnie. He was also content in possibly having a way out of the relationship. He would think about it some more, but he felt confident that ending this sham was the best thing for everyone.

He woke up about 30 minutes later and started the prep work for the desserts. He boiled the sweet potatoes and pulled out the rest of the ingredients for the pies and the cake. He grouped the ingredients in order by dessert and pulled out the measuring cups and spoons. Next, he pulled down the bowls and mixing tools. He was just checking on the sweet potatoes when he heard the garage door open. Moments later the door to the kitchen opened and the brood came in, all smiles and chattering away.

Malcolm loved the sound of that. He glanced at the clock; it was just after 3pm.

Strange, Bonnie was still sleeping. He would give everyone a few moments to get comfortable and then wake Bonnie up to at least welcome everyone.

"So, how was the shake place?"

"It was great! We brought you and Bonnie back some shakes. They had your favorite, German chocolate cake," Janae held the bag out to her dad. "And we got strawberry chocolate chip for Bonnie. She's here, right?"

Janae felt herself flinch as she waited for the answer and quickly turned away to place the shakes in the freezer.

"Hey! Yeah - Bonnie's taking a nap. I will go in and check on her in a few, then you guys can rest for a while and help me with dessert!" Malcolm went back to sorting out the makings for each dessert.

Micah, Katie, and Michael took off their coats and put them away. Janae hung out with Malcolm while he worked on the dessert prep. She knew her dad's system and helped him organize, getting the measuring cups and spoons ready for each dessert. She knew he was very organized and detailed when it came to cooking. They smiled at each other. It had been a while since they had worked together in the kitchen.

Micah, Katie, and Michael made their way back into the living room and sat on the couch. They chatted in low tones so they wouldn't wake Bonnie.

Bonnie was not sleeping exactly. She was standing just inside of the closet making an odd motion over and over again with her arms. Lethar and Kat were in the closet with her, directing her. After a while, she went back to the bed and got under the blanket and went back to sleep.

"Well, I am going to go wake Bonnie so she can see you all. Then maybe you can relax for a couple of hours, then we can have dinner and make the desserts for tomorrow.

The kids grew silent and the mood in the room shifted. They looked at Malcolm as if he was going off to wake a sleeping tiger. "Kids, it will be fine. I promise."

Malcolm entered the bedroom. Bonnie was already stirring. "Hey, you've been out for hours."

Bonnie heard Malcolm, but she was so tired. It took her a moment to respond. "Yeah, I don't know why I'm so tired. Are the kids back?"

"Yep, they're in the living room. Why don't you come out and see everybody? If you're still tired you can come back to bed." Malcolm sat down on the bed next to Bonnie and looked at her face.

She did look tired. She had dark circles under her eyes, and she looked a bit pale.

Malcolm took her hand and noticed scratches on the back of it.

Bonnie looked down and saw the scratches, "I must have done that in my sleep. I was having some really strange dreams."

"C'mon, poor thing. You probably are really tired." Malcolm rubbed Bonnie's head and helped her as she tried to get up.

Bonnie looked at the time and gasped. "I really was out for hours. I think you're right. I better get some more rest after I see the kids." She stood up and walked toward the door with Malcolm following her.

When she got to the living room, the kids were sitting there quietly, as if they were waiting for a grand entrance.

She went over to Katie first. "Hi baby! How are you? She kissed Katie's face and hugged her tight. It's so good to see your face."

Malcolm was puzzled. Hadn't she seen Katie this morning? Maybe she meant she was glad to see her while she was awake.

Bonnie went over to Michael. "Hi Michael." She stared at him for a moment, almost shy in demeanor. Then she leaned down and hugged him. "I'm sorry about yesterday. I want us to have a great holiday. Please forgive me," she whispered. Then she let go of Michael and smiled down at him.

Michael looked at his mom; she seemed sincere. She looked very tired, and she didn't have her normal color. He watched her as she moved on to Micah.

"Micah! You're a handsome man! You grew up so fast," she kissed him on the cheek and gave him a long but light squeeze.

"Hi Janae!" She paused as she took Janae in. There was no doubt, the girl was a beauty, even more so than her mother.

Bonnie felt the old tension rise and she fought it back down. She reached out and took Janae's hands. Janae stood-up so Bonnie could get a better look at her.

"Well, you're gorgeous! It's so good to see you!" She wrapped Janae up in a warm and genuine hug.

"Janae, I know we've never been close and it's all my fault. I was stupid and petty. I will be better. I don't expect you to forgive me right now or ever and that's okay, I just want you to know that I am truly sorry," she whispered.

She stepped back and looked at Janae with tears in her eyes.

Janae couldn't tell if she was for real or not, so she played along. Janae figured if this was a game it would reveal itself sooner than later. So, she nodded and squeezed Bonnie's hands. She hoped that it was not a game.

"So, what's everyone been up to? How is school? How were your flights?" Bonnie sat down on the couch between Katie and Michael. She took Katie's hand and listened as the kids caught her up.

Malcolm called out for the chicken and watched the scene from the kitchen. Bonnie laughed and talked with the kids. She was really engaged. She asked thoughtful questions and listened to each of them as they answered. Maybe she was turning over a new leaf? Maybe it was a holiday wonder? A Thanksgiving Day miracle?

Bonnie looked at Malcolm and smiled. She still looked tired. He was starting to get worried; this wasn't one of her usual cries for attention. She didn't look well at all.

"Hey Bon, you still look a bit tired. Do you want to go back to bed? I'll bring you a plate once the food gets here," Malcolm prodded.

"I am tired. I'm glad I got to see you all for a while. Malcolm is right. I better get some rest. I will come back out once I get my energy back," she smiled at the kids, lovingly. It was all new to everyone in the room.

She stood up and started walking to the bedroom.

Michael followed her. "Mom, are you okay?" They were in the bedroom with the door closed behind them.

"You look sick, are you sure you're okay?"

"I just feel really tired. I might be coming down with a cold. I stayed outside..." she paused to catch herself from telling the truth, "On the balcony too long last night after you left."

She paused again, "I had a chance to do some real thinking, about everything. I really want to be a better person. I know I haven't been the easiest to deal with at times. Well, most of the time." She laughed nervously.

"I just need to get some rest. If I'm not better in the morning, I will go to the emergency room; that will be the only place open on Thanksgiving."

"Okay, let's get you into bed," Michael tucked his mom in for the first time ever. He kissed her on the cheek. "Remember, you promised to go to the hospital if you're not feeling better. I am going to hold you to that."

"Okay, honey. I will keep my word. Now, go and enjoy the evening with everyone else. I will be fine."

Michael hesitated. "Malcolm said he would come check on me when the food arrives. I'm fine, honey. Don't worry about me. I'm just tired." Bonnie assured him.

"Okay. See you tomorrow if not sooner." Michael left his mom's side and went to the door. He looked back at her and exited the room, closing the door behind him.

Michael went back to his seat in the living room.

Everyone looked at him as he re-entered the room.

Everyone was quiet. They waited for him to speak.

"Well, I don't know. Seems like Cruella has left the building. I don't know what to make of it," Michael explained.

"Let's just enjoy it. Maybe she's coming around. Maybe she has, you know -" Michael interrupted Janae.

"Feelings?" He couldn't help himself.

"No, I was going to say, "Maybe she's grown," Janae looked at Michael and shook her head.

"Well, whatever it is, I'm with Janae," Malcolm replied. "Let's enjoy it." And with that, Malcolm jogged to the kitchen to start working on the desserts. Janae and Katie were close on his heels. Janae made the cake batter while Katie chopped up walnuts for the sweet potato pie. Malcolm and the girls laughed and talked.

Michael and Micah would wander in the kitchen every few minutes to "volunteer" for tasting. Then Micah took his turn at bat making the apple pie. In no time, the kitchen smelled of cinnamon, butter, apples, and dough baking. Katie and Malcolm made the sweet potato pie together.

Dinner arrived just in time for them to put their desserts in the oven. They gathered at the dining room table and laughed and talked until the oven timer went off. Then their dessert game faces were back on.

Michael stood back and emceed the event like one of the hosts on a reality cooking show. "Looks like Janae is struggling with getting those cakes on the counter. Micah seems to be handling the apple pie with ease and folks let me tell you - it smells glorious! Here come Katie and Malcolm with their sweet potato souffle surprise. It's gonna be a tight race folks. Let's take a break and see how the show ends."

Once everything was cooling on the counter, Malcolm went to check back in on Bonnie. Bonnie or the thing that was parading as Bonnie was standing a bit deeper inside of the closet again, making jerking motions with her back to the door. She could sense movement coming towards the bedroom, so she stopped what she was doing and got in the bed.

Malcolm reached the door just as Bonnie was settling into place. He opened the door, and she was laying in the bed prone. He walked over to her and nudged her.

"Hey Bon, are you hungry? You haven't eaten anything in hours," Malcolm could not hide the genuine concern in his voice.

Bonnie turned over and looked at Malcolm with the kindest pale green eyes. "Hey, honey. No, I'm not hungry right now. I think I may have a bit of a bug. I feel fine, I'm just really tired."

Bonnie could see the concerned look on Malcolm's face, and she reached up and touched the side of his face gently, "Don't worry, if I don't feel better tomorrow, I will go to the ER. Now go back and keep the kids company. Hug them all for me." She put her hand back down under the covers.

Malcolm kissed her on the forehead and tucked her in. He walked toward the door, completely thrown by Bonnie's kindness. He wondered if this was a trick. She rarely called him "Malcolm", nor had she ever been so genuinely kind. He looked back at the figure in the bed, and saw that Bonnie was already drifting back to sleep if she wasn't there already.

He went back out to the living room and sat with the kids. They laughed and talked for a couple of hours. Then they watched a movie. Katie and Janae frosted the cake. Then Malcolm put some finishing decorative touches on it. They covered everything up and went to bed.

Well, Malcolm was the only one that went to bed and slept. He heard the kids laughing and talking long after he was in the bed. He had to get up early and get the turkey started. The kids would handle the sides. He took a quick shower and hopped in the bed next to Bonnie. She was still knocked out and Malcolm fell asleep almost immediately.

CHAPTER 26

Thanksgiving

Dena was awakened by Liz jumping on her bed at 5 a.m. "The bird is in the oven!" squealed Liz. Dena giggled as Liz crawled under the covers with her. This was something they did all the time as kids. "The Detroit Thanksgiving Parade will be on in a few hours. In my younger years, I would've said, 'Let's go down and watch,' but it's snowing out so that's not happening."

Dena sat up at the mention of snow. She rolled over to the window and opened the blinds and to her amazement, white, fluffy snowflakes were falling from the still dark sky. She rolled back over to her sister and sat up in the bed, so she could watch the snow fall. "It's so pretty and peaceful," Dena said.

"You and your obsession with snow. It's just flurries today. It is really pretty." They sat and talked about their plans for the day and the day after. Time seemed to be moving fast. Their mom came in and joined them around 7am. She filled them in on all the local gossip and family news. It was wonderful to be home. Dena and Liz didn't realize how much they missed being home until they were back.

An hour later, they got up and got ready for the day. Dena would make the cornbread dressing, Liz the macaroni and cheese. Their mom would make peach cobbler for dessert. First, they would have breakfast and watch the parade, and call the family. It was shaping up to be an amazing day.

Kelly had spoken to Beth, and she forgave him on the spot. She agreed that it was a silly argument that had gotten out of hand and that she would love to have a Thanksgiving "do- over." She would be home on Wednesday and would be able to help with cooking and cleaning. "So, Babe, what are you going to do for dinner? I'm sure all the stores and restaurants will be closing early if they are open at all."

"Now honey, you know us country boys are always prepared. I have dinner with all the trimmings ordered and will pick it up in a few hours. Then I will sit in front of the TV and watch football or football will watch me," Kelly paused, "I know that you're impressed. I can tell from the silence. I hear this place that I ordered from has the best deep-dish pizza in the south, if that's possible."

Beth giggled, "Well, okay. As long as you have something to eat." Beth and Kelly talked for about an hour. The client she was working for had invited her to an extravagant Thanksgiving dinner being thrown by him and his partner. "It's going to be quite lavish, so I've heard. There are rumors going around that there will be peacocks."

"You're going to eat peacocks? That's just wrong. I don't think you should eat those beautiful birds," Kelly interjected.

Beth laughed and they talked some more. All was well, and she was so glad they had made up.

Malcolm woke up early and to his surprise, Bonnie was already up. He found her in the kitchen making coffee and scrolling through her phone. She glanced at him, "Morning; can't believe I slept all day yesterday."

Malcolm was a little puzzled. It seemed like the old Bonnie was back. "You didn't miss much last night. Most of the cooking is done. I was just getting up to put the turkey in the oven." He walked over to the refrigerator to get the turkey out while keeping his eye on Bonnie. She had turned away from him and was attending to the coffee maker by this time.

Malcolm pre-heated the oven and checked the turkey to make sure it had been seasoned properly. He looked over at Bonnie and said, "Are you hungry? There's fried chicken with sides in the fridge." He paused and turned his attention back to the turkey. He felt like he was staring at Bonnie and didn't want to make her angry.

"There is? I am starving!" Bonnie moved passed Malcolm and opened the refrigerator. She took out the chicken and picked out the sides she wanted. She grabbed a plate and started putting food on it. "Thanks Mac!"

Malcolm knew instantly that the old Bonnie was back. She is the only person who called him "Mac" and he hated it. Malcolm chose his next few words carefully, "How are you feeling? You still look a bit tired."

Bonnie put the food in the microwave and sneered, "I'm fine! Don't treat me like a child. I know we have a house full of them, but I am definitely an adult." Bonnie shocked herself. She hadn't planned on starting an argument and yet one was forming.

Just then, the oven timer went off letting Malcolm know that it was ready for the turkey. Malcolm covered the turkey up and put it in the oven. He looked over at Bonnie, who was watching her food turn in the microwave. "Are you sure you're an adult? Last time I checked, starting an argument because someone is concerned about you seems truly childish. But, whatever, you know best."

Bonnie turned and saw Malcolm glaring at her. The timer went off on the microwave and she pulled out her plate. Bonnie didn't know how to respond, so she poked at her food, pretending to check that it was ready to eat. She placed it back in the microwave for show.

"Are you going to eat in the bedroom?"

"Yes, I guess I will get some more rest since I look tired." "Good, I am going to stay in here and watch the turkey".

"Oh - and the kids saved a shake for you. It's in the freezer. But I guess that doesn't matter to you especially since you didn't ask about them." Malcolm reached into the drawer to get a knife to cut up the lemons for the fruit tea he was planning to make for dinner. He looked around in the drawer for the knife he had gotten used to cutting and chopping with but didn't see it. He figured it must have been in the dishwasher or dishrack and selected another one to do the job.

Bonnie froze for a second, then she picked up her coffee and plate and headed to the bedroom. She closed the door behind her and thought, "I will see the kids later. What's the big deal?" Then she remembered how worried Michael looked last night when he tucked her in. She remembered holding Katie's hand while on the couch. She remembered flashes of her conversations with Micah and Janae. "I must have been delirious, making promises to be a better me? That's not like me at all."

She took a bite out of the chicken, and it tasted like sand. Somehow, the years of guilt had gotten the best of her in this moment and there was little she could do to fight it off. She refused to cry so she ate her bland meal and drank the tasteless coffee while watching some meaningless informercial. Then she grabbed a book she had been reading and tried to focus on completing it. She couldn't concentrate and kept thinking of all the strange things that had happened to her in the last day or two.

"Am I psychotic? Something is off with me. Have all these years of master manipulation caught up with me?" Bonnie thought. She remembered that her job had a program where she could talk to a mental health care provider if she needed to. Then she shrugged off that decision. "I am still me. No one has been hurt, namely me." Then she put her plate on the nightstand and fell quickly back to sleep. She had strange dreams again. Dreams about fat cats with fur so silky it looked oily. She dreamed of orange eyes again, and of falling. She tossed and turned while dreaming and in the corner of the room the orange eyes appeared again.

Malcolm set the timer on the oven and laid down on the couch. He decided he would watch this new documentary he had been hearing great things about. He opened the blinds to the balcony and grabbed a throw to wrap up in. He turned on the TV and found the documentary. The volume was down low so he wouldn't wake the kids.

The apartment was completely silent for the most part. He could hear some noise coming from the room he shared with Bonnie. It sounded like the TV but everyone else was still asleep. He had to remember that the kids were here and to try not to have squabbles in front of them. There was no denying that the tension between him and Bonnie was still there. Was she putting on a show for the kids so they would think things were good between them? It's possible.

Malcolm pulled out his phone and texted his nephew, James. James was renting the house in California while going to school. Malcolm figured he should go ahead and find out how James was doing and if the house needed any attention as it would probably be home to Malcolm within the next couple of months. He knew it might be too early to send a message, but James was an early riser and was probably already awake. He glanced at the clock on the phone, which read 5:37am. Malcolm was right. He received an answer minutes after the first text was sent.

Around 7:30am, Micah joined Malcolm in the living room. He found his dad texting on his phone. "Hey Dad! Happy Thanksgiving! The turkey smells great!" Micah sat down on the opposite end of the couch his dad was sitting on.

"Hey, son! Happy Thanksgiving to you. I was just about to check on the bird." Malcolm stood up. "I was just texting your cousin James to wish him well and to check and make sure the house was fine." Malcolm walked to the kitchen and checked on the turkey. "Looks good." Malcolm made his way back to the couch and saw that Micah was studying him.

"So, you're checking on the house? I was out there before I came here. The house is fine. Gutters need cleaning – James and I will do that once I get back on Sunday morning. So, what's really going on?" Micah sat back on the couch and continued to study his father.

"Nothing, I'm just checking on the house. I appreciate you and James taking care of it." Malcom looked outside the balcony door. "Okay, it's no secret. Things have never been great between me and Bonnie." Malcolm sat down on the couch and looked at Micah. "The last argument we had a few days ago while Michael was here pretty much sealed the coffin shut." Malcolm paused, "She doesn't treat you and Janae well. Her own kids don't want to be around her. I feel like none of you would have to go through this if we broke up. Especially, Janae." Malcolm looked away from Micah.

"All of you kids are great. There shouldn't be any reason for me to defend any of you when you haven't done anything wrong. The truth is that Bonnie is abusive and manipulative." Malcolm paused again, "I know that you and your sister see that. I know that's the reason that both of you left the house the first chance you got. That hurt me so much. That my own kids don't feel welcome in their own home. And not just you two, but her own kids?" Malcolm shook his head, "I think the only reason Bonnie has them come over is because I'm there. It's like a big show and honestly, I am tired of it."

"Wow Dad. I don't know what to say. "Micah looked over at his dad. "We just want you to be happy and if you're not, we will respect any decision that you make. Don't make any decisions based on our happiness. We are all fine."

Malcolm nodded and sat back. He restarted the documentary. They both watched in silence. Janae came in about 30 minutes later.

"Katie is just waking up. Micah - I thought you or Michael were going to sleep out here on the couch."

"Yeah, Michael let me have the bed and decided to put a sleeping bag of sorts on the floor. It was a, uh, cozy."

Janae smirked, "Cozy, huh? Okay." Then she caught a strange look on Micah's face that said there was a story or two to be told. She plopped on the couch across from her dad and Micah and started watching the documentary. "I saw this already. It was really good."

They sat and watched in silence. Katie popped into the living room and sat on the couch with Janae. She was still a bit sleepy, as pre-teens tend to be. She cuddled up with Janae and pulled one of the throws over them both.

The documentary was over by then. They turned on one of the many Thanksgiving Day parades. They saw that the Detroit Parade was just starting so they watched it.

"Is there a parade here today?" asked Katie.

"No, they have a Christmas parade but that won't take place until sometime in December," answered Michael. "I looked it up before I came."

"Man, what? Are you in sleeper mode?" Micah turned with everyone to see Michael plopping down in the chair in the corner. "Seriously, are you an assassin in training?"

"Could be," Michael yawned and turned his attention to the parade. "The turkey smells really good. How long until - "

Michael's question was cut off by a shriek coming from Bonnie in the bedroom.

Everyone paused to hear what was going on. Malcolm jumped to his feet and ran to the bedroom. Michael followed him with Micah close behind the two of them.

Janae held Katie on the couch. "Don't worry, Bonnie is probably having a bad dream."

Malcolm entered the bedroom first and saw Bonnie standing in front of the closet pulling what looked to be tattered clothes from it.

"LOOK AT THIS! WHO DID THIS?!" Bonnie shrieked.

Malcolm walked over to the closet and saw that more than half of every piece of clothing in the closet had been shredded in some way. Sweaters, pants, shirts, skirts, and dresses either had holes, jagged cuts or slits in them. He stared into the closet in shock.

Bonnie continued screaming, "WHO DID IT? THIS WASN'T LIKE THIS YESTERDAY WHEN I GOT HOME! IT HAD TO BE ONE OF YOU!"

Michael couldn't help himself, "It was probably moths.

You know they grow them big here in the south."

Micah looked down and snickered silently despite himself.

They both instantly regretted their actions.

Malcolm instinctively stepped in front of Michael and Micah. He could see that Bonnie was close to becoming wholly unhinged. He didn't think she heard what Michael had said and he was thankful for that.

Janae had just appeared in the doorway to make sure everything was okay.

"YOU DID IT, DIDN'T YOU? YOU HAVE ALWAYS HATED ME! SO, YOU DID THIS TO GET BACK AT ME!" Bonnie was in a complete rage by now.

Janae shook her head and looked around the scene to try to make sense of what had happened.

Malcolm turned and faced the kids, "All of you go back to the living room now. Bonnie and I will figure this out."

"NO, NO! DON'T TRY AND PROTECT THEM. ONE OF THEM DID THIS! I KNOW IT WAS HER!

I KNOW IT!" Bonnie attempted to lunge at Janae, but Malcolm stood firmly between Bonnie and the kids.

Malcolm ushered the kids out and closed the door behind them. He locked it for good measure. He didn't know why but he felt that a locked door was needed. He thought cautiously about how to approach Bonnie. He walked toward her and gently moved her aside, so he could get a closer look at the clothes. Not only were the clothes ripped to shreds but there were deep, long marks in the wall behind the clothes. He pushed the hangers apart so he could get a closer look. Claw marks? Nothing that big could have been in the closet without somebody hearing or seeing something.

"Bonnie, stay here. I'm going to check the rest of the apartment."

Malcolm started with their bathroom. He closed the door behind him and then checked the bedroom. He looked under the bed and checked the bedroom balcony exit.

He left the bedroom, closing the door behind him and went to the living room where the kids were. "All of you stay here." Malcolm circled the room and checked the balcony exit off the living room. He then went into the kitchen and out the garage door exit. He checked the garage, under the cars and inside. He looked in the trunks. He came back upstairs and went to Katie and Janae's room next. He looked under the bed and into the closet. He checked the guest bathroom, then the laundry room and storage closet. Lastly, he checked the room that the boys had stayed in. There was no one else in the house.

He suddenly remembered the outdoor storage closet which they kept locked. He grabbed the key from the kitchen and went to search it. He unlocked the door and checked inside. There was nothing. He went back to the living room. He had to tell the kids something.

"Well, it looks like someone broke into the house and shredded Bonnie's clothes." Malcolm stood there looking at the kids. "It's really strange, they didn't take anything, and they only messed with Bonnie's clothes." Malcolm thought as he talked. He didn't want to say what he was thinking out loud because it didn't make any sense.

"Hey! Why don't you go grab some breakfast for us all from one of the restaurants around here? Most places are open for breakfast this morning." He grabbed his wallet and gave Micah a wad of bills. "You know what we like; be sure to get some fruit into those bodies." He saw that the kids were still in their pajamas and said, "Don't worry. The kids wear their pajamas everywhere here. You look great!" He moved the kids toward the door and gave Micah the keys. "Be careful and give me about 30 minutes before coming back." Malcolm closed the door behind them.

He waited until he heard the garage door open before moving further into the kitchen. He checked the turkey, puttered around the kitchen for a moment, then he went to the bedroom to talk to Bonnie.

"Well, there is no one else in the house." His eyes roamed over the room looking for clues and he saw none.

"I told you! It was her! She did it! She hates me!"

"Bonnie, Janae didn't do this. When would she have had the chance to do it? Someone has been home the whole time she's been here. Be logical." Malcolm sat down in the chair Bonnie used for her desk.

Bonnie had pulled the shredded clothes out of the closet and piled them on the bed. "She could have done it while I was out yesterday or while I was asleep! You always take her side."

"She was with me and the rest of the kids the entire time she was here yesterday. Do you think either one of us would have slept through something like this?"

Malcolm raised his voice, "The truth is that you're threatened by her, and I can't understand why. My daughter - all the kids - have been nothing but kind and good anytime they are with us. So, what is really going on Bonnie?"

Bonnie was stunned. Malcolm had always defended the kids, but he had never spoken out directly against her. She didn't know how to answer since she clearly was not in control of the situation.

"In fact," Malcolm continued, "The only people that would have had the opportunity to do this would be either you or me. I was home by myself yesterday morning and you said so yourself - the clothes were fine when you got home." Malcolm waited for a response.

Bonnie had no response.

"That leaves you Bonnie. You were the only one in this room alone for an extended amount of time."

Bonnie looked at him in complete terror. Did she do it?

Was she sleepwalking again? How?

Malcolm got up and walked over to the bed where Bonnie was sitting. "You know a knife is missing from the kitchen, right?

Malcolm reached around Bonnie and turned over her pillow. Sitting squarely underneath where the pillow was laying was the missing knife from the kitchen. Malcolm picked up the knife and carefully placed it on the nightstand next to the plate.

"Do you have anything to say?" Malcolm stared down at Bonnie.

Bonnie shook her head. She had absolutely no idea how it had happened. Her smug, controlling self had completely left the building. She sat on the bed completely horrified. Scared of herself and not knowing what she was capable of.

"Bonnie, you are going to listen to me for once. I don't know what is going on with you. I don't know if you did this for attention and I don't care. What I do care about is the fact that you, once again, tried to create friction between me and my daughter. This can't continue."

Malcolm gently picked up the knife and plate and walked toward the door. "I suppose that none of these clothes can be repaired. I'll bring some trash bags in. You need to start thinking about how you are going to apologize to Janae and how you will make this up to the rest of the kids."

Malcolm was just closing the door, "And Bonnie, we are going to have a nice, family meal with no dramatics. If you can't be pleasant, then please stay in this room. We will talk about this again once the kids have left for California."

Bonnie sat on the bed shaking in fear and anger. She got up and walked over to the closet to examine the damage more closely. She had examined her side of the closet even. She turned on the light, so she could get a better look. She was trying to make sense of what happened. Her side of the closet was the closest to the door. None of Malcolm's clothes were touched; they hadn't been knocked on the floor in what must have been a very violent exchange.

She examined her clothes closely and tried to imitate the motions that would have needed to happen for the clothes to have been slashed. To her horror she realized that it had to have been her that did it. The way the cut marks started and ended matched her height perfectly. She reached back and touched the marks on the wall. They were deep and jagged. She stared at the wall and clothes for a few moments when she suddenly felt nauseous. There was a smell coming from the crack in the wall, she thought. She put her face closer to the crack and the smell seemed to be lighter. She moved deeper into the closet to try to figure out where the smell was coming from. It became stronger the further she moved in. She felt lightheaded and decided that she needed to sit down before mentally attacking what happened. She turned off the light and looked back into the dark closet in disbelief. That's when she saw the orange eyes again, they were staring at her. Had they been there the whole time?

Bonnie knew she couldn't scream. She had already caused enough trouble for one day. More than enough. So, she did the only thing she could do. She stared back at the eyes and within moments, she fainted. She landed on the heavily carpeted floor in the closet. The closet door closed with her on the inside. She was out for less than a minute and when she awoke the eyes were gone. She realized she was sitting in a pitch-black closet, alone. She knew she had left the door open so who closed it?

Sleepwalking again? It had to be. She was certainly stressed beyond measure at this point. She picked herself off the floor and exited the closet. She closed the door firmly behind her. Just then Malcolm came in with the plastic bags. He dropped them on the bed and left the room without saying a word. He wouldn't even look at her.

Bonnie knew there was no way out of this, but maybe she could play this to her advantage. Surely, Malcolm couldn't leave her if she had some sort of mental breakdown. That would buy her time to make everything right again.

She got up from the bed and started filling the bags up with the ripped clothing. Tears rolled down her face as she discarded her favorite red sweater. She was planning to wear it for Thanksgiving dinner. There were clothes laying in the pile that had been given to her by her late mother. She felt her spirit sink even lower. The tears started to fall hot and fast now.

"What is happening to me?" she said it out loud. "Am I going crazy for real?" She sat down on the bed. She grabbed a pillow and held it to her face. She began wailing into the pillow hoping that the kids and Malcolm wouldn't hear her.

No one heard her, no one came to check on her. She finished putting the clothes away and went to take a shower.

She stepped into the bathroom and looked at herself in the mirror. She was pale and the dark circles under her eyes had returned. Her eyes were puffy and red from crying as well. She stared at her reflection and saw something dark colored in her hair. She reached up and recoiled the moment her hand touched the dark spot in her head. It looked like a streak of black hair going from the center of her head over the right side of her face and down to her shoulders.

It was the same black and oily cat hair she had cleaned up before. She tried to untangle the clump of hair from her own and found that she could not. She yanked and pulled, and it seemed to be stuck in her head. She grabbed a vanity mirror to try to see how it was tangled in her hair. She gasped and realized that it was in fact a part of her hair!

Bonnie calmed herself down while turning on the shower and grabbing some clothes to wear before going out to see the kids. She got in the shower once it was warm and thoroughly shampooed her hair. Once she was done, she leapt out and dried her hair with the hair dryer to see if the black, greasy streak was still there.

To her dismay, the streak was still there. Bonnie finished dressing and carefully pulled her hair back into a ponytail, hiding as much of the streak as she could with her normal colored hair.

Malcolm and the kids were sitting at the dining room table picking at a cold breakfast of sausage biscuits and hash browns. The mood was somber and dark. Malcolm looked at the kids' sad faces and said, "Hey, we are going to have a great day! It was just a misunderstanding. Bonnie just isn't feeling herself."

Katie, who looked the most worried of all, slowly got up from her chair, "I'll be right back." Without hesitating, Katie walked straight to her mom's bedroom. She didn't have a plan or a speech. She just wanted to see her mom and the closet for herself. She arrived at the door and let herself in. Her mom was coming out of the bathroom. She had on some yoga pants and a long sweatshirt. Her hair was tied up in a bun which was new. Katie felt awkward, but she pushed through her nervousness and sat in the chair in the corner.

The bedroom closet door was closed so she couldn't see the damage. But she did see three big trash bags filled to stuffing on the bedroom floor. Katie looked at her mom and her mom stared back at her.

"So, Mom. We haven't talked alone in a while. I thought this might be a good time."

"Did Mac-Malcolm send you in here? Is this a one-on-one intervention?" Bonnie huffed and fiddled with her hair before sitting on the bed across from Katie.

"No, Malcolm didn't send me in here. But I'm worried about you. I've never seen you like this before." Katie continued to stare at her mom. "Something is going on. What is it?"

Bonnie looked at Katie. Katie appeared to be staring into Bonnie's soul. She knew she couldn't tell Katie the truth. Bonnie herself didn't know the truth. She couldn't tell her daughter that she thought she was seeing, seeing what? Well, seeing demons with cats. She couldn't tell her baby girl that she thought she might be taking a lunch to go sleepwalk in the woods. So, she lied.

"Honey, can you keep a secret?" She looked at Katie with her serious face on. She realized that the sociopath in her was bordering on being psychotic. "I didn't want to tell you or your brother, but things haven't been great between me and Mac-Malcolm. I know it's my fault- I pushed Malcolm to move here because I thought it would help our relationship. I thought if I had him to myself, I could mold him into what I wanted and then we could be a happy family." Bonnie purposely looked down at her hands. "I've been feeling very depressed lately. I went to seek some professional help and they put me on some medication to balance out my moods."

Katie watched her mom carefully. "I think I mixed up the dosage and it caused me to spiral. I think that's why I was so tired last night." Katie sensed that her mom needed an ally and she felt like she was being pitched to. "I have a call into my doctor. I'm going to try to get in tomorrow to see if the dosage can be adjusted."

Katie listened and wondered how her mom could gloss over the closet incident.

"I guess the medicine made me a bit manic and I lost control. Baby, I'm sorry if I scared you. It scared me too." Bonnie looked at Katie with tears in her eyes, "I haven't taken any of it today and I will only take half the dosage if I start to feel really bad." Katie continued to watch her mom.

"Well, why don't you come out and watch some of the Thanksgiving parade on TV with us?" Katie stood up and reached her hand out to her mom. She didn't completely believe the story that her mom was telling her so she decided to play along until she could figure out what was really going on. There was always a method to her mom's madness even though most of the time the madness made more sense than the method.

Bonnie took Katie's hand and scooted off the bed. She led Katie to the door. "Mom, do you still have that quilt that grandma made for us? I would really love to wrap up in it while watching TV." Bonnie turned and beamed at Katie.

"I sure do! It's in the bench in front of the bed. I can't believe you remembered that." Bonnie watched as Katie walked over to the bench and opened the leather cover. She saw that the quilt was close to the top. She reached under the comforters on the top to grab the quilt. She began to pull, and it became snagged on something. Katie took a second look, and it was a box with a familiar name on it. She shifted it a bit and pulled the quilt out of the bench. She flipped the other comforters on top of the box in a way so that she could get a closer look at the box without tipping off her mom.

"Ok, I've got it. Let's go grab a seat on the couch." Katie could sense that her mom was hesitant about going out to face everyone. "C'mon Mom. This blow up was only an eight on the Bonnie Goes Crazy scale." She hoped her joke would lighten her mom's mood. It seemed to work.

Bonnie took a small step toward the door and reached out for Katie's hand for courage. The walked out of the bedroom and into the living room where Micah and Michael were sitting. Janae and Malcolm were in the kitchen preparing the side dishes for the big meal. The mood changed as soon as Bonnie entered the room.

"Hey, I uh... don't really know what to say. Janae, I am really sorry. I was a complete jerk and wrong and I hope that you will forgive me eventually. I understand if you don't want to. I was completely out of line."

"Micah and Michael, I don't know exactly what came over me. I've not been feeling like myself lately," she turned to address the young men. "I have a call into my doctor and hope to get in to see him tomorrow. I don't want to ruin today with a trip to the emergency room − I know that I need some help and I am taking the steps needed to get it."

"Mmmm-Malcolm- I hope you can forgive me too. I was awful - I know it. I own it. I hope it never happens again."

Malcolm was stunned. First off, Bonnie didn't look like herself at all. Her hair and clothing weren't what he was used to seeing on her. He took a breath and read the room, "Well, let's just move on with the day and see where it goes from here." He looked at the clock in the kitchen. It was 11:00am. He and Micah still had a bit of cooking to do before they could sit and socialize. They were really enjoying each other's company and bonding over cooking.

Katie led Bonnie to the couch where they sat down together. They watched TV silently as the parade gave way to one of many of the football games to be played on Thanksgiving.

Michael wasn't really into football. So, he watched silently and played games on his phone. He wanted to call his dad, but it was still a bit early on the west coast. His phone dinged with a message and Michael went to read it. He smiled when he saw it was from Katie. He looked over at her and saw that she was purposely looking at her phone with no intent of looking at him. So, he read the message. He was a bit confused by it, but he decided to go with the flow. He pretended to play with his phone and kept a watch on Katie and his mom. He saw Katie whispering excitedly to their mom who seemed a bit skeptical at whatever was being discussed. Katie kept working on her and eventually his mom appeared to come around.

Bonnie got up and squeezed Michael's shoulder as she made her way to the kitchen. She stood across the island from Janae and said, "Hey, Janae...I was thinking, you know tomorrow's Black Friday and I could use some new clothes. I was thinking of switching up my style a bit. Would you mind coming shopping with me?" Bonnie braced herself and then she continued, "It would be a good time for us to connect. I really want to make this morning up to you, please say 'Yes'.

Janae looked at her dad and then back at Bonnie. "Uh, that's really generous of you Bonnie. I don't know, let me think about it."

Just then Katie chimed in, "Michael, you could go with them." Katie knew that Janae was afraid of being alone with Bonnie.

Micah watched the scene play out. He looked at Katie incredulously and Katie frowned for a second and then winked at him. Then Micah looked at Michael, who was rolling his eyes unseen by Bonnie and Janae.

"Yeah, I'll go! Probably a good time to get started on Christmas shopping," he said without turning around. He looked at Micah and smirked.

"Well, ok. I would be glad to help you shop. What time should we head out?" Janae smiled at Bonnie.

Micah couldn't help picking up on the fact that some kind of plan was in place. He looked over at his dad who was working furiously on cooking and was completely oblivious to what was going on. He figured that Katie or Michael would clue them in once they had a chance.

Janae and Bonnie worked out the details for their shopping trip while Michael and Micah continued to exchange glances at each other. Katie submerged herself in her phone.

"Hey Katie, we better call Dad." Michael got up from the couch and went over to where Katie was sitting, so they could make the call.

Their dad picked up the video call on the third ring. "Hey Dad!" Katie and Michael sang out.

"Hey kids! How's it going? You been down to the honky tonks, yet?"

Michael and Katie laughed and chatted with their father while Bonnie hung out in the kitchen with Malcolm and Janae.

Micah waited for Katie and Michael's dad to talk to the rest of the kids. Paul was a nice guy. In fact, he was a lot like his dad, personality-wise. He could see why things didn't work out between Paul and Bonnie.

"Hey, where is everybody else? Micah? Janae? Where are you hiding?"

Katie took the phone over to Micah so he and her dad could talk. Then over to Janae once they were done.

Even though Paul suspected that Bonnie had left him for Malcolm, he wasn't quite sure if Malcolm knew that was the case. He really grew suspicious of this, because Bonnie would never let him, and Malcolm be alone. Paul had no ill-will toward Malcolm. The marriage was over long before Paul knew of Malcolm's existence even though the timing of everything was questionable.

Paul chatted with Bonnie and Malcolm, well mostly with Malcolm. He was a bit taken aback at Bonnie's appearance, but he figured the move had changed her and he hoped that they were happy. Paul knew Malcolm was a good man and he knew that the kids really cared for Malcolm. Nope, there was no need for any animosity between them.

He also knew that Bonnie would still go completely bonkers from time to time, and he had a sense that something had happened judging by everyone's behavior.

He knew he would get a call from Katie and Michael if things were going badly.

"Hey Dad! Let me show you my room here. I'm sharing it with Janae." Katie took the phone into her room and had a private conversation with her dad. When she came out, the conversation had ended, and she gave a nod to Michael and sat back down on the couch.

Bonnie went over to the freezer and grabbed the milkshake the kids had gotten for her the day before. She grabbed a spoon and a straw and walked back over to the couch where Katie was sitting.

Malcolm and Janae finished up in the kitchen and heated up some of the leftover chicken and sides for lunch. They bought the food over for everyone to enjoy and then they watched Christmas movies, talked, and laughed until it was time for dinner.

CHAPTER 27

Dena

Dena and Liz were setting the dishes on the table while their dad cut the turkey. Their mom was in the kitchen loading up the serving dishes with food.

Both Dena and Liz spent the day enjoying their parents, while cooking and texting with their beaus. And now it was time for the big meal.

Once everything was in place on the table, the family sat down, held hands, and bowed their heads while their dad prayed aloud. Then they ate and talked until they couldn't do either anymore.

All four helped clear the table. Dena and Liz washed the dishes even though their mother tried to stop them. They cleaned the kitchen and then they all sat together in the family room. Their dad eventually fell asleep and so did Dena, Liz, and their mom after a time.

They had big plans to visit family and friends the next day and they were really excited about it.

CHAPTER 28

Kelly

Kelly enjoyed his deep-dish pizza while watching the football games. Beth, Maddy and Joey had called throughout the day. Kelly was glad to hear from all of them even though they couldn't be with him for the holiday. He did feel a bit of sadness being on his own. But when it felt like the sadness was getting too strong his phone would ring and push the sadness away.

Not only did Beth and the kids call. He got calls from various friends and family members. It was as if the people closest to him knew he needed to hear from them. The last call came in at about 7pm and lasted for 45 minutes. By the time he hung up, his phone needed charging, his ear was ringing, and his heart and soul were full of happiness.

He was charging his phone when he noticed he had a bunch of text messages. He cleaned up the living room and went to take a shower before responding to the messages. Once he had finished responding to them all, including one from Ms. Dena, it was 9pm. He decided it was time to go to bed. He didn't know who sounded the alarm to have everyone reach out to him today, but he was glad that they did.

He had a big day planned for tomorrow. He was going to put up the Christmas tree and decorate the apartment with the things Beth had purchased. He would also start on his Christmas shopping via the online Black Friday sales. He hated going anywhere near a mall or shopping center the day after Thanksgiving.

CHAPTER 29

Bonnie, Malcolm, Micah, Michael, Janae and Katie

Janae and Katie set the table. Michael and Micah gathered in the kitchen to line up the dishes on the counter so they could do a buffet-style serving. Malcolm carved the turkey while Bonnie poured the drinks.

Once everything was ready, the "family" lined up, ladies first, to fill their plates up and then one by one they sat at the table. No one ate until everyone was sitting. Then the feast began.

Malcolm made a shrimp and crab dressing that was so delicious it was almost gone by the time the meal was over.

Everyone talked and laughed, and Bonnie seemed to be a different person. She was really trying to be kind with the kids and Malcolm.

Katie was quiet and seemed to force herself to participate in the conversations from time to time. Micah picked up on it and was sure it had to do with whatever Michael and Katie were up to. He wanted to know but felt like maybe it was something that was to stay between Michael and Katie and yet he felt uneasy about it.

Once dinner was over, Michael and Micah agreed to do the dishes. "It's only fair. It's not like I cooked at all - I would really love to learn how." Michael looked at Malcolm when he said this. "Do you think you could show me the basics? "

"Of course, I will. It's not as hard as you think," said Malcolm. "I will show you something simple to make before you leave and then we will pick up the lessons the next time you visit or by video chat. You let me know." Malcolm smiled.

Micah looked at his dad and then at Michael and smiled warmly. To him it felt like they were really bonding. Not that they hadn't bonded before, it's just that Bonnie seemed to want to keep some distance between all the kids. He guessed it was a "divide and conquer" strategy. It had worked up until now.

Janae and Bonnie were sitting at the table going over the stores they would shop at the next morning. Micah listened as they made their plan to get up and out early. They mapped out the stores they would hit first and what items they were looking to buy. Janae used her phone to check out the store sites so they wouldn't waste time searching the store aisles. "Bonnie, we will have your closet back in order in no time!"

It was eight o'clock when Janae said, "Well, I guess I better go to bed. Big day tomorrow morning." She stretched and said goodnight to everyone and headed to bed.

Katie watched from the living room sofa as Bonnie made her excuses for bed not long after Janae. Bonnie came over to her, kissed her and gave her a squeeze. "Thank you, Baby. I hope this shopping trip helps." Bonnie looked at Katie and kissed her again.

Katie looked at her mom. She wanted to hug and kiss her back, yet she sensed that her mother hadn't changed at all and that she was hiding something big.

Also, even though the person looking at her seemed to be her mother, it didn't feel like her mother. Katie chalked it up to her mom hardly ever being affectionate. And this weekend her mom had been in overdrive, up one day and down the next. Katie looked at her mom and saw a flash behind her eyes. She kissed her mom's cheek. "I hope that you and Janae will become great friends."

Bonnie went off to bed after that.

Malcolm and Micah were in the kitchen when Michael came over to Katie with two plates of chocolate cake. "So, little sister, what have you gotten me into?" asked Michael. "I already have visions of me having to hold endless bags of clothing and purses tomorrow. This better be worth it."

"Michael, something is not right. I'm not sure yet. But I will tell you as soon as I figure it out." Katie looked at Michael with a worried look. "I saw something that I don't think I was supposed to see, and I can't let it go. I think whatever it is will pretty much be the end of this relationship between Mom and Malcolm."

Michael picked at his cake with the fork. He took a bite and it tasted like nothing. "Well, that's just great. I felt like Mom was trying to change, but if you feel like this is an act and she is still manipulating Malcolm then -"

"I think she's done more than just manipulate Malcolm. This is way beyond that. I need to put the pieces together before I say anything more."

"What can I do to help?"

"I need to figure out how to get Malcolm out of the house for a while. Or if I can't, I will have to tell him the truth and I'm not sure what the truth is."

"Well, I can ask him to come with us tomorrow. Or maybe he would like to spend some time with Micah; they haven't had any time together yet."

"That is a brilliant idea. I will suggest they go out and do something tomorrow while you're out shopping with Mom and Janae."

Michael winced at the idea of shopping. "Man, this better be worth it. I almost hope you're wrong."

Katie finished her cake. It was rich and chocolatey. She got a glass of milk from the refrigerator to chase it down. "So, what are you two up to tomorrow?"

Micah and Malcolm looked at Katie. "I don't know Katie, sounds like you're trying to get us out of the house. Where are we going?"

"I still want to go to the wax museum at the mall with everyone. Maybe we can do that later tomorrow. Don't you and Micah want to hang out a bit? I have some homework to do tomorrow morning. Not much - I just didn't want you to think you had to stay in the house because of me."

Malcolm looked at Micah. "Well, there is this museum filled with European classic cars we could go check out if you want."

Micah looked at Katie. He saw her raise her eyebrows slightly and took the bait. "Yeah, that sounds like fun. I don't have anything planned. - Let's check it out."

From there, Micah and Malcolm planned out their morning at the museum.

Malcolm went to bed about 9pm. Bonnie was fast asleep. He noticed that the TV was on one of the music channels again. This time it was on a country station. He knew that Bonnie hated country music. She must have rolled over on the remote. He went to the bathroom to wash up before bed. He didn't see the pair of eyes looking out from the closet. He would not have seen the outline of the black cat on the floor of the closet.

Malcolm could hear the rest of the kids making their way to bed. The last couple of days had been stressful. He hoped the rest of the weekend would go smoothly. He slid into bed and found the remote. He turned the TV so he could check out the football recaps. He drifted to sleep, unaware that they were being watched from inside the room. Once he was fully asleep, the channel changed by itself back to the country station.

Morning came quickly. Bonnie, Janae, and Michael were up and out of the apartment by 4am. Well, Michael tried to be up. He climbed into the backseat and hoped that they would have at least a thirty-minute ride to the outlet shopping mall in Lebanon. It was still dark out, so he had no problems falling asleep instantly as the car made its way to the mall.

Katie woke up about 5:30am. She heard someone rumbling around so she got up to check it out.

Malcolm was in the living room, wearing sweats and doing stretches. "Hey Katie! I'm going on a run. I should be back in less than an hour." He kissed her on the forehead. "I have my phone if you need me." Malcom exited using the stairs to the front door. "I'm going to leave the door unlocked. It's pretty safe around here." Except for when your mother has a knife. But that's old news, he thought.

Providence! That was the only word for it. It had to be providence! Katie checked on Micah and found him still asleep. She went into the living room and grabbed the quilt her mom had brought out the night before. She folded it up neatly and headed to the bedroom to put it away. She closed the door behind her and went over to the bench. She put the quilt on the bed and opened the bench. She hesitated for a moment, her courage took over and she reached into the bench to find the box she had seen the night before.

It didn't take long for her hands to find all three boxes. She pulled them all out and placed them on the bed. She turned on the lamp to make sure she was seeing what she thought she was seeing. And she was seeing what she thought she was seeing. She saw three boxes addressed to Malcolm, Micah, and Janae from Donita Adams. She knew that Donita was Malcolm's wife. She knew that Donita had been gone for years. There were no dates on the boxes so she couldn't tell how long her mom had been holding on to them.

Katie went back to the bench to see if there was anything else. She found her mom's gun which was not a shock. She decided to put it somewhere else for now. She didn't know why she felt the need to hide the gun, but she felt like it was best to be safe rather than sorry. She took the gun and put it in Malcolm's sock drawer.

She was about to pull all the quilts and comforters out of the bench when her knuckles scraped against what felt like a balled-up piece of paper. She grabbed the paper and pulled it out. It was a letter addressed to Malcolm from Donita. She didn't read it but, she looked at the date and saw that it had been written in mid-August. She smoothed the letter out and put it on the bed with the rest of the boxes. Then she sat in the chair across from the bed and tried to think of what to do next.

The answer came to her quickly. She would wake Micah up and show him the boxes. He could at least look them over and open the one that belonged to him if he chose to.

She leapt from the chair and ran to the room where Micah was sleeping. She knocked loudly. "Come in." She was surprised to see that Micah was awake, sitting on the bed playing a game. "Ok, Katie. What are you up to?"

"I need to show you something. It involves you and I don't know what to do. Please come with me."

Micah followed Katie to the bedroom and saw the packages laying on the bed. "The middle one is addressed to you. I wanted to make sure of what I was seeing, so I had to wait until Malcolm was gone."

Micah walked over and picked up the package. It was light. He looked at the address information and furrowed his brow. He picked up the other boxes and examined them. "How did these get here?"

Katie explained how she saw the one with his name on it last night, and then how she found the others just then. Micah listened and nodded. Everything made sense now. Katie then handed him the letter from Donita. Micah took it and looked at it. "Well, this is not a real surprise. Mama sent letters to me at school over the past few weeks. I even met her for lunch before coming here. Honestly, me and Janae met her for lunch."

"So, Bonnie must have retrieved these before my dad could see them." Micah thought for a moment. "It's no secret that Bonnie feels threatened by my mom. Who's to say that my dad is even willing to forgive my mom at this point?" He looked at Katie and saw that she was worried.

"Yes, your mom was wrong for keeping this from my dad. I know he will be mad about it but I'm not sure it will be something they break up over. Besides, even if they do, you're still my little sister. We grew up together. Nothing will change that."

"Should we tell Malcolm when he gets back?" Katie was almost in tears.

"Yes, don't worry Katie. I will tell him. It won't be as bad as you think. Go on back to bed and try to put this out of your mind for now. I will wait for my dad."

Katie and Micah left the bedroom, closing the door behind them. Micah went to the living room to wait on Malcolm, and Katie went to her room. There was no way she was going to be able to sleep. She checked her emails and text messages to see how her dad and friends were doing. She tried her best to keep her mind occupied. This had sealed the deal for her. She would not live with her mother -not after this.

Fifteen minutes after Micah had sat down in the living room, he heard the front door open and saw his dad emerge from the stairwell.

"Hey, son! You're up early. The sun is just now coming up." Malcolm saw the serious look on Micah's face and said, "Can this wait until after I take a shower, or do we need to talk about it now?"

"Let me give you some background and then you can decide. It's not all bad but it's going to be a shock."

Malcolm sat down and braced himself, "Ok, what's going on?"

Micah told him everything, about how Donita had contacted both him and Janae. How they had been texting and writing letters. He told his dad how they met her for lunch before coming to Nashville. He watched his dad's reaction.

"Ok, well, I'm glad she's okay and that she has reached out to you. I hope that you can have a good relationship with her now. Thank you for telling me." Malcolm sighed, "That wasn't too bad, I -" Malcolm glanced at Micah's face. "There's more, isn't there? Okay, let me have it."

"Dad, come with me. I want to show you something." Micah led Malcolm to the bedroom and to the boxes. He picked up the letter from the bed and handed it to his dad. "Katie found the boxes in this bench this morning. She was putting away a blanket. She found the letter too. We didn't read it."

"I know you need some time to read the letter and take this all in. I'm going to make some cereal for me and Katie." Malcolm sat heavily on the bed with his mouth open in shock as Micah had predicted. Micah left the room and closed the door behind him.

Malcolm read the letter. in it Donita apologized and said that she was sad and sorry that she left him and the kids the way that she had.

She didn't expect him to forgive her, but she at least wanted to be a part of the kids' lives. She hoped that she and Malcolm could one day be friends again. She was in recovery and counselling. Donita had moved in with her older sister, just outside of Los Angeles. She had started an online business designing clothes and planned to open a storefront early next year. She said she wanted to show Malcolm that she had been stable for a while so he wouldn't worry about her while she was spending time with the kids. She hoped he was happy and well. She had no intentions of interfering in his life but, she had to be in the kids' lives again no matter what. She even said she was willing and ready to sign divorce papers if that's what he wanted. She was surprised he hadn't tried to reach her to do just that in the past. She left her phone number, email address and her business website information and ended the letter with another deep heartfelt apology and with a private phrase they used to say to each other.

Malcolm read the letter again and then a third time. He put it down on the bed and looked at the boxes. He picked up the one for Micah and held it for a moment. He did the same for the boxes with his and Janae's names on it. "I guess I can't ignore this any longer."

He wasn't mad, he was in complete disbelief. He looked at the date on the letter and put everything together. It all made sense. He had been "handled" and it was not a good feeling at all. He still wasn't mad, at least not mad at Bonnie. He was mad at himself for not seeing what was happening.

Had she been handling him the whole time? Of course, she had.

He got up and put his hand gently on the letter, then he went to the bathroom to shower, thinking the whole time. By the time he was halfway through the shower he had decided on what to do.

Once he was dressed, he picked up the box with Micah's name on it and took it into the living room. "Hey, why don't you go ahead and open this? I'm going to go have a word with Katie." He didn't want Katie to feel bad about what had happened.

When he reached Katie's room, she was sitting on the bed, finishing up a phone conversation. "Hey! I didn't mean to interrupt - I just wanted to talk to you for a moment,"

"No, I was just talking to my dad. I told him everything." She hesitated. She had been so emotional this whole trip. It was like she knew things were going to boil over and it seemed like they had.

"Katie, everything is going to be fine. I know you weren't sure about moving here with us and I'm sure this weekend has helped you make up your mind." Malcolm looked at Katie and put his hand on her shoulder. "None of this is your fault so don't feel guilty about any of it."

"It's not that," said Katie. She patted Malcolm's hand. She looked up at his kind face and said, "I just don't understand my mom. How could she do this? And why?" She took a breath. "I mean, I guess I know why but really, WHY?"

"I can't answer that honey. Only your mom knows why she does the things she does, and I don't think she's going to give any secrets away at this point."

Katie and Malcolm continued their conversation while Micah opened the box while sitting in the living room on the couch. He already knew what it was, or at least he had a strong feeling about it. He smiled as he tore open the box. Inside it was a scarf to match the sweater his mom had made for him when they met for lunch. it was dark blue with gold leaves sewn in. It was warm and soft and wonderful. At that moment, he missed his mom.

Both he and Janae had talked to her briefly and discreetly yesterday after dinner. Yet, he still missed her. He pulled out his phone and texted Donita.

"Okay, well, I talked to Katie. I am not going to make a fuss while you kids are here. This is something that me and Bonnie will work out after you leave, so not a word of this to her."

"Okay, Dad, I understand." Micah wrapped the scarf around his neck and went back to the bedroom to get in a quick nap. He stopped, "Dad, what about Janae? What about Michael?"

"Don't worry. I have that figured out." His dad grinned. "Nice scarf."

"Did you open your gift?"

"Not yet. I'm going to wait a bit on it." Malcolm looked down at his hands and Micah went to the bedroom.

All this drama and it was only 8am. Malcolm made his way back to the bedroom he shared with Bonnie to clean up. He put the box with his name on it back in the bench and covered it back up with the comforters. He took the letter and smoothed it out. He put it in his wallet. He took the box for Janae and put it in on the bed in the room she was sharing with Katie. Katie had fallen asleep.

He left the room and closed the door behind him. He walked back to his room and figured he could get in a nap as well. He closed the bedroom door behind him and got into bed. The sheets were cool and soft. Malcolm rolled on his stomach and reached his hand underneath the pillow only to be met with a sharp pain. He pulled his hand out and saw blood droplets forming on the tip of his index finger. He lifted the pillow and found his old friend the knife there. Again, the knife looked just as confused as Malcolm was.

"How the hell?" Was Bonnie planning to shred his clothes next? Malcolm was too tired to try to understand. He grabbed a Kleenex off the nightstand and wrapped up his finger. He put the knife in the nightstand.

Malcolm sat up and looked at his phone. He thought for a moment then made the call he had been considering making since this madness with Bonnie came out. Once he was done, he put his head back on the pillow and quickly drifted to sleep noting that the knife was not there last night.

Bonnie, Janae, and Michael came back home just before 9am. The apartment was quiet, everyone was still asleep. They were tired as well.

They put up their packages and went to their separate beds to rest before everyone else woke up.

Bonnie went to smoke on the balcony. She hadn't had a cigarette since the night of the dank bath and cat hair. Maybe this was a good time to quit. She looked at the half-smoked ember and put it out.

She went into the living room and took off her shoes. She grabbed one of the blankets and wrapped herself up in it. She was off to sleep in no time on the plush couch.

This was a good thing. It kept her from hearing Katie and Micah filling in their siblings on what had happened while she was out. Even though something else was listening the whole time.

Malcolm was the first one up from the morning nap session. He was starving, no breakfast served with two helpings of drama could do that to someone. He decided to make lunch for everyone, and he put the knife back in its rightful place. Turkey sandwiches with mashed potatoes and mac and cheese, Malcolm thought as he cooked. He watched Bonnie as she slept on the couch. She looked peaceful as she slept. So, he kept working and considered how he was going to execute his plan. He realized now that Bonnie was not only manipulative; she was dangerous as well. He had to play this just right.

Katie awoke and came into the living room. Then one by one the kids woke from their slumber and appeared. Bonnie was the last to wake up.

Lunch was ready. Plates were made and then served. Everyone sat around the table laughing and talking like nothing was wrong. Everyone pretended that all was well except for Bonnie who had no clue that her web of lies, and deceit was about to be destroyed. And so, it was like that until Sunday morning when the kids all left for California.

Bonnie stayed at home while Malcolm took the kids to the airport. Even though she wasn't alone. And at this point she knew better than to try to run from her "guests."

On the ride to the airport, he told the kids not to worry.

He had a plan, and everything would be fine.

"When are you going back to your house?" Katie asked, excitedly.

"Katie let's just see how things go. I want to take my time and make sure I do this the right way." Malcolm glanced at Katie through the rearview mirror while she was sitting in the backseat. "I don't want to hurt your mom's feelings."

Katie accepted his excuse. She hoped he would be back in California before Christmas. She was glad to be going home too. It was nice in Nashville, but something about the apartment gave her the creeps.

"I liked visiting, Malcolm, but have you noticed that your place is a bit scary at times?" Michael asked from the backseat.

"Really? How so?" asked Malcolm.

"Well, my earbuds would randomly change stations during the night. Even when I wasn't wearing them and no matter what I was listening to. Also, your cutlery would show up in the weirdest places. I found a knife in my backpack the first night I was there. And I kept feeling like I was being watched; that's why I slept with Micah" Michael paused for a moment. "I knew he would protect me! He's my hero."

Malcolm listened in bewildered silence for second, "I guess that settles it. The place is haunted. I can't deny it any longer."

The kids laughed. But Malcolm was serious. He thought of ways to ramp up his plan considering Michael's admission.

They made it to the airport and Malcolm said long goodbyes to them all. "Call me as soon as you land!" He stayed until they made it through security then he went back to the car. He had to admit that he was not in a hurry to go home. He pulled out his wallet and took the letter from Don out. He read it again then he leaned back in the car seat and cried. Then he did something he hadn't done in years. He prayed.

As coincidence would have it, Dena and Liz were exiting the airport while Malcolm was in his car. They used a ride-share app to get to Liz's apartment where Dena had left her car. They had had a wonderful time in Detroit. They were both a little sad to be back in Nashville, only because they missed their parents. They laughed and talked the whole way to Liz's place.

Liz helped Dena get her suitcase into the car and then Dena helped Liz get her suitcase up the stairs to her apartment. Once inside, Dena used the restroom and washed her face. When she came out of the bathroom, Liz was already cuddled up in a blanket and wearing her pajamas.

Dena kissed Liz on the forehead and said, "I better get home. I want to get some couch time in before going to work tomorrow."

"Aww, you can share my couch!" Liz said and put on her best sad, little sister face.

Dena laughed, "No, I have to go, besides isn't Jon coming over this afternoon?"

Liz sighed and nodded, "Yeah, I better get some rest. I'm going to have to cook and be fresh for him."

"So, you're going to nap and play video games before he gets here. I know you!" Dena and Liz both laughed.

Dena hugged her sister and said goodbye, then she made her way home. Sadness came over her as she entered the gates to the apartment complex. She stopped and picked up her mail before going to her apartment.

Once she had parked, grabbed her luggage, purse, and mail, she walked down the path to her door. She stopped when she saw something caught in a tree branch just outside her door. It was a large, long, black, greasy clump of hair. Gross!! Had someone lost their weave? Just disgusting. She had some napkins in her pocket and was able to reach up and gather the hair. To her surprise it smelled awful yet familiar. She didn't want to bring it inside, so she balled it up and left it in the corner outside. She would take it to the trash later.

She made it inside the apartment and flopped on the couch. She closed her eyes just to have a moment to herself before making her next move when she heard something coming from the bedroom.

Dena froze and thought, "Not again." She listened for a moment to try to make out the noise and realized that it was music coming from her alarm clock. It wasn't her regular station; She must have bumped up against it causing the station to change. The alarm was set to go off at 6am and it was just 7:15am so it made total sense.

She got up, took off her coat and hung it in the bedroom closet. She turned the alarm clock back to her normal station and then reset it. She decided to take a shower before putting on her pajamas. She prepped for the shower and as she walked past the blinds, she opened them. She was going to spend the entire day lounging on the couch. She went back to getting her pajamas ready when she realized she had seen something outside up on the hill. She turned around and saw her neighbor staring at her from her balcony.

Dena watched her for a while, thinking that she was mistaken. Maybe the woman was looking at something else and it just looked like she was staring at Dena. Dena shrugged it off and walked into the living room. She opened the blinds and saw that the woman had shifted to watch her in the living room.

"Let her watch. It will be pretty boring watching me watch TV." Dena picked up her phone and texted Liz, her parents and Chris to let them know she was safe at home. She went to take her shower and change into her pajamas. Once she was done, she picked up her phone and saw that she had missed a call from Chris. Her mom and her sister had texted her back. She called Chris and talked to him for about 20 minutes. They had talked off and on while she was in Detroit.

"Hey, Babe. Let's go see the new superhero movie coming out next week!" Dena agreed to the date and mentioned they could see it at the movie plex near her house.

"We can watch it in 4-D over here," she said excitedly.

"Yeah! Let's do that. You sound tired. I really missed you.

You go ahead and get some rest. Call me later," Chris said.

"Okay, I will. I am beat. I always get like that after flying plus we did get up really early to catch the flight." Dena walked back over to the window, trying to fight sleep. She looked out again and saw that the woman on the hill was still there staring at her. Dena watched her for a moment, not breaking contact and then the woman turned and went back into the apartment. Dena convinced herself that she was imagining things.

"Babe? You there? Did you fall asleep?"

"No, just window watching. I am going to lay down now. Call you later." They said goodbye and Dena looked out the window one last time. She thought she saw something moving against the balcony railing where the lady was watching her. It looked like a large black cat. Dena had never seen it before. She loved cats but this one looked strange, it had greasy, slick hair. She had never seen a cat with greasy fur before.

"Maybe it's wet," she thought. "I better lay down before I fall down." She sat on the couch, grabbed the remote and turned the TV on to lull her to sleep. She closed her eyes and let the TV watch her.

Bonnie also watched Dena from the balcony. She came back out with the cat and stared at her. She knew this wasn't her doing but she couldn't help it. Her "guest" had compelled her to do it. Dena had something that it wanted. Bonnie could feel what it was, yet she didn't know what to call it. She stood in a trance in the cold morning air looking into Dena's living room window. She could barely make out the sleeping form on the couch, but she knew she was there. So, she watched and watched and watched. She watched for nearly two hours. Then she went back inside to let the next shift take over watching.

Dena woke up about 9am, still a bit tired and hungry. She left the warmth of her blanket and couch to head over to the kitchen to make something to eat. As she rounded the corner to go into the kitchen, a lower kitchen cabinet door corner caught her in the shin. "Ouch! Dang it!" Dena grabbed her leg. She leaned against the wall and examined her leg. It was already tuning red and swelling. It wasn't bleeding but it hurt bad. She hobbled into the bathroom behind her to tend to her wound.

Once she was done, she went back into the kitchen. The cabinet door was still opened. She looked at it in disbelief. She knew she had checked the entire apartment before leaving for Detroit and everything was in its place, so how was this door open? She examined it for a moment, checking out the hinges to see if anything was out of order and found nothing. She sighed and closed the door.

She decided to make some comfort food. A tuna sandwich, chips, and a soda for breakfast. She put everything together on a plate and ate her meal while sitting on the couch. She was still tired, and this was not normal. Usually, after a nap and something to eat she was up and ready to go! She ate half the sandwich and only a few chips. Then she pulled the blanket back over her and laid down. It was still early, just a couple more hours of sleep and she felt sure she would be rested and ready to take on the rest of the day.

She didn't realize that she was still being watched by the four-legged creature on the balcony up on the hill. She was asleep in less than a minute and she dreamed of a wet darkness.

Dena woke up and knew that she had been asleep far too long. She grabbed her phone and saw that she had missed texts and calls from her mom, Liz, and Chris. She checked the time; it was noon. Not too bad but still much later than she had planned to sleep.

She grabbed the land line phone and called Liz first. "Hey, I guess the plane ride really knocked me out! I was not planning to sleep this long."

"I figured - I didn't want anything. I keep forgetting that your cell phone doesn't work in the apartment. Just wanted to let you know that the girls want to go to brunch next Sunday. You probably got the invite already."

Dena checked her phone and saw that the invite was there.

She went ahead and accepted the invitation.

"Yeah, I got it! I will be there. What are you doing?"

"I just came back from the grocery store. I'm starting dinner and having a bite to eat for lunch."

"Oh, what are you making for dinner? I hadn't thought that far in advance," Dena asked.

"Probably baked chicken and some sides. Hadn't decided yet. You okay? You sound tired and I don't know...something else."

"I am still a little tired and I banged my shin into an open cabinet door a couple of hours ago. Hurt pretty bad but at least the swelling is going down. I'm going to have a nice conversational bruise," Dena laughed.

"Oh, poor little shin! Want me to kiss and make better?" Liz made kissing noises over the phone.

Dena laughed, "I think I will survive. I better go. I still have to call Mom and Chris."

"Yeah, Mom and Dad are out. They went to some celebration at the church. Probably just text Mom and let her know you're alive."

"Okay. Thanks! Will do! Talk to you later. Love you little sis." Dena ended the call, took a moment for herself, and called Chris. She texted her mom while the phone rang for Chris.

"Hey! Have you been asleep all this time? I was wondering if you wanted to go to dinner tonight. Or I could bring you some dinner and we could watch a movie?"

"Hi, yeah! I would love that! What time should I expect you?"

"I can be there at 3:30. That way we can catch up for a while," answered Chris.

"Okay. See you then! Can't wait." Dena leaned back on the couch and looked at her nearly untouched sandwich and chips. She took a couple of bites of the sandwich and got up to shower and shave for her date tonight. She painted her toe nails a dark burgundy color and gave herself a facial. She hadn't seen Chris in four days, and she wanted to look her best. They were still in the beginning stages of dating where looks mattered.

She looked at her face in the mirror and saw that her eyes were puffy and dark circles were forming under them. She grabbed a facial cream known for solving this issue and put it on. Strange, she never had this problem from sleeping too much. She put on lotion and waited as the cream worked its magic. And in minutes she saw an improvement.

She went to her closet to pick out an outfit. Something casual and comfortable. She stood in front of the closet trying to figure out what would work best. She zoned out for a moment and when she came back to reality, she felt weird, like she was being watched. She went to the window and saw that her neighbor had gone inside, and the black cat stood watch on the balcony. "Great, now I'm paranoid." She closed the bedroom blinds to feel secure again. "No way the cat is watching me." Dena shrugged and went back to the closet.

She picked out a gray, cotton hoodie dress that went to her knees. She laid the dress on the bed and went to her jewelry box to pick out a necklace. She selected a short, delicate silver chain with a pearl pendant hanging from it and placed it on top of the dress.

She went and cleaned up the bathroom and pulled out make-up and perfume to prepare for tonight's date. Once she was done, she went back out to the living room to make sure everything was clean and tidy. She took the top off the candle on the coffee table and lit it so that the fragrance would fill the room. She picked up her glass and the plate with the remnants of sandwich on it and went to put it in the sink. To her surprise, the same cabinet door that she had bumped into with her shin was open again! She pushed it closed angrily and put her plate in the sink. She grabbed a screwdriver out of the toolbox in the laundry room and set about tightening the screws on the hinges of the cabinet door. They were pretty tight already, but a little more tightening couldn't hurt. She looked inside the cabinet to see if something had shifted to push the door open and of course everything was neatly placed inside. Nothing was pushing the door open.

Dena shook her head in disbelief and went back into the laundry room to put the screwdriver away. When she turned around the door was open again! She huffed and grabbed some electrical tape to shut until Chris got there. Maybe he could figure out what was wrong with it. "This place is falling apart!"

That's when she remembered the hair, she had balled up in a napkin that she had left outside. She went back to the bedroom, took off her robe and put on some sweats. She grabbed her keys, headed out the door, locking it behind her. It was sunny and brisk outside.

She grabbed the clump of hair still wrapped up in the napkins. She placed it in the small plastic bag she had in hand and walked to her car.

She looked at Kelly's place to see if he might be home. She hadn't heard from him since he responded to the Thanksgiving text she had sent. His place looked empty, even though she could see his truck parked in its normal spot from the path. She made it to her car and finished her errand of discarding the hair. It still smelled pungent, almost like a skunk, but in some ways worse.

She pulled back into her parking spot and took a minute to let her windows down to get the horrible smell out of the car. She walked down the path and made it back to her apartment. She was just stepping up to unlock her door when she saw that it was open!

She was terrified! Her phone was inside. She asked, "How?" again for the second or third time that day. She listened to see if anyone was inside and didn't hear anything. She thought about what to do and came to only one conclusion. She turned and walked back to Kelly's apartment.

She took a moment to build up her courage and knocked. Kelly came to the door in less than a minute. "Hey, Ms. Dena! Did you have a good trip?"

"Hey Kelly! Yes, it was good to see my family and friends. I hate to bother you, but can you check out my apartment? I could have sworn I locked my door and when I got back from dropping off the trash, it was open."

Kelly looked at Dena and nodded his head in silence. "Ms. Dena, I think that's pretty common around here. This whole place seems to be haunted. C'mon, let's see if you have a haunt or a hooligan."

They walked back down to her place and Kelly went in first. He turned, "Stay here just in case." Dena waited outside feeling silly and yet still having a feeling of being watched. She looked up at the apartment on the hill where her neighbor had been gawking at her and was glad to see that no one was there. She turned her attention back to her doorway and waited for Kelly to come back out.

"Well, it looks like it's a haunt," Kelly sighed and patted her on the shoulder. "Listen, I don't know what's going on in this place but it's not just happening to you. Make sure you stay in close touch with your loved ones and don't spend too much time alone in your apartment." Dena looked at him, somewhat leary, yet she took in what he said. "I know it sounds crazy but please just hear me out and keep on your toes."

Dena moved closer to the door, and she turned to thank Kelly.

"No problem. You can always call me or knock on my door. And I mean that."

Kelly started walking back to his apartment when he suddenly turned and looked at Dena. "I've been meaning to tell you something. I believe that I did come to your door the night you said I did. I just don't remember it. I'm guessing I was sleepwalking due to the medication, but I just can't be absolutely sure."

He shrugged, turned around and walked back to his place.

Dena took it all in and didn't know what to make of what Kelly had said. She walked back into her apartment and closed the door behind her. She made sure that both locks were secured before sitting back down on the couch. She wondered what else he had been through. She was a bit relieved that it wasn't just her, yet she didn't want anyone to live in fear. Maybe that's what's wrong with her stalker neighbor up on the hill. It was too much to take in all at once. She started to question all the bizarre events that had taken place since she had moved in. Her change in demeanor, doors opening on their own, spoons magically appearing, the hanger. But today was the weirdest day of all. She looked at the phone and thought about calling Liz or Chris. She didn't want Liz to worry, and she didn't feel she knew Chris well enough to spring this on him. She looked away from the phone and went to her office to get the bible.

She turned on her laptop to search for the appropriate passages and prayers. Once she found what she was looking for she noted them so she could bookmark them on her cell phone later. She read what she had found several times and began to feel better. It was 2:30 by then and she needed to start getting ready for her date with Chris. She picked up the phone on the table to call Liz and let her know that she had plans with Chris.

"That is great! Jon is on his way over here! Almost like a double date."

Dena hesitated. She wanted to tell Liz about what was happening, but she didn't want to sound crazy or to even believe what was happening herself. So, she laughed, "Yeah, almost. Well, I better get dressed. Text you later."

Dena hung up and got dressed. She decided she and Chris were past the stage where she needed to wear make-up on every date so, she put her make up away and went for the natural look. She was ready by 2:50pm and she had some time to kill. So, she sat on her bed and relaxed by closing her eyes and clearing her mind. Just for a moment. She took a few deep breaths to push out anxiety and to calm herself from the events of the day. She felt calmer and at ease. She had been feeling off ever since she stepped into the apartment. She figured the negative energy had gathered again and was laying heavy in the air of her home. She took one last deep breath and opened her eyes. She heard Chris knocking on the door a few moments later.

She could see him from the bedroom window. She laughed at herself, wondering if he saw her meditating on the bed. She got up and went to let him in.

Chris had a bag full of food in one hand and a gallon of sweet tea in the other. He was truly a Memphis, country boy. She hugged him and kissed his cheek before letting him in. "Wow! PDA's already, this soon in the relationship."

Dena gasped, "You just called this a relationship! I knew it!"

Chris shook his head and walked inside the apartment. He set the food down on the coffee table while Dena went to go grab the plates and cups from the kitchen. "Hey, since we're all boo'ed up now, I can ask you to fix things around the house, right?" Dena walked back over to the couch with the plate and cups in hand.

"I guess I can take a look at whatever needs a 'fixin, baby girl," said Chris. "What's going on?"

Dena laughed and said, "It can wait till after dinner. Let's eat before the food gets cold." And so they did, eating and catching up with each other before cuddling up on the couch to watch a movie. They talked more after the movie and by then Dena had forgotten about having him check the cabinet. She rested against his chest with his arms wrapped around her and felt warm and cared for.

Chris left around 9pm since he had to get up for work the next day. He gave Dena a long, close, tight embrace and kissed her deeply before leaving. He stepped away from her and sighed. Then he turned around to leave. He paused for a moment and turned back to her, "By the way, you know you're my girl, right?"

Dena smiled, "Yeah, I figured as much." She kissed him again and he left for home.

Dena went back inside and got ready for bed. She cleaned up the living room and put the leftover food and tea in the refrigerator. She turned off the lights, closed the blinds and made sure the door was locked.

She went into the bedroom and closed the blinds, forgetting she had closed them earlier. She turned on the lamp on the nightstand closest to the window and checked to make sure her alarm clock was set. She suddenly felt a chill wash over her and she turned around quickly. She looked at the window and she had the strange feeling that she was still being watched even though the blinds were closed. She reached over and turned off the lamp, then went back to the window. She lifted the thin, plastic window blind blade to see if her neighbor was still watching. And she was! She was sitting on the balcony, smoking a cigarette in the dark. Her body was positioned to face Dena's apartment. Dena shuddered and thought, "It's just a coincidence. She's having a smoke, nothing crazy about that."

Dena turned on the TV and went to the bathroom to brush her teeth. When she came back into the bedroom, she saw that the TV was on a cable music channel again. "This is starting to get annoying." She changed the channel to her favorite Sunday night zombie show and got in the bed. She texted Chris, who had made it home, then her mom and lastly her sister. Then she settled in to give her full attention to the show. She turned the sleep timer on during the commercial break and fell asleep not long after the show was over.

She was still being watched, even though her blinds were closed.

The large, slick, black cat was sitting outside her window, gazing at it, and making what could only be called "mewling sounds of an undead cat." The mewling became louder and louder until it woke Dena. She sensed that something was outside and heard the noises. She went to the window to check to see if an animal was hurt. She peeked through the blinds and saw nothing at first. The cat was gone, there was no sign of it at all. What Dena did see was what looked like gopher holes. She let out a loud sigh and went to bed. Her head was full of questions. The clock on her nightstand read 2:52am.

The next day she woke up achy and sore. Her arms were a bit red, and she had scratches on them. Her shin shouted in pain as she tried to get up. "What's happening to me? I'm falling apart." She laughed sadly and started her day.

She chalked the bruises on her arms to her handling the luggage yesterday. She figured she had probably overdone it. She saw that her shin bruise was turning a nice dark maroon color while she was in the shower. "Great."

She remembered the strange noises and the holes while she was brushing her teeth. She checked for the holes once she dried off, and they were there. It was not her imagination. "Guess I need to research gophers or moles. I wouldn't think they would be out right now. Late summer, early winter is the time for them." She dressed and went to the kitchen to grab some oatmeal. The cabinet was still taped shut but the tape was stretched and loose like the cabinet had been pushed from the inside. Dena sighed again and continued with her task.

She grabbed her coat and bag and left for work. She would look at the gopher holes again when she got home. It was just too much to deal with on a Monday morning. It was a Monday of all Mondays, which was expected but no one including Dena was prepared for it. It seemed that 4pm came quickly and Dena was worn out. When she pulled into her parking spot, she sat for moment to let the day wash over her. She zoned out and lost track of time. When she came back to reality, she was still weary and had lost twenty-five minutes. She dragged her sore, tired body from the car.

She was confused. She hadn't felt bad physically at work and now she was in pain. She hoped she hadn't caught a cold or something worse. She walked slowly down the path and went inside the apartment. She changed into her pajamas immediately, grabbed a blanket and laid on the couch with her phone. She texted her mom, Liz, and Chris to let them know she was home resting. She turned on the TV and music started blasting from the soundbar. She tried to turn it down using the remote, but it wouldn't work. She turned the TV off and turned it back on and again the music started blasting. "Oh no!" She jumped from the couch and ran over to the sound bar and disconnected it. She hit the remote again and watched the volume bar on the TV turn up to the maximum setting on its own. She turned the TV off again and checked the remote to see if the volume button was stuck. It was fine. She checked the buttons on the TV itself and they seemed fine. She turned the TV on again and again; the volume bar spiked from 0 to 50 as she watched. She quickly turned it off again. She did the only other thing she could think of. She squeezed behind the TV and unplugged it. She waited a minute and plugged it back in. She held her breath and turned the TV back on. All was back to normal.

Dena went back to the couch and pondered over what had just happened. Then she thought about the gopher holes, and she went out to look at them. They were still there. No signs of life in sight so she went back to the couch. She thought about the cabinet door trying to open on its own. Then she thought about the conversation she had with Kelly about him coming to the door on Halloween eve and not being sure he did it. "Oh Dena, you are going to drive yourself nuts. You are reading too much into this." She leaned back onto the couch and found something to watch. She texted with Chris, who was watching Monday night football and eventually she fell asleep, without wanting or eating dinner.

She woke up at 8pm and grabbed some of the leftovers from the meal Chris had brought over the night before, along with a soda out of the fridge. She made a plate and carried it back to the couch where she noticed the TV again was on some weird music station.

The remote was on the coffee table as usual. She put her food and drink down and changed the channel again. She asked herself, "Do you still think it's a remote on the same frequency as yours? No one is living upstairs or in the place next to you, so how is this happening?" But it didn't explain why it happened in the bedroom too. She stopped herself from going down the crazy path again and ate her dinner. She checked her phone while she ate and saw that she had missed messages from Liz and Chris. She responded to them and told them she was going to bed. Her mom had told her to turn in hours ago. She stayed up another 30 minutes after she ate and then put herself to bed.

She dreamed of falling in a dark slimy place. She saw orange eyes watching her fall and cartoon music notes floated around her, ushering her to what surely must have been her falling death. She heard a distant but shrill ringing background. The ringing became louder, bringing it to the forefront and waking her from her dream. Her home phone had just stopped ringing.

She checked the caller I.D. and saw that it was Chris calling at five in the morning. She called him back, worried that something had happened, "Hey Babe! So sorry to wake you. My car battery died. Can you come over and give me a jump?"

"Yes, give me ten minutes to get ready, and I should be there in 20 or so." She hung up the phone and jumped in the shower. She was out the door in eight minutes. She drove over to Chris', relieved that he was okay and thankful that he had pulled her out of that horrible dream. She made it to his apartment in record time. He got the car started. She marveled at him working on his car. It reminded her of her dad except Chris was wearing dress pants and a button-down shirt.

"Thanks Babe! I better get going. I'm already late. Text me and let me know you got to home or work okay." Chris kissed her on the lips. "It's great to see you again. Can't wait to see you this weekend."

"Ok, text you later. Have a good day at work." She smiled and pulled off, with Chris behind her. She decided to go straight to work since she would only be about thirty minutes early and then hopefully, she would be able to leave early.

Wishful thinking. She left work twenty minutes later than normal and again dragged herself home, dead tired. She didn't sit in the car this day. She nearly ran to the door and threw herself in. Again, the heaviness and weariness compounded as soon as she closed the door behind her. She kicked off her shoes and sat on the couch a moment to clear her head.

Then she got up to get the house phone so she could call her mom. Her plan was to call her mom while she made dinner. She kept the phone on the charger in the office nook next to the kitchen while she went to work. To her dismay, the phone was not on the charger. She checked the bedroom to see if she had left it in there. She checked the sheets, the nightstands, the dresser, under the bed...with no luck. She was tired and then she remembered that the charger had a button thingy that would tell you where the phone was if it was lost. She went back to the charger and pushed it. There was no sound. She waited and pushed it again then she walked around the apartment to see if maybe she could hear it. Still nothing. She sighed and went to grab her cell phone from her purse. That's when she remembered that she had left it in the car.

She sighed heavily, grabbed her jacket, and went out to the car. She saw the phone sitting in the cupholder where she left it and she saw a familiar shape under the passenger seat when she opened the door. She grabbed her cell phone first and then leaned down to get a better look at what was on the floor. She grabbed it and it knew that it was the home phone the moment she wrapped her hand around it.

"Am I losing my mind? How did this get out here?" She knew she was wide awake when she left that morning. She was positive that she had put the phone in the charger. Maybe she hadn't. She didn't know anymore. She was exhausted, her head hurt, her body ached mysteriously, and she was hungry. She grabbed the phones, locked the car, and went back into the apartment.

She called her mom and kept the conversation short, saying that her phone battery was almost dead. Which was true. She hung up the phone and put it firmly in the cradle.

She knew her mom was worried and made a mental note to text her later with something cheerful. Her head was hurting bad now and the room was starting to spin. She went to the bedroom and got in the bed. Just her and her cell phone. She texted Chris and her sister and went to sleep almost immediately.

It was dark outside when she woke up. Her head felt better but her body still ached, and she was still hungry. She got up and checked her phone. No new messages. She went to the kitchen and made herself a bowl of cereal and took it back to the bedroom. She sat in the dark and ate, still so tired. She grabbed some pain meds out of the nightstand drawer and drank a couple down with milk. She hoped that would stop whatever was coming over her. She decided to text everyone goodnight and go back to sleep. That's when she noticed she hadn't hit the send button on any of the earlier texts.

She threw her head back in frustration. She sent off the messages and told everyone goodnight. Then she laid down and went to sleep.

She didn't remember dreaming. But she did dream that night. She woke the next morning, got ready and went to work. She still felt terrible, but she soldiered on. At least she would be able to rest during the weekend.

It was late Thursday afternoon when she remembered that she had a date with Chris and brunch on Sunday with the girls. She hoped she would feel better by then. Her week went on with her still feeling achy and weak. By Saturday morning, she had given up hope of being able to go out at all which really disappointed her; she just couldn't find the energy to get up. She called Chris and told him she wouldn't be able to make it for the movie.

"Babe, you sound terrible. Why don't I bring you something to eat? Let me make sure you're okay," Chris responded.

"That would be so nice. I don't want to get you sick, too."

"Don't worry about that. I will be fine," Chris assured Dena. "See you in a couple of hours. I won't stay long so you can get your rest."

Dena agreed and was very happy to see Chris. He brought her favorite soup, salad, and eggplant parmesan, which she loved, and he hated. She laughed, "I know ordering this meal hurt your soul really badly."

"Yuck. I don't know how you eat that. I knew you liked it, so I got it for you." He kissed her on the cheek and led her back over to the couch and wrapped her up in a blanket. He served her the soup so she could at least get some of that down and they sat and talked for about an hour before he left. "Feel better, okay? I will call to check on you later." He kissed her on the cheek again and left.

Dena pulled herself off the couch and locked the door behind him. It was just 4pm but she was beat. She took some cold and flu medicine and went to sleep. She didn't dream. Or at least it didn't seem like she was dreaming. She seemed to be sleeping on the couch with her eyes open. She tried to move but she couldn't - her arms and legs would not obey the commands from her head. "I must be tired. I probably just need to go back to sleep instead of trying to fight it." So she relaxed, and the room faded away to darkness.

Dena was not really sleeping at all. She was in a type of trance. Her body sat up on the couch and reached for the remote to change it to a music station. He had done this before, trying out different stations to figure out which one suited Dena best. He was having a hard time figuring it out. Once the channel had changed, Dena's body got up and began to dance and not in the way that Dena would dance at all. Lethar found it hard to control Dena's movements today. It had a hard time taking her over all together hence Dena being able to see around her but not move. Call it a glitch if you will, a glitch called happiness, positive energy, or self-determination. But these made the best prospects even if they were difficult to take control of. Once Lethar was in, he was in.

Lethar didn't have the same problem with Bonnie. Bonnie already had malice and ill-will deeply rooted inside her. In fact, when he took over her body, she became much nicer. Dena was much more difficult, and he was getting tired very quickly in his attempts to hold her today, which was always the way with kind souls. He placed her back on the couch. He couldn't afford for her to shut him out completely. She had already started praying and that offered some protection to her while at home.

Dena's body went limp and fell back against the couch. She laid down and the blanket was placed over her. Her body slept as it would take her a couple of hours to recover. She woke up at 7:30pm and immediately reached for her phone. Missed messages from Liz and Chris.

She felt weak, but much better than she had over the past week. She called her sister first.

"Hey Liz! I'm feeling better! I think I can make it tomorrow."

"Good, I was getting worried about you. I've been trying to call you, but the call won't go thru for some reason. The line goes dead."

"Oh wow! How long has that been happening? I will have to call the company and see what's going on?"

"It started this past week. I kept forgetting to tell you. I guess it's okay. I mean you can get text messages and call out."

"Yeah, I wonder if Chris has been having the same problem? How strange? Oh well, so much for 'these smart phones'.

Liz and Dena talked and giggled for another twenty minutes before hanging up.

Dena looked at the clock. She had a thought as she called Chris. "Hey! I'm up! Feeling much better. You still want to see the movie?"

"I'm glad you're better. But don't you think you should take it easy?"

"I'm fine. We can catch the 9:20 show near your house. It won't be 4-D, but it will be pretty amazing!"

"Okay, but just the movie and I will come over there! A show starts in True Vision at the same time," Chris countered.

"Okay, see you soon." Dena rushed off the couch and got ready.

The rest of her weekend was wonderful. She met with the girls and had a great time. Yet on Sunday night, the heaviness returned and took over. She tried to push it away; she had felt so good lately, but she couldn't shake the darkness away. She thought it had to do with Monday looming so close and having to face work, still she didn't want to believe that either. Nevertheless, when Monday morning came, all the old aches, pain and sadness came with it. And so went the rest of her week.

CHAPTER 30
Kelly's Thanksgiving

Kelly's week after Thanksgiving celebration went very well. Beth got back early Tuesday morning. She came over and started decorating for the big dinner with Kelly's help. They worked together and reaffirmed their bond. The ugliness that had happened just a week earlier was not spoken of. They spent the night nuzzled together watching Christmas movies in front of the fireplace.

Maddy showed up late Wednesday afternoon, weak from fatigue. She hugged her dad. Kelly and Beth had a meal and a warm bed waiting for her. She had been working 16-hour days for the past week or so. She was exhausted. He appearance worried Kelly a bit; she looked like her mom on a bad day before she lost her battle with cancer. They fed her and put her to bed.

Kelly and Beth stayed up playing cards and listening to gospel music. It was around 8pm when there was a knock at the door. Kelly got up to answer it and chuckled after he investigated the peephole. He opened the door and there stood his son Joey! "What are you doing here? Boy, you are a sight for sore eyes! Let me look at you." Kelly took in his son, smiling proudly at him in uniform. He shrugged and gave him a bear hug.

"Dad! It's good to see you too." Joey came in and put his bag down in the other spare bedroom after greeting Beth.

"Where's Mad?"

"She's sleeping. She got in a few hours ago and pretty much went right to bed," said Kelly. "Well, fill us in. How are you? What's new?"

And so, Joey filled in Beth and his dad for hours.

Thursday morning was here; it was time to get their Thanksgiving do over in gear. They spent the day as families do during a regular Thanksgiving – talking, cooking, eating, laughing, watching some football and Christmas programs. It was wonderful and so was the rest of their weekend, for the most part. The only thing that convinced them that this was not a real Thanksgiving was the calendar. And who looked at calendars anymore?

Saturday morning, Kelly and Joey saw something strange. They were headed to the old house to see if the new owners had changed anything. They stepped outside and saw Bonnie staring down into Dena's apartment very intently. Kelly was worried and walked down the path to Dena's house to make sure that everything was okay. He instinctively tried the door - it was locked. He didn't smell smoke or see anything out of the ordinary.

He looked back up at the strange lady on the hill. "Hey! Is everything alright? Do you see something?" She was dressed in sweats that hung off her body. Her hair was a bright orange color. Kelly couldn't tell if it was bad dye job or if she did it on purpose.

Bonnie jumped at the unfamiliar person speaking to her. She suddenly realized what she was doing and said, "Everything is fine. Sorry, I just zoned out for a moment." She looked down into Dena's apartment and could just make out her figure lying back down on the couch in odd, almost robotic movements. She shivered; she realized what had been happening to her. "It's controlling both of us," she thought. She hid her terror from the neighbors. "Cold out here. Have a great day!" Bonnie almost knocked over the table while trying to turn around and run back inside. She closed the balcony door behind her and sat on the couch. Malcolm was out again. He was spending less and less time at home which worried her. Had he found someone else? Or did he not want to be around her anymore? The latter seemed to fit better and that made her sad. Sad and not mad. She was confused by this. Then she had a fit of panic and ran to the bedroom to check the bench in front of the bed. She opened the bench slowly and carefully, placing her hand gingerly inside reaching downward until she felt the top of one of the boxes she had hidden away. The panic subsided and she re-positioned the blankets to ensure it stayed hidden. "The best place to hide something is in plain sight." She was starting to feel like her old self.

She had a thought, "Maybe I should try to talk to the lady that I've been staring at. Maybe we can figure this out together." Bonnie scoffed at herself. She hadn't realized that she was scoffing at a part of her that had just recently awoken during this dark time in her life. "It's got her now and I am free. She will have to fend for herself." In that instant, Bonnie went back into her trance while sitting on the bed. Falling into the wet sticky darkness that clung to her in her waking nightmares.

Kelly and Joey watched as the lady on the balcony turned and walked inside. Kelly was uneasy, so he went back and checked Dena's apartment one last time. He glanced inside and saw her sleeping on the couch. She seemed peaceful, so he turned away and vowed that he would check on her in a day or so.

"Dad? Everything okay? What was that lady trying to see into that apartment?'

"Yeah, just checking on my neighbor. She's nice. Wanted to make sure nothing odd was going on." Kelly and Joey walked up the path to Kelly's truck. Kelly still felt uneasy, something about the woman's behavior seemed eerily familiar. He had shaken off the feeling by the time they had made it to the truck. He felt happy again, his kids and his lady were home. He wanted to enjoy this time before they all had to leave again.

Malcolm was spending his time at the office this Saturday. He made every excuse not to be at home since the boxes had been discovered. He needed time alone to think and plan. He had made a lot of headway. He could get his old job back in California at the first of the year. He had a week to give them an answer. The house was in fine shape. He would have his nephew stay as long as he needed. There was plenty of room for Malcolm, the kids, and his nephew. He reached for his wallet and pulled out the crumpled-up letter from his wife. There was no denying it, his heart was with Donita. She said she wanted to be friends. He had emailed her after he put the box back in the bench. He didn't want Bonnie to know her secret, well her lie, had been discovered. Donita responded just hours later and here he sat looking at the phone, afraid to call her as planned. He closed his eyes and tried to relax. He had no clue of what to say. He opened his eyes, picked up the phone and called her. He was still not ready to trust Don yet and who knows? She might not want anything more than friendship. He looked at the letter again and knew that wasn't true. He felt sure that she was still in love with him. He knew what to say as soon as he heard her voice. They talked for hours, and he felt even more sure about the changes he was about to make. He called the kids and checked in with them. He and Donita had agreed to wait to tell the kids that they were speaking again.

Malcolm put the letter back in his wallet carefully, then he went home. He found the closer he got to the apartment the slower he drove. He stopped and went to the electronics store, then to the grocery store, and then to get gas, even though the tank was nearly full. Finally, he went home. It was already dark outside.

He put the groceries on the counter and went to tell Bonnie that he was home. He found her in the bedroom, sitting in the dark, listening to heavy metal of all things. "Hey, I'm going to make dinner."

"Do whatever you want. I'm not hungry." Then she reached for the remote and turned the music up louder. Her voice was vacant and cold.

"Bon, I'm worried about you. You don't eat much lately; you seem tired most of the time. I thought you were going to the doctor." Malcolm walked into the room and turned on the lamp.

"There is nothing wrong with me!" hissed Bonnie. "Now get out and make your precious dinner, Mac!

Malcom winced at the final insult of being called "Mac", left the room, and closed the door behind him. That was the first night he slept in the guest bedroom. There was no chance he would ever share a bed with Bonnie again. The attraction was completely gone. He didn't know if it was the constant manipulation or the fact that she was now just a horrible person to be around. He knew something was off, she wasn't dressing like herself. She had died her hair while he was taking the kids to the airport, and it had come out a bright orange color with weird dark streaking in some places. He knew she was embarrassed because she didn't leave the house without a cap or a scarf on. He went to the kitchen and made dinner. He made enough for Bonnie. He knew she loved crab cakes. He was still trying to figure out the best way out of this. Every idea he came up with seemed to be mean and hurtful to Bonnie. He wanted to be civil even though she had played him every step of the way.

He sat down at the dining room table and thought while he ate. Then he began to plan in a definitive manner. He decided on dates and packing. He was going to accept his old position and put his notice in at his present company on Monday. It was more than clear that he needed to stop worrying about Bonnie's feelings as she never considered his at any point that they had been together. His planning continued.

Bonnie came out of her trance briefly. She bolted from the bed and ran to the bathroom. She looked at herself in the mirror and laughed, hysterically. Then she cried again. The music was still on in the bedroom; she knew that Malcolm couldn't hear her. She reached in a drawer and grabbed the black permanent hair dye. She couldn't afford to keep wearing scarves and working from home.

She knew this process would take hours, still it had to be done. She was conforming to Lethar, and she didn't even realize it. The black cat waited in the bedroom, sitting in between the closet and the bed. It knew that she was alone and soon Lethar would know.

CHAPTER 31

Dena

Dena's week was awful. It was crunch time at work and she had to get everything done by Christmas because everyone would start their vacation time then. She envied her coworkers who were able to take off two or three weeks at the end of the year. Her seniority had not built up enough to allow her to do that yet.

Chris was busy too and hadn't been able to text or call nearly as much. She felt like he was distancing himself from her and she prepared herself for the "before Christmas break- up." She felt sure that Chris was not that kind of guy and yet she wasn't positive. He said he was busy with work too. Which was probably true; they worked in the same field as luck would have it. "I am making something out of nothing. He is working on closing out the year like I am." She decided to take a break and start on Christmas shopping. She was done with her online purchasing after fifteen minutes. She went on with her day, buried under work and dragging herself home late again.

Her routine was the same, put on her pajamas, hunt for something to eat, lay on the couch for a couple of hours then go to bed. She wasn't staying in touch with her sister and her mom as much; she was just too tired.

Thursday evening came and just as Dena was about to put on her pajamas, she heard a knock at the door. It was Kelly! "Hey! How are you doing?" Dena invited him in.

"Hey Ms. Dena! I just wanted to check on you. I saw you walking by, and you looked dog tired. How are you doing?"

Dena sighed heavily, "I am beat. Work is super busy with Christmas coming up but I'm okay."

"Well," Kelly thought hard on what he was going to say next. He looked around her apartment and saw that it was brightly colored and furnished. It was a calm and happy place. "I just wanted to check on you. I hope you're taking my advice about not staying by yourself in this place. It seems like pain and sadness will settle in on a body if you sit too still here."

"Kelly, I never thought about it like that. I do feel better when I'm at work," Dena pondered. She laughed, "And I have not been fond of work lately."

Kelly laughed. "Well, I just wanted to check on you like I said. I'm flying out tomorrow. Call me if you need me. And, uh, have you noticed..." Kelly trailed off. He couldn't believe what he was about to say. He saw Dena looking at him intently, waiting to hear what he had to say. "Well, have you noticed your neighbor up on the hill staring down at you?'

"Oh my gosh! Yes! I thought I was imagining things or that maybe she was daydreaming? But you saw her too?" Dena took in the information. "I don't want to keep my blinds closed because it gets so dark and gloomy in here. I will pay more attention and really give her something to see." Dena saw that Kelly was very serious.

"What do you think it means, Kelly?"

"You don't know her, right?" Dena shook her head. "Well, she looked like a cat about to pounce. That's the best way I can describe it. I don't know what she could have seen from up there, but she zeroed in on your place like she could see through the walls."

"Okay, Kelly. Do you think she's a stalker or do you think she's unbalanced? Should I report it to the office?"

Just then, the cabinet door that had been bound with duct tape swung open and shut with such a force that both Kelly and Dena jumped.

Dena looked at Kelly with fear in her eyes. They walked slowly over to the cabinet. Dena turned on the light so they could see and of course there was nothing to see. Dena reached down and checked the hinges. The door and hinges were intact. The tape that was keeping it held shut was ripped in tatters. Kelly moved in front of Dena and looked at the cabinet. He opened it slowly and saw that it was pretty much empty. There was no sign of an animal lurking inside. Kelly closed the door again, "You got any more of that tape?"

Dena already had the tape in her hand. Kelly triple taped the cabinet on all sides. When he was done, he said, "Check it every so often and if it starts to loosen, put more tape on it. We could use glue, but

I don't want you to lose your security deposit." Kelly pulled on the door, and it wouldn't budge at all. "You can always call me or come over if.... if anything really scary happens."

Dena nodded, her brown eyes big and wide. She started to walk Kelly out and she grabbed her house phone to call her sister. "I never asked you. How's your back? You seem to be completely healed."

"Funny thing. My back is fine. Doctor said that he wants me to come back for a few more visits. He can't see any bruising from the surgery, and I feel ten years younger." Kelly studied Dena. "Tell you the truth, I think this place was the cause of my back problems. Weird stuff would happen when I was alone. I would lose track of time and my back hurt something awful."

"How did you stop it?"

Kelly pointed to Dena's bible. "That helped a lot. That and staying close to Beth and the kids worked wonders. Now, Dena, remember what I said. Don't stay in this apartment by yourself too much. I'm flying back Monday night and you have my number. I'd give you the key to my place, but I don't think sleeping next door would help." He placed his hand on her shoulder and said, "I mean it! Call me if something really spooks you or you feel like you're in danger!"

"Okay, Pa!" Dena knew he was worried. But she barely knew him, and it felt comforting and strange at the same time.

Kelly winked at her, "Pa? My own kids don't call me Pa! I guess I better hobble myself back to my place. Take care of yourself."

Dena was watching him walk back to his place when the phone which was still in her hand rang. "Dena! I've been calling you for at least an hour! Are you okay?"

"Hey Liz! I'm fine. Is everything okay?"

"Yeah, I just wanted to tell you about the birthday party this weekend. I got worried when I couldn't get you on your cell or the house phone. Didn't mean to scare you."

"Liz, my phone hasn't rung all evening. In fact, I'm standing outside. I guess this is the only place I can get a signal. I'm going to have to call the cable company and have them come out. I'm paying for wi-fi and phone service and neither seems to be working."

"Good idea. I have to get back to work. I will text you the details on the party. Love you!" Then Liz was gone.

Dena didn't know why but Liz telling her that she loved her made her feel so much better. She took a breath and went back inside her apartment. She closed the door and walked over to the bible. She began to read the passages she had marked previously, and the air seemed to clear. She prayed for protection, strength, and guidance. Then she called the ultimate prayer warrior, her mom.

"Hi Mom! I just wanted to hear your voice. How are you?"

Dena's mom knew something was not right. "I'm good.

How are you?"

"I'm just a little tired. Work is wearing me out." Dena did not want her mom to worry.

Her mom was worried. She knew Dena was hiding something. She also knew that it would come out sooner or later. "Your Uncle Lee just left. I'm sure he would have loved to talk to you! Maybe call him later on or tomorrow. I'm working on planning my garden for next spring. Anything you want me to try and grow?"

"Hmm, I really like the tomatoes you had last year." Dena made a note to get her mom some gardening gear for Christmas. The women talked for about 45 minutes. It was almost eight o'clock when they said goodbye. "Love you, Mama."

"I love you too. I miss you and your sister so much! Maybe you can come home for Christmas?" Dena's mom felt sure she could fish out what was going on if she could get her to come home.

"I doubt it. We will be in Dickson for Christmas, but we will call before we go out there. Talk to you later."

"Okay, talk to you later, too." Dena's mom started praying as soon as the call ended.

Dena picked up her cell and texted Chris and her sister. She suddenly realized she hadn't eaten all day. She moved toward the kitchen and then stopped out of fear. Then Dena got mad, "This is my house. I pay the rent here. I'm going to the kitchen that I pay rent for and making my favorite meal!" Whatever darkness was lingering left the building temporarily. Dena made pancakes and turkey sausage for dinner, and it was marvelous. Then she put on her favorite pajamas and went to bed. She texted with Chris for an hour before saying goodnight. She texted her sister and mom and let them know she was in bed. And for the first time for a while, she made it to dream land. She got in the boat, and it seemed bigger and more luxurious this time. She leaned back and could hear the water softly hitting the boat. She felt at ease, and she slept better than she had in weeks. Unfortunately, by Friday night the gloom had returned, and Dena was back in a dark place again.

She was exhausted when she got home. She texted Chris and Liz to let them know she was home and that she was going to take a nap. And she did; she napped into mid-Saturday morning. She woke up on the couch, her body ached, and she felt dizzy. The sun was beaming through the closed blinds. Dena grabbed her phone and called her sister.

"Liz, I'm sorry! I don't know what happened. I fell asleep, I just woke up! Liz?"

"Dena, I was worried sick! I was just about to leave and check on you! The brunch has already started. Don't worry. I told the girls you had been really tired lately. Do you want to try and make it?"

Dena was standing in the mirror in tears. "No, Liz. I look awful. I've got dark spots under my eyes, and I look all puffy. I don't know what's happening to me."

"Don't worry. You are probably still tired. Take it easy and I will call you later." Liz could hear that something was wrong in Dena's voice. "Do you want me to come over? You don't sound like yourself."

Suddenly, Dena was angry with Liz, and she didn't know why. "NO! I'm not a child! I can take care of myself! I don't need you feeling sorry for me!" She hung up the phone and was instantly sorry. Why had she said those things to Liz? Dena sat on the bathroom floor and cried. She thought Liz would call her back then she remembered that she couldn't get incoming calls.

She called Chris, "Hey! I -"

"Hey Babe. Where you been? I had to go into work this morning. I'm going to be here all day. Big emergency with a project. You okay? You sound - I don't know."

"I'm okay. I just slept too long. I wanted to ask you. Have you had any problems calling me on my home number?"

"Yeah, I have. I meant to tell you that a while ago, but I kept forgetting. The phone will ring and then it will go dead."

"Okay, I will let you get back to work. I will call the company now and see when someone can come out."

"Good. I texted you about a hundred times. I was beginning to feel like you had ghosted me. Babe, I have to go. Call you - I mean text you, later."

"Okay." Dena sighed and grabbed her cell phone. She had 5 missed calls and 13 text messages. She started to answer Liz's texts, but she didn't know what to say so she didn't say anything. She called the cable company, and they could have someone out the Friday after next, in the afternoon. That was almost two weeks away. Dena was hoping for an earlier appointment, but on the bright side she would leave work early and start the long Christmas holiday weekend early.

She decided to take Kelly's advice. She got up, took a shower, and went to the gym to work out. Then she took herself to a movie and went to one of the nearby sushi places to pick up lunch and dinner. She was pulling into her parking space when the loneliness struck her again. She tried to shake it off but couldn't. She walked up the path and took a deep breath before opening the door. Once she was inside, she was gone.

Lethar didn't have Dena yet. But he was getting closer. He fed on her when he could - he kept getting interrupted with praying, bible reading and loved ones checking on her. He couldn't feed on her the way he wanted until she was completely alone and submerged in sadness and despair. He used Kat as much as he could to monitor Dena and Bonnie, while he rested in their lair. He had to get this one right. If he didn't, he would be stuck, tethered to this place forever. This human would more than please his master, Byleth.

Lethar worshipped Byleth and even took part of his name once he transformed from a human to the disciple of the demon Byleth, Demon King of Hell in which music plays before him. He remembered the night he summoned Byleth and the sweet horrors that came with it. He was weak and scared. And now, he was a protégé of one of the most powerful and disturbing demons of hell. Dena would be one of his most prized conquests. Better than Billy, better than Bonnie, better than any other soul he had captured. She was surrounded by love, and she didn't even know how strong and powerful a weapon it was. He didn't think she would figure it out. He let his protégé get Dena ready for what was to come. Kat had made great progress and he felt sure he would have Dena ready in a week or so. Until then he would feed on Bonnie. She was easy to access, and her spirit was already dark. Although lately, the goodness in Bonnie had tried to come forward but Bonnie was so stupid and selfish, she barely listened to it.

Lethar and Kat didn't have to rid Bonnie of her friends and family. She didn't have any friends here and it seemed like her family would soon abandon her. The man who lived with her seemed to care for her, but Lethar could sense a distance growing between them. Not much of a challenge - all he had to do was step back and wait. He came and went as he pleased into Bonnie's mind and soul, using Bonnie's closet as his base of operations.

Dena woke up on the couch. The sushi was untouched. Her cell phone was dead, and the house phone was nowhere to be found. Again, her body ached all over. She told herself that she overdid it working out earlier. The TV was on another weird rock station again.

She went to the bedroom and plugged in her phone. It was eight o'clock at night. Dena whimpered and then she cried again. "What is happening to me? I don't understand this. Maybe I need to see a doctor; I must have a virus or something." She stopped crying and pulled herself together. She salvaged what she could of her dinner and took a shower.

She had missed texts from everyone. She responded and said that she was tired and was going to bed. She would call everyone once she woke up.

She didn't wake up until noon on Sunday. She needed to find the house phone and she needed to call everyone.

She grabbed her cell phone from the charger and went outside in her pajamas and sneakers.

She started with her mom and that went well; then she called Chris.

"Hey Babe, surprise, surprise. How are you, sleepy head?"

"I feel like I've been hit by a truck. I'm going to call the doctor tomorrow."

"There is some bug going around. Maybe that's it. I'm at work again. I wanted to stop by, but it sounds like you need your rest."

Dena was disappointed. She really wanted to see Chris. "Well, you haven't had much of a weekend. You probably need to rest yourself." Did he really work all weekend? Seemed unbelievable. "Man, you missed all the games?"

"Ha - you know I recorded them all. I will catch up on them this week." Chris laughed. "Babe, I have to go but I should be leaving in the next hour or so. I will call you once I get home and settled in. Love you!"

"Okay, talk to you later." She hung up the phone and realized that he had said he loved her. That can't be right. We've only been dating a couple of months. "What is wrong with me? The man said he loved me and I'm questioning it. I'm losing my marbles."

She wanted to call Liz and tell her, but she still felt awkward considering their last conversation. So, she texted her instead. She was about to hit send when she felt like she was being watched. She looked up and there was her neighbor on the hill watching her. She looked completely different. Her hair was jet black and overly shiny. Like it was slicked back with black oil. She looked awful; her robe was hanging on her frame and her face looked sunken in like a skull. Dena felt like she was staring at her, and she didn't mean to. She felt bad for her, "Hey neighbor! How are you?"

Bonnie seemed shocked that Dena could see her much less speak to her. "H-h-hey! I'm good. How are you?"

"I'm well. I'm going back inside. It's a bit cold out here. See you later." Dena waved goodbye and walked back into the apartment. She turned her attention to finding the home phone. It wasn't in any of the obvious places, and she knew she had it yesterday when she got home. It wasn't in her bed. She didn't have the patience to search for it, so she went to the cradle and hit the phone locator button. She jumped as the phone started beeping loudly from behind her. She turned around quickly to find the source.

She took a step forward looking carefully and she realized that the phone was inside the cabinet that had been taped up. She froze in terror. She would have to pull off the tape to open the cabinet. There was no other way to get inside. Dena's knees felt weak, and she was breathing fast and hard. She used the wall to steady herself and stepped carefully towards the cabinet. She knew she would need a knife or scissors to get all the tape off. She would tape it back immediately after she got the phone out.

She stopped herself. This was going to require more planning. She grabbed a knife, scissors, electrical tape, and a flashlight. She went back to the cabinet and cut the tape with the knife. She didn't need the scissors. The phone was still beeping and was louder now that the tape had been removed. She slowly opened the door with her left hand while she held the knife in the other. She saw the phone flashing and grabbed it quickly, closing the door even faster. She had strips of tape at the ready and she used them to fasten the cabinet door tightly. She backed away from the cabinet and went to grab the bible from the office nook. Now was the perfect time for reading verses and prayer.

The bible was gone! She knew she had put it back on the shelf and she made a habit of looking at it every time she came home. Dena fought back tears and terror. She tried to find the strength to pray but her mind was working so fast to try to make rational sense of what was happening that she couldn't focus. Her hands were shaking, and she was starting to see spots. She grabbed the counter to steady herself and push her way out of the kitchen. She felt like she was walking through syrup. Her heart was beating strong and fast, and she could feel herself hyperventilating. She tried to calm down but couldn't. She still had the phone in her hand but the room was spinning by now and she couldn't make her body obey her so she could use it. Then she was gone.

She woke up a few hours later, barely remembering what happened before she passed out. Her front door was open, and she felt like she wasn't alone. She moved slowly, looking around the apartment to see if someone had come in while she was sleeping. She tried to remember if she had forgotten to lock the door.

She knew she had locked it. Something was in the apartment with her. She concentrated all her energy. She was going to run and go to Kelly's. She got up to run and was inches away from the door when it slammed shut! She put her hands up so she wouldn't hit it headfirst. But she did hit it and the force of her hitting the door knocked her out.

Lethar appeared out of the shadows. He looked down at Dena on the floor. His claws reached for her, but he couldn't have her yet. She wasn't ready but she was close. Kat had done his job well; Lethar didn't expect this kind of progress so soon. She should be ready in week. He picked her up and laid her on the couch but not before dancing with her. Yes, she was much weaker than before. He could smell the fear on her skin, and it was intoxicating. He fought with all his might not to take a sample, for that would ruin her all together. After he laid her on the couch, he watched her for a while then he and Kat left. But, not without Kat leaving something behind.

Dena woke up at 4am. She was still on the couch, weird music was playing. She turned off the TV and got in her bed. She knew that everyone was probably worried about her. She would deal with that once she woke up. She remembered that she couldn't find the bible and went to look on the shelf. Somehow, it was back in place. She convinced herself that she had imagined the whole thing.

She felt terrible and she couldn't sleep. She got up and ran a bath for herself. Then she went and grabbed the bible and read it while the tub filled up. The words were blurry, and she kept having to read the same passages over and over. It didn't make sense, so she put the bible down and climbed into the tub. She soaked for a while and then she washed herself. She thought and thought and thought. Then she tried to stop thinking. She tried to meditate and calm herself. She was almost to a place that resembled peace when she smelled something foul. She opened her eyes and looked around. "My God, now what?" She got out of the tub and dried herself off and wrapped the towel around herself. "Nope, not gonna catch me in just a towel today." She went to the bedroom and grabbed her robe, then she went to the kitchen to see where the smell was coming from.

Her first instinct was that it was coming from the cabinet. Thankfully, that was not the case. She stared at the laundry room door and knew it was coming from there. She opened the door and turned on the light and the smell hit her so hard that her eyes burned. She was about to step in and check the washing machine when she saw long, thick, black, oily strands of hair on the floor. She knew instantly that the hair was the source of the smell. It was familiar, like, like her neighbor's hair! Then she realized that she hadn't been imagining anything and that something was trying to take over the apartment and maybe even her. She thought about this as she reached for the rubber gloves and a bucket under the sink. She went to work cleaning up the hair and washing the floor. She could sense that she was being watched the whole time.

"I need to get out of here. This thing won't let me leave. I have to play along so that it will let me leave for work in a couple of hours, then I can escape." She dumped the soiled water into the sink and cleaned out the sink thoroughly. Then she threw the gloves away, closed the trash bag and put it near the front door.

She went to the bedroom and laid down. She pretended to sleep; she could still feel that something was there with her. She hoped she could fool it long enough so that it would leave. It worked. She could feel that something had left the apartment. She couldn't fight holding off sleep anymore and gave in. And she dreamed, not quite her normal dreams but close enough to know that she was free for now.

She heard the alarm go off and she hit the snooze button, remembering to stay in character. She didn't feel like anything was in the apartment with her, but she couldn't be sure. She hit the snooze button one last time for good measure then she got up and got ready for her day.

She was dressed and at the front door, ready to leave. She grabbed the trash bag and tried to brace herself without being seen by anything. She reached for the door and opened it. She was outside! She walked to her car at her normal pace. She knew that whatever was trying to take hold of her had been in her car. She felt like that was as far as it could go. She dropped off the garbage and went to work. She would call her sister as soon as she got to her desk.

She got off the elevator and made it to her desk. She logged onto her computer and that was the last thing she could remember. Lethar had her! She was his puppet. He couldn't take her soul yet, but he could control her with ease now. He allowed her to do her work, she talked to people like she normally would, but Dena had checked out.

She didn't check back in until late that evening. She found herself in her bed with her clothes on. She checked her cell and saw that she had sent messages to her friends and family that she hadn't remembered sending. She tried to text someone, but she couldn't. She tried to get up but couldn't. She tried to pray but her thoughts were so jumbled that she couldn't do that either. She didn't know what day it was, she felt like she had been in bed for some time. She kept trying to fight so she could get up, but nothing worked. She grew tired and slept.

When she woke up, both of her phones were missing. She ran to the door, but it wouldn't open. The windows were a dead end. She went to her laptop to send an email and her hard wire connection was out. She turned on the TV to see what day it was and was shocked to see it was Wednesday morning. She had had enough! She grabbed a cast iron pan and went to break the bedroom window. She held the pan like a bat, braced herself and swung with all her might. The pan stopped in mid swing and pulled itself out of her hands. It floated over to the bed and landed there gently.

Dena was completely alone. Kelly was gone. The unit above her was empty so was the unit where Valarie and Elise had stayed. Dena took off her clothes and put them in the hamper. Then she took a long hot shower thinking about what her next move should be. She put on some sweats and went out to the living room.

She had a pile of gifts that needed to be wrapped for Christmas, so she pulled everything out, grabbed the wrapping paper, scissors and got to work. She thought about each friend and family member as she wrapped their gift. She wondered if she would ever see them again. She fought back tears. The TV came on and hard metal music started playing. She went to grab the remote and it was missing. She turned off the TV using the buttons on the back of it and unplugged it from the wall. She went back to wrapping the presents and was almost done when she started to feel particularly low. She was going to a dark place. She could feel herself slipping away and it scared her more than whatever was trying to haunt her place. Then she was out.

That was how it went for the next two days, except each day her waking moments happened less and less. She didn't eat, her clothes didn't fit anymore, her hair wasn't combed. She would shower but she didn't feel clean. The smell was back, and she didn't have the energy to find the source. The cabinet door that had been taped shut was wide open. What did it matter? Whatever wanted in or out, was in or out. She was done crying but she was still miserable.

The only thing she had to keep her company were her thoughts and most of the time they were not comforting. She tried backtracking to how she got here. How did this thing enter her life? Was it always here? It had to have been. She remembered back to the day she moved in and the smell in the laundry room. She remembered the problems she was having with it being so cold in the apartment. Then she remembered all the rumors surrounding Gospel Billy. What happened to him? Is this what he went through? Is this the reason why he left?

It HAD to be! Dena shuddered. Did he get away? Or did this thing carry him off? Dena tried to remain positive and believed that Billy had escaped. Most of his things were gone according to the neighbors. Maybe she had a chance. Or maybe this thing was smarter now and knew better than to let her have a way out.

Dena sighed and tried to rest her thoughts but couldn't.

She wished she had something to be hopeful about.

She wished that she had gotten a Christmas tree, that probably would have given her some joy. She tried hard not to think about her sister and her parents. She missed them so much. She figured the thing that was keeping her hostage was talking to them and that scared her. She wondered if they would be able to figure out that it wasn't her. What if it was telling them horrible things? Things that would hurt them. The thought of that hurt her soul and she pushed it away quickly. The thought of her parents and her sister hurting broke her heart.

Kelly had flown out already and she couldn't remember when he would be back. She tried to listen to the wall that connected their apartments every so often to see if he was in. She never heard anything. And she wondered even if he was there would he hear her?

It was Friday morning now, the day before Christmas Eve and she was supposed to go to Dickson on Sunday for the family Christmas dinner. She figured she wouldn't make it there. She could feel the darkness coming again but this time she felt mad.

How dare this thing come into her home and interrupt her happy life? It hadn't even had the courage to show itself! It had cut her off from her family, friends, and Chris. Poor Chris, what must he think? She couldn't even begin to explain this to him. And that made her even angrier. She was not going to let this thing have her. What could she do? Then a thought came to her. I can end this on my own. I can make the choice on how I want to go out.

Then she got up and took a shower. She did her hair and put on some make-up. She got dressed. She went to the office nook; the bible was missing again, and the internet connection was still out. She sat down at the nook and grabbed a notepad to start writing her farewells to her family and friends. She hoped they would understand and not think that she was crazy. She tried to explain that this was the only thing that would give her back control. She hoped that God would forgive her. She finished her notes and placed them with the Christmas presents.

Dena walked to the kitchen to get the butcher knife she had once used for protection. She had just wrapped her hand around the handle when there was a knock at the door.

It was the cable company! Dena stood stock still for a moment.

Was this a trick? She dropped the knife and found the strength to run to the door. She unlocked it and opened the door with ease. She didn't think for a moment that it would open.

"Hi! I'm here to work on the wi-fi and the phone line." Dena didn't hear a word he said after that. She watched the stranger come into her house and go over to the computer to start working. The tech was cheerful and talked about the weather and Christmas. "Nice bunch of presents you got there."

"Thanks," said Dena. Her voice was hoarse from not speaking in days. She watched as he worked, and she saw that her phone was in the cradle again. She tried not to run to it, but she couldn't help herself.

She picked it up and was about to call her sister when she heard a voice from the front door.

"Dena! Oh my God! Dena!"

Dena turned and saw Liz, "Liz! Hey! The cable guy is here to fix the phone." Dena took Liz by the hand. "I will be just outside if you need me."

"Sure thing!" The tech went back to work.

Dena wrapped her arms around Liz and held her tight for minutes. She cried and cried. Liz was crying too.

"Dena, what happened? I've been trying to reach you for days! Mama and Chris were worried to death."

"Oh Liz, I don't know where to begin. Something got inside of the apartment and inside of me. Please believe me! I've been stuck in the apartment for days. My phones disappeared and the internet was completely out. I couldn't get out. It wouldn't let me leave. I couldn't even break the windows!" Dena stopped and searched Liz's face to see if she thought she was crazy.

"I know you're not crazy. I believe you!" Liz held her sister's hand. "What do we do?"

"Whatever it is, is gone right now. I don't think it knows I'm out. I think it could keep me in but it's not strong enough to physically keep other people out." Dena paused. "Can I come stay with you until I figure this out?"

"Yes, let's pack some bags and get you out of here!"

The sisters went inside and gathered up the presents and put them in Dena's car. Then Dena packed two bags. As she packed, she noticed that her cell phone and charger were on the nightstand in their normal places. It had all been some sort of trickery. She grabbed them and threw them in one of the bags. The cable tech was just finishing up.

"You're all set now. The router was faulty, so I replaced it.

You have a Merry Christmas."

"Thanks! You do the same." Dena walked the tech out and used her key to lock the door. Her hands were shaking.

"C'mon! Let's get out of here!"

Dena and Liz got in their cars and raced across town to Liz's apartment. She was beyond the reach of Lethar at Liz's place, and she finally felt free. They unpacked Dena's car and went upstairs.

When Dena was able to let her guard down, she began to cry. "Oh Liz, I don't know where to begin. I kept blacking out, then I would wake up, but I couldn't move! I wanted to call you, but I couldn't because I was being silly and full of pride. Then I couldn't call anyone after the phones disappeared! Then this thing kept playing this horrible music." Dena stopped to catch her breath.

"I am going to make you some tea. Wrap yourself in this blanket and then we will figure this out," Liz went to the kitchen and turned the kettle on. She got some cups ready and then came back to Dena.

Dena sat on the couch thinking. She looked so small, wrapped up in the blanket. Liz went over and hugged her again. "Okay, start from the beginning and tell me what happened."

"It was after we got home from Thanksgiving that I started feeling lonesome, but it would only happen in the apartment mostly. Then I started blacking out and I can't remember a whole lot except that the phones disappeared and so did the bible. I was so confused that I couldn't pray or think clearly."

Dena jumped off the couch and ran to the spare bedroom to get her cell phone. She called out to Liz, "What made you realize something was wrong?"

Dena came back with the phone, fumbling with it to get to the home screen. She sat back on the couch.

"Your texts were strange - they didn't sound like you at all after a while. They were short and kind of cold. You know you always pick up the phone when you need details on anything and I don't know... there was none of your personality in the text," Liz answered.

"It was really strange not to hear your voice. I know you were mad at me, but you would still call Mama or Chris. That's what scared me! That nobody had talked to you. None of our friends and family had talked to you even though you continued to text."

Liz looked at Dena, "I was starting to think someone had stolen your phone and you were being held hostage. And you really were BEING HELD HOSTAGE!" Liz shook her head in disbelief.

"How did you and Chris manage to talk to each other?"

"Dena, he was worried too. He came to my job and waited for me to come out one night. He recognized me from the picture in your living room." Liz tilted her head, "You know, oddly enough it wasn't a bit stalkerish. He's a really good guy!"

"He was so concerned about you. He said he felt like he had scared you because he said he loved you. He just wanted to know that you were alright."

"He did tell me he loved me, and I didn't say anything!! I remember now. He did it so fast and...and oh my God! I remember now!"

Dena told Liz about the neighbor staring at her and how Kelly came by to check on her. She told her about Kelly saying that he may have come to her apartment late one night and even mentioned losing track of time. She told her about the advice Kelly had given her and how she wished she had listened. Then she told her about the cabinet. She told Liz about the weird black cat and the awful hair, then she gasped. She finally put it together.

"Liz, when I got home from Thanksgiving there was a clump of greasy, black hair hanging from a tree. I wrapped it up in a napkin and threw it away. Later, I saw a cat with the same greasy hair, and it did not seem friendly. It was on my neighbor's balcony - the one who was watching me - then one day I found a bunch of the same hair in the laundry room. It stunk and I had to use a ton of cleaner to get the smell out.

Liz! It was the same smell that was in the laundry room when I first moved in. I think the cat is the key to this."

Just then the teapot started to whistle. Liz got up to make them tea. She had made chocolate chip cookies the night before and brought them over with the tea.

"But Liz - how did you know to come at the moment that you came? I mean, I was close to taking myself out of the game. I was desperate, confused and so lonely. I thought that this thing had taken my phone and was saying horrible things to everyone I knew and loved. Liz, I wrote notes to say...to say..." Dena looked down at her lap. Then she picked up her cell phone and started scrolling through her messages. She could tell with each person exactly when it was not her texting. What was disturbing was that some of the texts had gone out before she was locked in the apartment.

She got to Chris' messages and decided on several things. "Well, I'm gonna need a new phone. The devil has been texting on my phone...can't use it anymore. I need to call Mom, Dad and Chris. But what do I say?"

"I told Mom and Dad that you were fighting the flu, but I know Mama is going to come down here if she doesn't hear from you soon. I told Chris the same thing and he said you seemed to be fighting something for a while."

Dena pulled up her work emails to see if she had been fired. She saw an email from her boss sent on Monday evening congratulating the team for doing such a great job at meeting their deadline earlier than expected. As a special thank you he had given her the rest of the week off to get a start on her Christmas vacation. Dena looked up at Liz and smiled.

"I will call my boss first," she thought.

And she did. She thanked him for the time off and wished him and his family a Merry Christmas. He thanked her for calling and told her that she had done a wonderful job getting everything in order before the end of the year.

"Well, I still have my job. The devil is good at administrative work. That's good to know."

Liz laughed. "You don't actually think it was the devil, do you? He's been busy. Sorry, sis, but this seems beneath him. Maybe it was a middle management minion or something."

They both laughed at that. They didn't know how close to the truth they were.

Dena had texts from Kelly. His last one said that he would be back Friday afternoon since his trip had been cut short and that he would stop by. She called him next. "Kelly, I am not at home. Let me put you on speaker so my sister can hear you. I'm staying with her."

"Dena, what in the world happened?"

Dena told him what happened and then waited for his response. "I told you not to stay in that place by yourself! That is just awful!

I'm so glad you made it out of there." Kelly had just pulled into the apartment complex. "I am going to go take a look at your place while I have you on the phone."

Liz and Dena could hear Kelly walking down the path. "Well, the neighbor lady on the hill is looking at your place. My gosh! Her hair is jet black now! She looks scared to death!" Kelly walked to Dena's door and tried it. It was locked tight. He made a show of knocking so that the neighbor would think that he was really looking for Dena. "Hey! Have you seen the woman that lives here? I haven't heard from her in a while?"

Bonnie jumped at the sound of his voice, "No." Then she turned and walked back into the house.

"Kelly, do you see a black cat anywhere?"

Kelly looked around, "No, but I see slimy, black hair stuck to the guardrail up on the hill. Why?"

"I know that loud music has been playing at least on one occasion when you weren't at home. Did that happen a lot? Were there times when you were watching TV and the channel changed to a music station?

Kelly, who was starting to walk back to his place, stopped in mid-stride. "Yes, it happened all the time. I never could figure out why."

Was there a weird smell in your place when you first moved in? Like, I don't know, cabbage and something else?"

"Yes. I thought the neighbors before me cooked cabbage to death. This is related to what happened to you. I mean to us?" Kelly realized that this was more than an illness and mood swings.

"I think so. Listen, I've got some explaining to do with some more family and friends. Please take the same advice you gave me. I really wish I had listened. Keep your bible close and your family too."

"What is it?" Kelly asked.

"I don't know. And to be honest I don't want to know. I am just so glad that we all figured out that something was wrong before it got too far. Be safe." Dena ended the call.

Kelly turned around to head to his place and paused to make a call, "Hey Beth, I think I'm going to stay the night at your place tonight. I think it's time we come up with a more permanent arrangement, too. I'm on my way." Kelly hung up and went back to his truck. It was getting dark, and he would much rather sort anything regarding his apartment out in the daytime and with other people around. "Hell, I don't need drama on Christmas Eve, no one does." He checked the glove compartment for the engagement ring he purchased for Beth before Thanksgiving. He had planned to give it to her tomorrow but tonight felt like a better time to do it considering everything.

Liz stared at Dena in complete disbelief. "Dena, the place is haunted or possessed. I'm just remembering what happened in the woods, how the temperature was never comfortable, oh my God Dena! The fire next door to you!"

"You're right Liz! Elise said she was positive that the stove was turned off and the fire department couldn't find anything wrong with it!" Dena thought, it all makes sense now. It confirmed that it wasn't just happening to her but to anyone in that area. That explained how it got into her car. It could travel short distances.

She wondered how far it could go. Did it follow her? She decided to set a trap of sorts.

"Let's call Mom and Dad." Liz used her phone and put the call on speaker.

"Hi Mama!"

"Dena! I was just packing to come down there! We were worried sick about you. Are you okay? Are you better? Are you hiding something?"

"Mama, I can't explain it now and I would love it if you and Daddy would come down and spend Christmas with us. I don't have to be back to work until Tuesday. I'm at Liz's place now. I'm sure we can have it ready in time for you."

"We aren't coming down there! A snowstorm is coming in! We are about to get seven inches of snow. It's going to be a white Christmas here." Her dad chimed in from the spare house phone. "How are my baby girls doing?"

And that was enough to melt Dena completely. Tears rolled down her face and she felt herself choking up.

Liz took over the call. "We are fine, Daddy; we are going to relax tomorrow and go to Dickson on Sunday. Jon and Chris are coming with us. We are going to have a sleepover and talk all night long."

"How is it a sleepover if you are going to talk all night?" Liz and Dena laughed at their dad's joke. They spoke to their parents a while longer and then made dinner plans.

"Well, I guess I better call Chris. You invited him to Dickson for Christmas?"

"Of course, I did! You love him and he loves you! I know it," Liz countered.

"I can't argue that. Liz, I am not going back to that place by myself again!"

Dena took the phone into the other room and called Chris. "Babe, you okay?" he asked. "You in the hospital? What's going on?"

"I'm getting better, but it was touch and go for a minute. Something tried to take me over but I'm getting back to my old self." Dena paused. "I can't wait to see you on Sunday. Are you nervous about meeting all of my family?" They talked for almost an hour before saying goodnight. Dena knew that she loved him and vowed to tell him when she saw him on Sunday.

Dena and Liz stayed up making plans on how to get Dena's stuff out of the apartment. She would stay with Liz until she could find another place. They were both happy about it; they missed living together.

And a wonderful Christmas was had by all. That is by all except Bonnie, Lethar and Kat.

CHAPTER 32

Bonnie Without Malcolm

The week after Kelly's late Thanksgiving and the evil invasion of Dena's apartment, Bonnie had gone back to being her old mean self. In fact, she was three times as mean as ever. She knew that whatever was trying to take her over was busy with the girl at the bottom of the hill and she was relieved for the most part. But, in some ways, she felt like a jilted lover. This thing had come into her home and invaded her most precious space, her body, and then left on a whim. She was attracted to it because she couldn't control it. She couldn't guess how to make it bend to her will or even how to manipulate or hurt it. She had never experienced this before. She knew she was crazy for entertaining the thought of being drawn to something that terrified her and she became frustrated with trying to understand it. To pass the time, she decided to make Malcolm's life a living hell.

After all, he had taken the kids' side against her with the closet fiasco, not believing for one second that she was not to blame even though she was caught almost red-handed. How was she to know that one of the kids didn't put the knife under the pillow? It had to be Janae! She was so sneaky! Slinking around her like a snake, trying to put her son Michael under some kind of spell. Well, Janae wasn't here so Malcolm would have to feel her wrath! Funny thing was that Malcolm was rarely at home.

He said he was working on some big project that needed to be finished before Christmas. Then in his free time he would play basketball or go to a movie without her. He would ask her to come and tell her she needed to get out of the house, but she wouldn't listen. She would start an argument with him as soon as he came in the door. "Where have you been? Are you seeing someone else? I know you are! You're just as sneaky as she is!"

Malcolm tuned her out as he walked into the guest bedroom that he had made his own. He took off his sweaty basketball clothes as she berated him from the bedroom door, not hearing a word she had said. Once he was down to his underwear, he turned and looked at her. She was still yelling about who knows what. He saw that she dyed her hair jet black. It looked wet like some of the wrestler's hair on that Monday night show. He walked toward her calmly and she flinched. He had never in his life ever hit a woman and he wasn't going to now. But her flinching let him know that he needed to act on his plan immediately. She already thought he was seeing someone else, so that can be the reason why the relationship fell apart. He went to the bathroom to take a shower and locked the door behind him. He just needed for Bonnie to be out of the house for a couple of hours so he could flee.

Truth be told, he was going to work and working on only one project. The rest of the time he spent putting his plan into action. He had talked to all the kids and told them that it was over and that he would be home for Christmas. He decided to slow down on his communication with Don. This was not the time to bring her into the mix. Bonnie was too unstable, and he wanted to be settled in before trying to see if there was any life left in his marriage to Donita. He felt sure there was, but he needed to be discreet.

He got out of the shower and went to check the mail. He didn't know if it was luck or God, but a recall notice was in the mail for Bonnie's car. She was supposed to have gotten it taken care of before they left for Nashville and thankfully, she hadn't. "Hey Bon! Did you see this recall notice on your car? You need to take it in as soon as possible!"

Bonnie came out of the bedroom and snatched the notice out his hand. She glared at him before reading the notice. The dealer listed for her car was more than thirty minutes away and the repair would take at least two hours. "Fine, I will do it the day after tomorrow. I will call and make the appointment. If you cared about me, you would take it in like a real man should."

"Bon, you never want me to touch your car. I'm respecting your wishes. You have a good night." Malcolm went into his new bedroom, closed the door behind him and locked it. He didn't want Bonnie running in there wielding a knife at him. He was right to lock his door because Bonnie was standing outside of it with a knife in hand.

Thursday couldn't have come soon enough. This was the day that Bonnie would take her car in for the recall repair. She had gotten the earliest appointment possible and left the house at 6am so she would be sure to be the first in line.

As soon as she left, Malcolm got up and packed the gym bag he had in the spare bedroom with everything he could cram in it. He pulled out his suit bags and two large suitcases. He packed all his clothes, shoes, hats, and toiletries. He took any keepsakes that he brought with him from California. He packed his laptop, speakers, and video game.

He was able to fit all the large suitcases in the trunk. He put the other bags in the backseat. The car was ready to go. He had already topped off the tank. All he had to do was leave. Yet, he wanted to make sure that Bonnie knew why he was leaving.

He went back into the apartment, into the bedroom he had shared with her and pulled out the now empty box that Donita had sent to him. He went into the guest bedrooms and found the empty boxes that were sent to Janae and Micah. Bonnie never found the boxes as Malcolm did most of the cleaning during the holidays. He placed all three boxes on the coffee table along with the empty envelope that held the letter from Donita. Then he placed a letter on top of one of the boxes for Bonnie.

He swept the apartment one last time and headed toward the door to the garage. He had his keys in his hand and he remembered to take off the apartment key and put it on the table. Then he went down and got the gate pass, placing it on the table. He went to the car, opened the garage door using the fob and dropped it in the night dropbox at the office with a note as he left.

He had a lot of free time over the past few days, so he went to the office and explained that he was moving out and that he wanted to pay the rent for the next four months. His name was not on the lease so there were no complications there. It was much easier than expected. And just like that, he was on his way back home to California. He would call the kids in a few hours once he had put a couple of states behind him.

One person he did want to call before leaving was his counterpart at the client company. "Hey Chris! It's Malcolm! Hey! I didn't want you to hear it from someone else, but I quit and I'm moving back to California."

"For real? Man, I'm sad to hear that, but I know you were having a rough time at home here. So, that really was our last game of ball the other night? I wish you had said something or let me buy you a going away beer."

"I know but I had to leave when the moment was right, and that moment was now! How are things going with you and your girl? Were you able to get ahold of her?"

"No, I did meet her sister and she was just as worried. She hadn't heard from Dena either and that's not like her. I don't know what to do. I just hope that she's okay."

"Man, I hope so too. She sounds like a great woman. Hold on to her. Well, I will be in touch man! I'm glad I met you; not too many black men in our line of business out here, it was good to see you sitting at the table."

"Same here! You be safe! I will talk to you soon!" Chris hung up the phone. He was the only brother at the table now. He was sad, but he had been there before. "Dena, where are you?" He texted her this morning like he normally did, and she answered but it just wasn't like her. He hoped and prayed he would hear from her soon.

Bonnie arrived back home about 10:30am. She saw that Malcolm's car was gone and assumed he had gone to work. She entered the apartment and the first thing that hit her was the sound of loud heavy metal music. She thought her guest was back and she went to seek it out. As she passed by the living room, she saw that the coffee table was covered with boxes. "Sweet Malcolm, I guess he still loves me. Christmas presents, already!" She moved closer to the table and her feeling of satisfaction turned into fear and then rage.

"He went through my things and found what I took from him and the kids! He took the letter from his ex-wife! But is she even his ex?" She saw the keys to the apartment. She saw the letter from him and sat down to read it. It was simple. It was over, he was done. No point in dragging it out. He knew she had been lying to him from the beginning, even before hiding the gifts from Don. She needed help and he hoped she would go get some.

"Well, looks like those chickens have come home to roost, Bonnie." She didn't cry, she was beside herself with anger and confusion. She had lost all control of her relationship, her kids, and her mind.

She grabbed her cell phone to call Malcolm, not knowing what she would say. She dialed his number and he picked up on the second ring.

"Malcolm, can't we talk about this? You can't just go like -"

"Hi Bonnie, you know that this has been over since before we moved out here. The rent has been paid for the next few months. I can't take it anymore and I'm not putting my kids through this anymore. This is the last time we will speak. I hope you have a happy life." He paused and waited for her response.

"No! NO! NOOOO! You think you can leave me? You're not going anywhere. Come back home now! NOW!!"

Malcolm let her rant for a couple of minutes and then he said calmly, "Bonnie, this is the last time that we will speak. Find a way to be happy. You know you weren't happy with me. Being in control does not equal happiness. Goodbye and I am blocking your number." He hung up the phone.

Bonnie screamed and then she tore up the empty boxes. The music in the background became louder and distorted. She pounded the walls and left sizable holes in the drywall. She threw anything that was in reach and was at the height of her rage when darkness fell over her. She was falling again, into the dank, slick darkness.

The next few days were a blur. She had found herself standing on the balcony staring at the apartment where her guest was spending his time. "Great, even an evil entity is cheating on me. At least he left his cat." She remembered finding herself on the balcony again and that there was a strange man watching her stare into her neighbor's apartment. She started to become afraid of when he would come and take her over; something in the darkness was terrifying her and she hated it. She knew she had been crazy to think that this was interesting or attractive. In and out she went day in and day out. She didn't bother to try to call anyone. There was no one to call. Her kids wouldn't want to talk to her until Christmas and that was still a day or two away. She couldn't remember.

She found herself standing on the balcony talking to a strange man again one morning. He was asking if she had seen the woman that lived in the apartment lately; she answered softly, "No." She turned and went back into the apartment. She closed the balcony doors behind her. She could feel that her guest had left and had taken the cat.

"Must have gone to see where his other conquest was. Guess she found a way to get away," Bonnie thought to herself just for a moment. She went into the bedroom and found the gun in the bench. Somehow, it had mysteriously returned to its exact original hiding place. She took the gun out of the holster and shot herself in the head without a moment's hesitation. She fell back on the bed, finally free of it all.

Word of her suicide spread through the complex quickly. Kelly heard about it the day after Christmas. He called Dena to tell her what happened. "Kelly, I almost killed myself too. I thought she had a family."

"No, she was alone every time I saw her. I hadn't even seen the man too much since after Thanksgiving.

"Hey," Kelly changed the subject. "I proposed to Beth, I'm going to move into her place as soon as possible. So, there is some good news. We survived, we made it out, by God's grace. Don't ever forget that."

"Yes, but I'm sorry that anyone was hurt at all." Dena paused, "I'm moving out too. I'm going to live with my sister for a while before I find a new place. I'm going to put all my stuff in storage until then. I'm going to the rental office tomorrow afternoon to start the process and get out of my lease."

"I am glad to hear that. Well, you stay in touch, dear lady. I am so glad to have met you! Your kindness probably saved my life a time or two. Goodbye." Kelly smiled as he put down the phone.

Dena was sitting with Liz, Jon, and Chris on the day after Christmas. It was a lazy Monday, early afternoon. Dena told them what happened to her neighbor up on the hill. "Her name was Bonnie. I just can't believe it."

"Bonnie? Her name was Bonnie?" Dena nodded at Chris' question. One of the guys I worked with was with a woman named Bonnie. He just left her because their relationship wasn't working out." Chris thought about, "It can't be." Then he picked up the phone and called Malcolm.

"Hey Malcolm! Happy Belated Christmas! You alright? You make it back to LA okay?"

"Hey Chris! Yeah, man. I'm made it home okay. Damndest thing happened, though. Bonnie killed herself! The apartment complex called me and told me yesterday. I'm completely shook. They said they had reports from several neighbors that she had been acting strangely - coming out on the balcony, barely dressed for hours at a time. They said she was staring at the apartment where some woman lived at the bottom of the hill." Malcolm paused for a moment.

"Michael and Katie are dealing with it, but I think they are still in shock. Sorry to drop this on you but I still can't believe it! She just didn't seem like she would- I don't know."

"I'm so sorry, man. But you said she had been having problems for a while. I know you tried hard to help her. Malcolm, did you stay at The Oaks on the Glen?"

"Yeah, oh no. Please tell me it wasn't on the news. I don't want anyone picking over Bonnie's death at a time like this. The kids are already in a state of shock, they don't need the media involved."

"No, man. It hasn't been on the news that I know of. I don't know how to say this but uh, the apartment that Bonnie was staring at belonged to Dena! I contacted her. She's here with me now." Chris hesitated again. "Look man, I know you've got to go and take care of the kids and yourself. I'm sure you will need to come back here to take care of some things. Call me and we can go to lunch. I'm deeply sorry about this - I don't know what to say."

"Thanks man, I will reach out once we have some plans in place. I may not be the one handling it. Bonnie's dad will probably want to take care of it. He's a bit closer, lives in North Carolina. I barely knew him, isn't that crazy? "Malcolm paused this time. "I don't know what to say about Bonnie staring at Dena's apartment. I might have seen Dena one time in the short time I was there. Small world. I gotta go man."

"Yeah, talk to you later."

Malcolm hung up the phone and looked over at Micah and Janae. He was never happier than at that moment. He wondered if Bonnie might have tried to take his life as well. Micah and Janae were texting with Katie and Michael to comfort them. They felt relieved strange as it seemed. They knew it would be a while before Katie and Michael would get to a place of peace and they wanted to be there for them. They were equally stunned and in disbelief about all of it. Katie had just told them that she had hidden the gun in Malcolm's sock drawer. She had forgotten to tell him. Surely, he wouldn't have put the gun back in the bench. How did it get back there?

Chris looked at Dena in utter amazement. "That was the lady that was staring at you on the balcony, right? Small world."

"Small world," Dena agreed. She got up from the couch and picked up her old cell phone which she had left out as bait for the evil being and threw it away.

CHAPTER 33

Lethar

Lethar was in deep shit! Not only had he lost his prized conquest, Dena, but he had lost the source in which he fed upon, Bonnie and his back-up source, Kelly. Within days he was starving. His gray scales had begun to crack and fall away. He hid in the closet of Bonnie's old place; he knew it would remain empty for a long time. Not many people wanted to live in a place where a human had taken their life. It was a great place to hide and regain his strength. But the timing was terrible. It was Christmas and every apartment nearby was filled with happy souls that were impenetrable. His work fared better when his victims were alone. The fullness of the season overflowed into the empty unit where he hid. It drained him of his power. Before long he couldn't travel. He couldn't even leave the closet on most days. Kat tried to find an animal or something to feed on but there was nothing.

His master, Byleth, would not be pleased at all. He had failed again in bringing him a soul that was full of goodness. He didn't even have Bonnie's raggedy soul as a back-up. He was going to be punished for this and it would be exquisitely, horrible. He sat and waited in the dark for something to happen. For Byleth to come or for a new neighbor to move in. There were now five units that might hold a decent prospect. He just had to wait.

CHAPTER 34

Epilogue

And what of Billy the Kid? He's still wandering around in the forest just across the road that leads to the path where Dena and Kelly lived. He roams the woods, not sure of where he is going or where he has been. It's been said that he's been roaming all this time. There and not there. Terrorizing trespassers that venture in too deep. Waiting to guide those that were sent by Lethar, although this was unknown to Lethar and Kat and there didn't seem to be any hope of any souls coming his way anytime soon. This was his charge. His doom. Always remembering the orange eyes with the huge black pupils that glimpsed into his soul and had broken his mind forever.

For more information or to contact the author, please visit her

website at: www.booksbyginnydavis.com or

email Ginny Davis at: booksbyginnydavis@gmail.com

Made in the USA
Coppell, TX
03 March 2022

74426190R00188